LILLIBULLERO

Though Nick did not l
already gone, and by th
moment carrying Lory I
on his way to Ams
disguised as a common s... was William Herbert, who had been Rear-Admiral of England and Master of the Robes until he had been closeted by the the King and dismissed for answering as a protestant. He carried a letter to the Prince of Orange, signed by seven of the highest and most influential men in England. They pledged their fortunes and their lives to his service, if he would but come to them quickly and in arms.

Also in Arrow by Robert Neill

THE GOLDEN DAYS
WITCHBANE
MIST OVER PENDLE

Robert Neill

LILLIBULLERO

ARROW BOOKS

Arrow Books Limited
3 Fitzroy Square, London W1

An imprint of the Hutchinson Publishing Group

London Melbourne Sydney Auckland
Wellington Johannesburg and agencies
throughout the world

First published by Hutchinson & Co. (Publishers) Ltd 1975
Arrow edition 1977

Made and printed in Great Britain
by The Anchor Press Ltd
Tiptree, Essex

ISBN 0 09 914830 7

When Royal James possessed the Crown
  And Popery grew in fashion,
The Penal Law I hooted down
  And read the Declaration.
The Church of Rome I found would fit
  Full well my Constitution,
And I had been a Jesuit
  But for the Revolution.

The Vicar of Bray, verse 2

The Original 'Lillibullero'

The words of the famous old song were written in 1687, a year before the Revolution, by Thomas Wharton, a noted Whig of the day, apparently as a satire on Tyrconnel's administration in Ireland. They did not at first attract much notice, but a year later, by one of those whims of popular fancy that no one can explain, the song leaped into undying fame as the battle cry and marching song of almost every protestant in England. This 'foolish ballad', as the contemporary Bishop Burnet called it, had an effect 'not to be imagined but by those who saw it. The whole army, and at last the people, both in city and country, were singing it perpetually. And perhaps never had so slight a thing so great an effect.' Wharton is said to have boasted, in later days, that he had 'sung a King out of three Kingdoms'.

He must have been greatly helped by the gay and swaggering tune, generally attributed to Purcell, that someone had the wit to put to his words. The attribution, however, is a little doubtful. The tune first appears, called a 'Quick Step', in a collection of tunes published in 1686, but no composer's name was attached to it. Purcell certainly knew it. He used it as a ground bass in 1689 and again in 1691, but by that time, of course, he could not have helped knowing it. Everyone in England knew it. So it may have been his own tune from the beginning, or he may merely have been using the tune he knew. The custom of the day would have allowed him to do that.

R.N.

Contents

1 The Officer in Green 1
2 Nemesis 9
3 The Almoner 24
4 The Summer of Fear 37
5 The Bishop of London 47
6 The Occasional Conformist 55
7 Judith 67
8 Royal Indulgence 81
9 The Whispered Doubt 91
10 Order in Council 104
11 The Water Gate 111
12 Trinity Sunday 122
13 The Warming Pan 128
14 King's Bench 135
15 The Flooding Tide 142
16 Signs of Storm 151
17 Lillibullero Bullen-a-la 158
18 The Protestant Wind 166
19 Royal Headquarters 177
20 The Unexpected 185
21 The Broken Hope 196
22 Twelfth Night 206

1 *The Officer in Green*

The Precentor of Wells Cathedral was standing in the organ loft, staring helplessly at the wreck of the organ, at splintered wood, battered and dented pipes, and a pool of green paint that had been splashed across the keys. Yesterday the organ had been a thing of life and glory, pealing triumphantly for St Peter's Day, and now it was a wreck. The shrill neigh of a horse came suddenly from the nave, which might have been startling enough in a cathedral, and the Precentor did not even turn his head. He thought that he too was a wreck, that it would be months before all this was put to rights, and that a cathedral without an organ would be little better than a dissenters' meeting-house.

'Rebels,' he muttered to himself. 'And Whigs. Green.'

He meant the Duke of Monmouth's men. It was Tuesday, June 30th, 1685, and three weeks had passed since the Duke had landed at Lyme, calling on all good protestants to join him against a papist King. Now they were being forced steadily back, and during the afternoon they had begun to straggle into Wells, where they had thought the cathedral a fit place for their horses. Many of them were dissenters who would grant no place in worship to anything as elaborate as an organ, and they had shown their doctrines by the damage and their politics by the splash of green. Then they had turned to the old painted glass in the Lady Chapel windows, hurling stones at it, shouting with delight as fragments came tinkling down, and they had grown so excited, so ripe for any mischief, that one of their own officers, Lord Grey of Wark, had stood through the length of the afternoon before the altar, sword in hand, to keep it from desecration. Now they had gone, and the cathedral was quiet except for the fidget of horses and the chatter of a dozen men who were doing the stable work. The Precentor climbed on the organ stool, balancing precariously as he peered at the battered pipes, trying to see if the reeds were broken.

'Creighton!'

The voice came suddenly from the choir below, and he all but fell from the stool as he turned to see two men standing by the stalls, one middle-aged like himself and in the same clerical black, the other much younger. He nodded vaguely, and then stumbled down the stair to the transept below. They came down the north aisle to meet him, and the elder spoke abruptly.

'What's it like up there, Creighton? Is there much damage?'

'Much!'

High in the transept wall the clock broke suddenly into its chime for the hour, and its iron horsemen, riding noisily round, cut short his indignation. He had to wait till they had finished before he could snap his answer.

'Can't you see for yourself, Holt? It's worse than I could dream of.'

'Nonsense.'

The retort was brusque. Dr Holt was the cathedral Chancellor, and he had to think of the whole building, not just the organ. His eyes turned to the aisle again.

'I can show you worse up there,' he said. 'Have you seen the Lady Chapel windows?'

'No? I – '

'You wouldn't, I suppose. Organ only, for you. Come and look.'

He led up the aisle and into the retrochoir. Dr Creighton followed, and then stood open-mouthed, staring in horror at the tall east window where the glowing colours of the richly painted glass were spangled with little stars of white where the stones had broken through.

'Look at that,' said the Chancellor tersely. 'Then not so much about the organ, please. We may have a new organ, if we have to, but we can't have new glass of the fourteenth century. And we can't match it either. What's happened to the silver? Do you know, Burnaby?'

'Safe. Or it should be.' The younger man, who was still standing with them, answered crisply. 'The Communion plate's in the Bishop's moat, hung in a bag on a string.'

'Your work?'

'No, the sacrist. He kept his head very prettily, and he was just in time. The only trouble was the verge. It was too long to go in the bag, and he hadn't time to hang it separately, so he put it on the organ stair, just behind the door. It's quite out of sight, and not a place where anyone would go looking.'

'We must do something for that sacrist. But we'll just make sure it's safe.'

He went stumping off, leading back to the transept and the organ stair. He opened the door, looked behind it, and brought out the verge, the long glittering staff of intricately worked silver that was carried in front of a dignitary as he entered or left his stall during a service. He looked it over carefully before surrendering it to the Precentor, who was holding out a hand for it. Then he turned again to Mr Burnaby.

'You're probably right,' he said gruffly. 'It'll be as safe there as anywhere, so it may as well go back there. Now, what's it like in the nave? Creighton, when you've finished staring at that thing, will you put it back?'

Without waiting for an answer he walked through the great inverted arch into the crossing, and from there he looked down a nave that was littered with buckets, tangles of hay, and blobs of dung. The aisles, north and south, were filled with tethered horses, and the men who had been seeing to them were now standing in talk, looking as if they had no more to do and were ready for further mischief. The west doors were open, letting in the golden sunlight of the summer evening, and showing horses grazing on the green outside. In the doorway, exactly in the pool of light, a man was standing alone, still and silent. He was young, in mud-splashed boots, and coat and breeches of simple grey, but he had also the sash of vivid green which some in that army were using to denote the rank of officer. Dr Holt stared truculently at him.

'I'd like the rogue better,' he growled, 'if he'd set these clod-polls to swill that dung away. Creighton, where are you?'

He had raised his voice, and the idle chatterers in the nave turned to look. Dr Creighton, perhaps startled by the shout, came hurrying into the crossing, still clutching the silver verge, and looking as if his thoughts had been far away. A shaft of sunlight, coming through a clerestory window, fell on the verge, turning its silver glitter into gleams of dancing light, and one of the watching men gave an excited shout. That was enough, and at once, between greed and curiosity, the whole group of them came rushing forward. Dr Holt stood his ground pugnaciously. Dr Creighton, in something near panic, swung the verge above his head and brought it down with a thump on the first man's head. Mr Burnaby tried to get in front of him, and the rush of men knocked both of them off their feet, with the verge clattering noisily as it hit the hard stone floor. Men were shouting everywhere, and for a moment it was pandemonium till another voice broke in, angry and imperious. The officer in the green sash, who had been watching from the doorway, had come to their help and was laying about him vigorously with the flat of his sword. With that, and the authority of his sash, he stopped the brawl, and then, before the bewildered men had well understood what had happened, he told them curtly to be out of the cathedral, and at once. They stared mutinously at him, and had small comfort from that. His sword twitched suddenly, with the point towards them, and one of them began to move slowly towards the door. In sullen silence the others followed, until one of them noticed the silver verge still lying on the flags, gleaming against the stone. An itch for plunder did the rest, and he snatched it up, gave an excited yell, and went racing with it to the door. The others went clattering after him, greedy for their share in this, and abruptly the cathedral was quiet. Dr Holt stood breathing noisily, and then turned to the young officer.

'Thank you,' he said brusquely. 'I don't like rebels, and therefore I can't like *you*, but I'll thank you all the same. That was timely.'

'Call it needful.' The young man's voice was crisp and pleasing. 'I didn't join this to spoil cathedrals, and – '

He stopped short, and suddenly he was still and tense as he stared at Nicholas Burnaby, who was standing as still as he. Recognition had been mutual. They had been law students together, first at Oxford and then in the Temple, and friendship had been strong between them. Burnaby, the son of a moderate Tory, had continued in the Temple until he had been called to the Bar some three months ago. But Lawrence Leclere, an ardent Whig, had had to get out of the country in a hurry after being implicated in a seditious pamphlet against the then Duke of York. He had been heard of in Amsterdam, and now he was back again, in a green sash.

The clang of a bell broke in, a single stroke as the clock in the transept chimed the quarter, and it was a welcome diversion. Dr Creighton, just on his feet, spun round as if startled, and even Dr Holt turned his head. Nick Burnaby left them to it and tried to think quickly. He must talk to Lory Leclere, urgently and at once, and the first need was to be rid of these two well-meaning prebendaries before they learned too much.

A burst of bawling and shouting, from somewhere outside the west door, provided a pretext. Leclere, very tense and silent, swung round to it at once, his hand falling again on his sword, and Burnaby spoke in a whisper to Dr Holt.

'Get him away, sir, quickly.' His glance indicated Dr Creighton. 'If those fellows are coming back – the ones he hit with the verge – there could be any sort of trouble. Get him to his house, and I'll see to things here.'

'Oh?' Dr Holt glanced at the door, then at the still unsteady Precentor. 'It might be wise. Are you sure you can manage?'

'Yes, of course. But quickly, please.'

'For a young man you have some grains of sense. Come along, Creighton. Out this way. You'll be better with your wife. *This* way.'

He was vigorous about it, taking Dr Creighton firmly by the arm and leading him out of the nave, into the transept, and then to the stair just beyond it, by which they could leave the cathedral. Burnaby went with them and saw them safe into the Chain Gate, the covered passage that would take them across the street beyond and put them safely on the way to their houses. Then he turned, and at the foot of the stair he found Leclere waiting for him.

'Lory!' he said quickly. 'What are you doing here?'

'I'd have thought it plain enough.'

'It is, while you wear that thing.' He eyed the green sash with distaste. 'Are you mad?'

'Not now. Only when I engaged in this business.'

'At The Hague, was it?'

'Yes, and I thought Monmouth was a competent soldier. I was none too happy about it, because I didn't like the look of the others, but they pressed me hard, saying they must have me.'

'Why? You aren't a soldier.'

'No. But it was planned to land in this west country, where I'd know the ground. I'm of Bridgwater, you see.'

'So you are.'

He had forgotten that detail. The Lecleres had been Huguenots who had come to England more than a century ago, after the massacre in Paris. Being skilled weavers they had settled first in

Taunton, where weavers abounded, and had then moved to Bridgwater, where they had prospered enough to send Lory to Oxford. But certainly he would know the west country, which might be useful to Monmouth.

'I see.' He looked steadily at Lory. 'And how are things now?'

'Can't you guess? Monmouth turns out to be just a handsome puppet with a winning tongue. He bewitches these country clowns, and God knows what he's leading them to.'

'You sound as if you've lost hope.'

'So would you, if you'd seen what goes on. I feel I'm in a trap.'

'Then get out of it, pray.'

'How?'

'You've a horse, I suppose? Ride him as soon as he's rested, and get away from here – a long way from here.'

'Desert, do you mean?'

'I certainly do. You might then be of use another day.'

'But – '

'Lory, what's your work in this army? Do you command some company?'

'No. They call me an aide, which means I'm a sort of talking map, telling them where places are, and how the roads run.'

'Then you aren't deserting men who follow you, which I admit would have been difficult. A talking map can go.'

'Nick, be sensible. Where do you think the King's forces are?'

'Somewhere near Shepton Mallet. About five miles away.'

'And do you think they won't have patrols out on all the roads? I'd merely be taken tonight, instead of in a few days' time.'

'Oh!'

It seemed all too likely, and for a long moment Nick was put to silence. The royal army was commanded by one of the King's favourites, the Frenchman Louis Duras, who was now Earl of Feversham, and no one thought him very competent. But his second-in-command was Brigadier-General Lord Churchill, who was said to be very competent indeed, and would surely have seen to it that cavalry patrols were out and properly instructed. They would question anyone who went riding out of Wells just now, were he Lory Leclere or – as a quick thought came – the courier who must be sent urgently to the Bishop after these events in the cathedral. At once the two thoughts merged, and Nick spoke easily.

'They won't take you, Lory. They'll stop you, no doubt, and ask your business, but you'll be a diocesan courier, riding to the Bishop. He's in London just now, for the House of Lords, but I'll write to him at once.'

'*You?*' Leclere's voice sharpened with surprise. 'What *are* you talking about? And what are you doing here?'

'Oh – ' Nick suddenly remembered that he had not explained it. 'I was called to the Bar in March, but I'd had a fever in the winter, and I was advised to be out of London for a while. A friend of my father, Lord Mumford, recommended me to the Bishop here, who needed someone for legal work, his diocesan Chancellor being sick. So I came for six months, and I've had enough to do. But I'm employed by the Bishop, you see, not the Chapter, so it's quite proper for me to tell him of trouble in his diocese. That will make it an authentic letter, and you an authentic courier.'

'Yes, but – '

'Listen.' Nick waved for silence as his fertile mind had another thought. 'This Lord Mumford is in favour with the King, a Gentleman of the Bedchamber, *not* the sort of man a rebel would take a letter to. So you'll take one, and that also will be authentic. He may even be pleased to have it.'

'Why?'

'It might make him first to the King with news of this, and that can be useful to a courtier.'

'Hmm!' Lory's tone suggested that he had no wish to be useful to a courtier. 'And you think these letters will get me past patrols?'

'Yes. I'll give you one also for my father, who's in London as a Parliament man, and I'll write all the letters with some good loyal sentiments, in case some officer insists on reading them.'

'Suppose it's just a sergeant, and he can't read? I'd be sent to headquarters to be identified.'

'What if you were?' Nick was sharp on it, and then he stopped suddenly, as if a further thought had come. 'That's exactly what you'd better do, Lory, from the outset. Ask for the headquarters.'

'What!'

'Listen. My young brother Harry is in that army, in the Foot Guards, and I know his Colonel too, which is very convenient. So I'll write to him also, and you'll ride straight at the first patrol you see. Tell them you've letters for Colonel Crosedale and

Lieutenant Burnaby, and wish, therefore, to be taken to wherever the Foot Guards are. You'll hardly be refused, and the letter to Crosedale will be genuine, asking that Harry may visit me here if possible. But I'll ask him in a footnote to see that you are not delayed unnecessarily, since your letters to Mumford and the Bishop are urgent. That should do it.'

'You seem to think of everything.'

'A good habit. And when you're in London you'd better not stay till someone recognizes you. Deliver these letters, and then go down to the Pool and find a ship for Holland. Have you money?'

'Enough for that. But I should be thanking you, Nick.'

'I want you for another day. Now then – ' He was incisive, with a note of command. 'Get rid of that sash, if I'm to walk the streets with you, and then we're for my lodging. I'll write the letters while you have an hour or two of sleep, and you can be away at first light – and I'll breathe better when you're gone. I'm not used to this sort of thing.'

'No?' Lory looked steadily at him. 'By the way things go, with King James, you'll soon have more than this to get used to.'

2 *Nemesis*

It seemed to go smoothly. Lory, well mounted, was away at four o'clock with the letters, and Nick Burnaby was left to wait through the day for news, fairly sure that no news would be good news. The rebel army, continuing its retreat, began to leave Wells, but it was slow and clumsy, and through the morning the cathedral was a tumult of men and horses. Nick went on waiting, thinking now that if the King's regiments continued to advance he might soon see something of his brother, or of Colonel Crosedale.

But the royal army slipped past Wells without coming in, and the citizens sighed with relief, thinking that dragoons might have been even worse guests than rebels. In the cathedral Dr Holt was busy. Since, he said, they had no Dean – by which he meant that the Dean was an absentee, seldom seen in Wells – he must take this upon himself, and he quickly had everyone he could muster sweeping and scrubbing, clearing away dung and picking up broken glass. The sacrist washed and cleaned the plate, and Nick Burnaby, with his own work at a standstill, gave what help he could to Dr Creighton. But everyone was waiting, sure that a battle was imminent and that news must come soon.

They waited till the following Monday, when a man came riding in with a letter from the Mayor of Bridgwater. The Duke of Monmouth, it said, had marched his men out of Bridgwater on Sunday evening to make a night attack on the royal army, which was encamped some three miles out. He had all but succeeded, but not quite, and there had been bitter fighting in the small hours of Monday morning. But with the coming of daylight the King's trained troops had soon made an end of it. The rebels had been utterly routed, and now they were scattering everywhere, pursued by the Dragoons and Life Guards. The Duke of Monmouth had ridden from the field, but it was thought that he could not for long evade capture.

That was the letter. But the courier looked unhappy, and when he had been given a cup or two of ale he had something of his own to say. He was a Bridgwater man, and he had been just opening his house that summer morning when a horde of fugitives from Monmouth's defeated army began to stream into the town, all of them weak and exhausted, and some in worse shape than that; and after them, within minutes, had come the pursuing cavalry, riding exultantly, resplendent in their uniforms, with swords lifted high and flashing in the sun. They had burst into the town as a great roar of hooves, and at once, without a moment's pause, they had hurled themselves upon the terrified fugitives in the streets, wielding their swords savagely. For a few short minutes, said the man, all hell had been loose in the town, made worse by the appalling noise, the hooves and swords, the shouts and cries, and the screams of the watching women. Then, as suddenly, it had ended as the cavalry went roaring into the open country again, continuing their pursuit. The town seemed empty, and the noise sank to the gasps of the dying and the stifled sobs of the women.

But the man had worse to say. He gripped the table as if he would steady himself, and then he spoke miserably. On his way to Wells, he said, he had deviated a little from his direct route to pass through the village of Weston Zoyland, which had been Lord Feversham's headquarters, and he had soon regretted his curiosity. As he neared the village he saw that rough gibbets had been erected, a line of them to fringe the road, and already men were cutting trees and digging holes for more, local men, working under guards of soldiers. He was stopped and questioned, and then allowed to ride on, to find that near the village a dozen men were already hanging, stiff and bloated in the summer sun. He had turned sick at the sight, and had kept his eyes to the ground, riding blindly into a village where the bells of the church were pealing joyfully – again with a guard of soldiers to keep the ringers at it. Again the courier was seized and questioned, and when he was at last released he had lost no time in putting that accursed village behind him, riding hard, as he said, to put the place out of sight. He shuddered, and asked that he might stay a night or two in Wells.

This was readily granted, and by nightfall there were few in Wells who had not heard his tale, and fewer still who liked it. Even Dr Holt, who had been as extreme as anyone in his insistence that nothing justified rebellion, and that rebels must be caught and punished, now began to have some doubts. Hanging men like that, he told Nick Burnaby, was too hasty, and it was the leaders of a rebellion who should be hanged, not the simple folk who had followed them. Nick pointed out, as a lawyer, that there was as yet no Commission of Assize, and therefore no authority to hang anybody. The army, he thought, had acted in disregard of both law and decency. Privately, he was hoping desperately that Lory Leclere was now safe away.

By the next morning Dr Holt was saying that rebellion was none the less rebellion, that they should rejoice that this one had been quelled so quickly, and that it was their plain duty to arrange a service of thanksgiving in the cathedral for this happy event. The canons were still discussing this, with the Precentor stubbornly maintaining that no proper thanksgiving service was possible without the organ, when another man rode in from Bridgwater, this time with a letter to the Chapter from the Bishop of Winchester. Dr Holt read it to the others. The Bishop wrote from Lord Feversham's headquarters, where, he said, he had been acting as chaplain. He was now starting homeward, and wished to lodge for a night in Wells; and he hoped, also, to have some part in the thanksgiving service that they would undoubtedly be arranging.

That, of course, put an end to the argument, and the service was promptly arranged for the next morning, the Precentor being firmly told that he must find what music he could; there must at least be a Te Deum. The canons were looking a little happier now, for this bishop was no stranger to them. Before being translated to Winchester he had for many years been Bishop of Bath and Wells. He had been liked by all of them, and at this moment they thought they needed all the advice and support he could give them.

He came into Wells that evening, rumbling in his coach-and-six to the porch at the end of the market place, where the canons waited to receive him as he entered the precincts. But in the streets he was hardly noticed, for the people of Wells had now something else to think about. Two companies of Dragoons had ridden in during the afternoon, had quartered themselves in the city, and had at once started a hunt for fugitive rebels and their sympathizers. They had questioned the Mayor, the constables, the clergy, and the members of the Watch, and then they had taken to stopping men in the streets and to searching suspected houses. Already there were tales of a score of men arrested, and there was now such a fear in the town that men were finding it wise to keep off the streets. Nick Burnaby stayed in his lodging, hoping that no one had seen him take leave of Lory Leclere in the first light of a summer morning. But all was well, and when, at the end of the afternoon, an officer in scarlet knocked at the door, he was not a Dragoon. This was the uniform of the Foot Guards, and his brother Harry.

Harry seemed pleased with himself. He settled at once, dealt quickly with a glass of wine, and then stretched lazily. The Guards, he said, were already on their way back to Westminster to resume their normal duties, and they had camped for the night a mile or two from Wells, which had given him the chance for this brief visit.

'We halted early,' he explained, 'and just as well too. Everybody's tired. The Colonel, by the way, sends his regrets that he won't see you. He says he's too busy, but I think he's just too tired. He thanks you, though, for that letter you sent him the other day.'

'Oh, by the courier?' Nick was carefully casual. 'I'm glad he found you. But I hope he got away quickly? His letters to London were important.'

'Oh yes. Crosedale did as you asked. He sent a corporal to see the fellow clear.' Harry stretched and yawned, as if he had heard enough of this. 'We'll be glad to be back in quarters. It's been all marching lately, and sleep where you can. No comfort anywhere.'

'I thought that was a soldier's life.'

'It is. But that doesn't make it comfortable.'

'How did the battle go?'

'Oh – ' Harry yawned again. 'They didn't give us a lot of trouble, though I must say they made a better fight than you'd expect from clodhoppers. That was while it was dark, of course. They weren't any use when it was light enough for musketry, and we just finished them off.'

'Did you? Then what's this of men being hanged without trial?'

'Nothing to do with us. We don't do that sort of work.'

'Somebody seems to be doing it.'

'Kirke, perhaps, and his Tangier rogues. But for us, we didn't do it, so I can't tell you. What's the family news?'

'Oh – there isn't any.' Rather reluctantly Nick accepted the change of topic. 'I was hoping you could give me some.'

'I can't. Father's still in Westminster, and he doesn't like the way things go. He wants to get home for the summer, and he can't while Parliament's busy, so he keeps growling about papists everywhere. One of his awkward moods. Have you heard from home lately?'

'Not for a month.'

'I'm wondering about John. I expect he's in one of *his* awkward moods too. Or if he isn't, he will be when he hears about this battle. You know how he dotes on Monmouth.'

Their elder brother had once been in the Duke of Monmouth's service, as a gentleman in attendance, and had formed a deep personal affection for him. A little later, when the Duke had showed some alarming signs of setting himself up as a legitimate heir to the throne, John had had to turn instead to the service of his father's friend, Lord Mumford. That had been some five years ago, and his family hoped that he had now forgotten Monmouth. Harry had evidently some doubts about this, and Nick was inclined to share them.

'That Act of Attainder has probably upset John already,' he said. 'The one they passed the other week, as soon as Monmouth landed. You know what it means?'

'Chop,' said Harry briefly.

'Exactly. Will Monmouth be caught?'

'Very likely, with the hunt they're making for him.'

'Then that will be the end of him. There'll be no need for a trial. The Act makes him formally guilty of treason, so it will just be the axe, and perhaps pretty quickly. Which will *not* please John.'

'And if he learns that Father voted for the Act, as I expect he did, that won't please him either. Ah well – ' Harry got cheerfully to his feet. 'It's a good thing he's married. Doraty will have to cool him this time.'

'If she can.'

'What are wives for? But it's time I was off. I only had two hours.'

'I'm sorry. If you get any family news, let me have it.'

'How can I, when they don't write to me?'

'Have you written to Mother, by the way? Because if you haven't, you'd better tell her you're safe. She's bound to be worried about you, after this battle.'

'Do it for me, will you? I can't write while we're marching, and you'll need something to do. A quiet sleepy life you must have here.'

'Like you at Westminster.'

The service of thanksgiving was held the next morning in a cathedral which had been cleared of dung and broken glass, but had not been repaired, so that scars and damage were to be seen everywhere. A sultry wind was coming through the broken windows, and Nick thought everyone looked as unhappy as he was, as if none of them could forget what was now being done in the villages of a stricken county. The Bishop of Winchester, preaching the sermon, dutifully said all the proper things about obedience to an anointed King, and looked all the while as if he wished he were somewhere else. Dr Holt, who read most of the prayers, looked grim and unhappy. Dr Creighton, bereft of the organ and reduced to some viols and a couple of flutes, could put no heart into what should have been a triumphant Te Deum. The Jubilate was even worse, and the whole service, as one of the canons said afterwards, began to sound less and less like a thanksgiving and more and more like prayers at a hanging.

His quip had a ghastly sequel. The cathedral had been filled with people by the hundred, perhaps thankful, perhaps troubled, or perhaps just prudent, and the way home, for most of them, was across the green and through the towered porch into the market place. They went streaming through, and then they found that at the other end of the market place their way was blocked by a double line of soldiers. They could go no further, and behind them another party of soldiers blocked the porch, preventing a return to the green. They were held in the market place, and then, to a great roll of drums, five pinioned men were brought, one by one, to the balcony of an inn and hanged. Not till the last of them had ceased to writhe and twitch did the drums stop rolling. Then the soldiers marched away, the bodies were left hanging, and citizens were free to go to their affairs or their dinners, as might best please them.

Nick Burnaby had been caught in the crowd, for his lodging was in the market place, and he knew at once that he could not dine in a room that faced that balcony. He turned, feeling sick and angry together, and went hurrying back in search of Dr Holt. He had seen men hanged before, but they had been condemned after proper trial and process of law, which was different; and nobody need watch at Tyburn who did not wish to.

Dr Holt, disturbed in his house as he was making ready for dinner, asked brusquely what the trouble was. He was told in angry words, and for a moment he seemed disbelieving. He had to hear some of it again before he fully grasped it, and then the angry rasp came into his voice.

'It's beyond bearing,' he snapped. 'These army officers – '

'They've no authority – '

'Never mind authority. They've also no sense, no decency, and no respect. I mean respect for God, and for the people here too. They prepare all this while we are in service, and then they let it loose as people leave the house of God – their thoughts, we'll hope, being of his goodness and mercy. Come away to the Bishop. They may listen to him, if not to us.'

He meant the Bishop of Winchester, who had stood high in the favour of King Charles and was believed now to be in the favour of King James. He was lodged in the Bishop's Palace, his old home, and Dr Holt snatched at his hat and led there at once. His Lordship was already at dinner, but he nevertheless came from it to hear them. Then he was less hopeful than they had expected.

'Here too, in Wells?' he said. 'It was the same at Bridgwater. They were hanging men the morning after the battle, and I went at once to Feversham to get it stopped – and I failed entirely. The man's a Frenchman, and he couldn't understand what I was objecting to. He kept saying he was there to crush rebellion, and this was the way to do it. Certainly I'll speak to the officer commanding here, but if he has his orders from Feversham, I doubt if I shall move him much. Come along, Holt. You may as well be with me.'

They went away together, and Nick spent the next half-hour pacing the terrace at the end of the Bishop's garden. It was at least secluded, and out of sight of that market place, but when they came back and he hurried to meet them, he knew without asking that they had failed.

'As I expected,' snapped the Bishop. 'He has his orders and will obey them. So I'm going home as soon as my horses can be ready, and from there I shall write to the King. At need I'll go to see him. Meanwhile, I think you should write from here direct to your own Bishop. He, after all, is in London, and can go at once to the King.'

He was away in his coach within an hour, and Nick settled in the Chancery Office, which was within the Palace, to write to their Bishop in London. But he wasted his time. He had finished it, and he was just leaving the Palace to take it for Dr Holt's approval, when a clatter of hooves on the bridge across the moat made him jump quickly aside as the Bishop of Bath and Wells came riding in, not in a coach-and-six like his brother of Winchester, but sitting a horse like any simple gentleman, and attended by only a single servant. He looked pale and tired, and Nick hurried to hold the horse and help him from the saddle.

'Thank you, Burnaby.' He spoke quickly, making no attempt at dignity. 'I'd have been here sooner, when I had your letter, but the King kept me at hand, and it was only yesterday that I had leave to go. I've made what speed I could.'

He looked as if he had been riding hard, and he was not a man built for that. He was of not quite fifty years, of less than middle height, spare and lean, with a soft and delicate face which was given strength by the dark and luminous eyes, vivid with inner life. He was clean-shaven and wore his own hair, which had now turned grey with some wisps of white. Even in his dress he made no show of being a bishop. He had coat and breeches of simple black, good stout riding boots, and a wide-brimmed hat which, with instinctive courtesy, he had already pulled off, even to Nick Burnaby. Nick, hat in hand himself, stood almost rigid. In his three short months in Wells he had come to a regard for Thomas Ken that went past mere respect. There was an unearthly quality in the man, something of God, as an ageing country vicar had once been heard to say.

'Tell me – ' The Bishop spoke again in the same quick voice. 'Tell me how it is now with the cathedral, and with my people here.'

'My lord – ' A quick thought came that the Bishop was here in response to his earlier letter, the one that Lory Leclere had taken when the rebels were in the cathedral. 'A building, my Lord, can be put to rights, or most of it can. But some of your people – cannot.'

'Oh?' Concern showed at once in the Bishop's face. 'Come in, Burnaby, and tell me of this.'

The outcome was that the Bishop, white with anger, could barely be dissuaded from going at once in search of the officer commanding, and it took some plain speaking from Dr Holt, who came hurrying as soon as he heard of the Bishop's arrival, to convince him that this would be a waste of time. Then he said he would ride the next day to Bridgwater to see Lord Feversham, and again he had to be told that the Bishop of Winchester had tried it already and in vain. Finally, he declared that he would ride back to London tomorrow and see the King, and he was not to be put off by being told that the Bishop of Winchester was to appeal to the King. In a matter of his own diocese he would go himself, he said, and personally see the King. On this he was adamant, and the most he would concede, when they both told him he was too tired for it, was that he would not start early; he would have a long night's sleep, and start, perhaps, at mid-morning. Nick offered to ride with him, to give what help he could on the journey, but he declined even that.

'It is kindly offered,' he said with his quick and winning smile, 'but you may serve me better if you stay in Wells. Write to me at once, please, if there is more of this, or if matters get better or worse. God be with you.'

However courteous, it was dismissal, and Nick had to accept it. He walked slowly from the Palace, and when he came to the archway called the Bishop's Eye, which would take him into the market place, he all but stopped, dreading what he might see beyond. He made himself go through, and then, in surprise, he stopped completely. The market place, usually thronged with strolling and chattering people in a summer evening, was wholly deserted, as if it were now a place to be shunned and on which no one could bear to look. He made himself look, and at least the bodies had been taken from the balcony. He was spared that horror, but he felt uneasy, almost a trespasser, as he hurried to his lodging, keeping against the wall and going almost on tiptoe lest his footfalls break the quiet. His room faced the balcony, and he would have his supper with his back to the window.

But on his table he found a letter waiting, rather to his surprise, for the postboys had not been seen in Wells these last unhappy days. He recognized his father's writing, and when he slit it open he saw that it was dated July 4th – last Saturday – which meant that Lory had made good riding; and so, perhaps, had the post-boys. But it was a thicker letter than he had expected.

It began with his father's comments on his own letter, about the rebels in the cathedral:

. . . disgraceful, and I do not see how Monmouth can profit by permitting such conduct. But the King's forces must be close at hand, and I hope that by this time you will be free of the rogues. Like all others here, I await news, and I pray that your brother Harry may be spared from hurt. God keep you both, and Colonel Crosedale too.

But I have other news for you. On Wednesday last our old friend Richard Law died at his house in Tower Street here, cujus anima requiescat. *He was of seventy-five years, and I think he had found little to live for since the death of his wife last year, yet I am sad at his going, as I am sure you will be. You will have memories of his kindness and his hospitality.*

The funeral was done yesterday, in St Dunstan-in-the-East, the church he had attended for more than fifty years, but the moment was unfortunate. The King had just prorogued Parliament, leaving everyone to ask why, and what he means to do next. There was much consulting among us, on whether we might now depart to our homes or should stay in London to be on hand, and there was the same unease in the City. Many, therefore, were not at Richard's funeral who would have wished to be, and so, by way of mending matters, a memorial service to him has been announced for Wednesday next, the 15th, also in St Dunstan-in-the-East.

This touches you. For after the funeral, Mr Thom, his attorney, opened and read his will. He has been generous indeed. He had gained a considerable fortune, and since he had no children the bequests to his friends are large. Among them he has bequeathed five thousand pounds each to me and Sir Nicholas Culley, one thousand pounds each to our wives, separately from us, and one thousand pounds each to you, your two brothers, and Tom Culley. This is surely a generosity which puts all of us under an obligation to be present at the memorial service on the 15th. Pray give thought, therefore, to whether you can by any means have leave from your duties for some few days while you journey here.

I am writing similarly to your mother and John, to Harry, and to Nick Culley. Likewise to Tom Culley; though as he is now in service as a Lieutenant in the Resolution *frigate, and said to be at sea, I have little hope that it will reach him in time.*

Nick gave thought to it at once. Richard Law, a woodmonger in London, had been known to his father for a quarter of a century, ever since the plotting and scheming that had led to the Restoration, and Nick himself, when he had been a law student, had found much of hospitality and shrewd advice at the house in Tower Street. He had come to a genuine affection for Richard, and he now felt a true regret at the loss – together, as he noticed, with an excited happiness at the thought of that legacy. A thousand pounds could transform life for a beginning barrister who must expect some lean years while his name was becoming known. But what mattered at the moment was that to attend the memorial service he must ask leave of the Bishop, who had just told him to stay in Wells, writing letters to London.

He went back to the Palace an hour later, and found the Bishop pacing the terraced walk by the moat, singing his evening hymn to end his day. But he listened courteously, and then at once went beyond mere permission. He asked Nick to ride with him when he himself set out for London tomorrow, admitting that he was indeed tired and would be glad of a younger man with him. Nick accepted, and he was therefore at the Palace again the next morning with his horse, his valise, and a strong feeling of relief that for the next few days he would be away from that market place.

They took it easily, Nick being very sure that the Bishop was in no state for hard riding, and by Friday evening they were some little way past Andover, and still some sixty miles from London. Here the Bishop called a halt at a roadside inn, where he was evidently known. He was given a deferential welcome, and the innkeeper led them up the stair at once. But then, as they were standing by the open door of the Bishop's room, the door of an adjacent room was pulled open and a man stepped out, big, tall and well proportioned, perhaps nearing sixty now, but still strong and vigorous. He turned as if to go down the stair, and then he stopped short, staring hard at Nick.

'What the devil!' he burst out. 'Are you for London too, young Nick? Old Richard, is it?'

'Why – ' Nick began to make sense of it. This was his godfather and his father's old friend, Sir Nicholas Culley, and that mention of Richard Law had given the clue. Sir Nicholas, too, must be on his way to the memorial service, and since he lived near Salisbury this would be a likely road for him to take; and he could as well have chosen this inn for the night as any other. But there was an immediate problem. Sir Nicholas was the most good-hearted of men, bluff and kindly, and almost always cheerful; but he was not always tactful. He was often noisy and impulsive, and at this moment Nick had the Bishop to think of too, who was tired and troubled, and perhaps not at his best for dealing with anyone as overpowering as Sir Nicholas Culley. It would need careful handling.

'Why, yes.' Nick set himself to do what was plainly needed. 'I must certainly attend this service. But, my lord, permit me – ' He had turned quickly to the Bishop. 'Here is Sir Nicholas Culley, to whom I have the honour to be godson. And, sir – the Bishop of Bath and Wells.'

'*Who?*' Sir Nicholas stared for a moment at the dusty boots and the plain black coat, and then he was suddenly making his deepest bow. 'My lord, I'm honoured indeed. Your most faithful and devoted servant.'

There was a fervour in it that went beyond politeness, and it derived from his early days. Sir Nicholas had raised himself in the world by his loyal service to the late King, but he had not been of gentle birth. His father had been a singing man in a cathedral choir, and young Nick Culley had been brought up in the cathedral and its school for choirboys; and the deep devotion to the Church that this had given him had included some high notions of the respect due to bishops. He was getting elderly now, a man of fifty-nine, but he had not lost that early teaching. If anything, it was stronger in him now, harder and more rigid.

'Sir, you say too much.' Dr Ken mustered a courteous smile as he answered. 'Too much for my unworthy self. I am delighted to meet you, and the more so since Mr Burnaby speaks of you as his godfather.'

'Oh – ' Sir Nicholas beamed with delight and tried to look modest. 'His mother being sister to my wife, which makes my wife his aunt, they chose me for the work. Which is why he is Nicholas, as I am.'

'Ah, I see.'

'I'd heard of him in your service, my lord, and was glad of it. Better for him by far than Westminster Hall or that wicked Old Bailey. But, my lord, since we are so happily met, may we not meet for supper too? Will you do me that honour?'

He sounded eager, and he was at once supported by the hovering innkeeper, who was quick to promise the best of suppers to guests so eminent as a bishop and a knight. Dr Ken was too good-natured to refuse, and Sir Nicholas beamed again and looked ready for any tactless blunder. His nephew, knowing him, wondered what his talk would be like at supper.

Yet by the time they came to it he had changed. His usual

ebullience had gone, and he looked a troubled man, with little to say beyond some courtesies until the meal was at an end. Then he pushed back his plate and came at last to what was in his mind.

'My lord,' he said quietly, 'are they true, these tales from your diocese of men already hanged, and before a judge has left London? Are they true?'

'I fear they are. Nor can I prevail to make an end of this. Which is why I now haste to London, that I may plead with the King for my unhappy people.'

'God speed you in that, my lord, though I doubt you'll succeed. He's vindictive, our James, as I've cause to know.'

'Sir Nicholas, please! What talk is this?'

'The truth, my lord. And I've no pleasure in speaking it.'

'Then why, indeed, speak it?' There was gentle reproof in the tone. 'For I have no pleasure in hearing it. And indeed, Sir Nicholas, I could wish not to be put in mind tonight of what I must take to the King. It's too sad a tale. May we, then, speak of something else?'

'Willingly, my lord. I – '

'Do you also go to this memorial service – for Mr Law?'

'Just that, and I hope many others will be there. He was one of those happy few who are liked by everyone. Is that a gift from God?'

'From God indeed, but perhaps not a gift. Has it not to be earned?'

'Well said, my lord.' Sir Nicholas sounded as if he were brooding on something. 'Who else will be there, young Nick? What of your brothers? Where's John, just now?'

'At home. That's to say, he's in the dower house with his Doraty. When my father's in London, for Parliament, John cares for the estate.'

'It's time he learned, if he's to inherit it. But is he now called to London?'

'I think so. My father said he'd written to him also.'

'The devil he has!' He sounded almost disgruntled, and then he turned again to the Bishop. 'Have you heard that Monmouth's been found?'

'The Duke? No, I – '

'On Wednesday, in Cranborne Chase, after a great hunt for him. He was taken to Ringwood, and I suppose he'll go to London.'

'Oh?' There was sudden anxiety in the Bishop. 'And what then, do you think?'

'You can guess as well as I, my lord. He's headed a rebellion, and he put out a Declaration about James that even I thought a foul thing. Best pray for him.'

'Indeed I shall. So should we all.'

Dr Ken looked troubled, and he fell silent as if his thoughts would not leave him. He sat brooding, and then in some few minutes he roused himself and asked that they should forgive him for leaving them; he was tired, he said, and must seek his rest. They assented dutifully, and in the fading summer light Nick went with him to his bedroom door. For a moment they looked at each other.

'Good night, my lord. I shall pray for your rest. The Lord be with you.'

'And with thy spirit. Burnaby, we must never question the goodness and mercy of God. But we may ask it, on a stricken man.'

He shut the door, and Nick went down the stair to find Sir Nicholas sitting very still, toying with his wine. He seemed to be brooding, and he was not in a hurry to speak. Then he looked up.

'I shouldn't have talked of Monmouth,' he said slowly. 'It's upset him. But I didn't think, and it was all in my mind after we'd been talking of John, called to London. You can remember, I suppose, that fondness he took for Monmouth?'

'Oh!' Nick began to see the point. 'We thought of it the other night, Harry and I.'

'It's a pity your father didn't think of it too, and then use his wits.' The old indignation was coming to Sir Nicholas's tone. 'He wrote to John, you say? So John will now be on his way to London, and Monmouth's on his way too, from Ringwood. They could arrive about the same time – with the whole town talking of Monmouth and what's to happen to him. And *that's* the moment when your father brings John.'

'But my father couldn't know of this when he wrote.'

'He could have done some guessing, I suppose? But he didn't, and all we can hope for now is that they won't be in a hurry to bring Monmouth to trial. Then John can attend this service and be packed off home before they start.'

'There may not be a trial. There's an Act of Attainder, and the King can just sign a warrant.'

'Good God!' Sir Nicholas jerked upright. 'Go to it, do you mean, in a day or two?'

'It would be lawful – but not likely, surely, in that haste?'

'Ugh!' The grunt expressed his doubts. 'Can you guess what it would be like in London? Nothing else to talk about. Folk in thousands going to Tower Hill, and a procession of coaches with Monmouth. Then hawkers in the streets with last dying speeches – that sort of thing. What would it do to John?'

'Drive him near mad.'

'And this is the moment when your father calls him to London, thinking only of Richard Law.'

'But what can we do?'

'Pray for a miracle. For if it happens like that, we shall have John driving *us* near mad.'

3 *The Almoner*

Sir Harry Burnaby, sitting with a glass of wine while he waited for dinner at Sunday noon, was pleasantly surprised when Sir Nicholas Culley came striding into the room, hearty and buoyant, and looking very much his old self.

'Ha, my boy!' was his greeting. 'I thought I'd find you here. A glass for me, please. You've a room bespoken for me?'

'Of course I have.'

'I came with your Nick, by the way. We met at an inn, and rode together. Ah, thanks! You've a nose for a good wine, Hal.'

They were in the Bell, in the Strand, where Sir Harry always lodged when Parliament was in session, and he was well enough known there to get the best of wine and service. Sir Nicholas tasted, and again nodded his approval.

'Your Nick will be here soon,' he explained. 'He had his Bishop with him – Ken – and he's taken him to Ely House. He hasn't a town house of his own, so he'll lodge with the Bishop of Ely. Is there any word of Tom? He's hard to write to.'

He meant his only son, who was a lieutenant in the Navy, and usually at sea and out of reach of letters. Hal Burnaby nodded.

'I did write to him. I sent it to Pepys at the Admiralty, asking him to do what he could, and I'd a note back that he'd done so. I like Pepys.'

'Everybody does. But, Hal, what's the news here? Anything about Monmouth?'

His tone changed suddenly, becoming sharp and urgent. Hal looked surprised, and then answered him carefully.

'Something, though it's still private. I heard service this morning in the Abbey, and Mumford was there with his wife. We had a word afterwards. Mumford's still very much of the Court, quite close to the King.'

'What did he say?'

'Monmouth is coming up under guard from Ringwood, and he's expected here tomorrow morning. But they won't take him through the City, which is perhaps wise. They'll take him to Vauxhall, and then he'll go by water down to the Tower.'

'And after that?'

'What do you expect?'

'What anybody would. But it's awkward. When's your John due here?'

'Any day now, if he's bestirred himself.'

'Just in time for Monmouth, and whatever's to happen to him. So how will he take to *that*? Has he forgotten Monmouth?'

'Oh!' Hal looked back at him in dismay. 'Nick, I hadn't thought of this.'

'I'm glad you see it now.'

'Of course I'd no notion of this when I wrote to John. I hadn't even heard of the battle then.'

'Never mind that. But this service for old Richard is on Wednesday, isn't it? So you'll have to send John home again on Thursday morning, and what we must hope for is no announcement before then about Monmouth and what's to happen to him.'

It was disturbing, and it took Hal to Whitehall Palace the next morning in search of news, though this was no longer as easy as it once had been. The late King Charles, affable to everyone, and with an exact understanding of who his supporters were, had always given him friendly notice, and occasionally private audience. But King James was a great deal less affable, and Hal Burnaby, like many another, could no longer expect to be noticed. But, like any other gentleman of good name, he still had access to the Palace, where he might walk in the Galleries and the Privy Garden, chatting, hearing gossip, and having, perhaps, a word with one of the King's ministers.

This, therefore, he did that Monday morning, and within a half-hour he thought he had learned all that was to be had; and it was interesting. The Duke of Monmouth was still expected at Vauxhall before noon, but he had now written to the King, asking for audience, and this had been granted. His barge, instead of going direct to the Tower, would first put in at Whitehall, where the audience would be given in the lodging of Mr Chiffinch. That seemed an odd place, but Mr Chiffinch was still a very confidential servant, and it would perhaps give privacy and informality to the audience. Hal went back to the Bell and told this to Nick Culley, whose forehead took a wrinkle as he considered it.

'What the devil?' he answered. 'Is he going to pardon Monmouth?'

'How should I know?'

'By using your brains. Can he see Monmouth, see him and talk to him, face to face in a small room, and then send him to the axe? Could he?'

'Surely not.'

'Exactly. He couldn't, and nor could anyone else. It wouldn't be decent. So all should be well, and if nothing's done to Monmouth, John will go off home again all sweet and happy, no trouble to anyone.'

'Oh, I see.'

'I thought you would, if you tried.'

He sounded pleased with his good understanding. But towards the end of the afternoon young Nick Burnaby went to Ely House to ask if all was well with Dr Ken, and he came back looking troubled. Dr Ken, he said, did well enough, and he had been that morning to Whitehall to make his plea for some spirit of mercy in his diocese. The King had promised to look into the matter, but would say nothing more positive than that. He had gone on to say that he was glad to have Dr Ken back in London, since he might soon have work of importance for him; and what this meant had emerged in mid-afternoon when a gentleman-in-waiting had come to Ely House with a royal command. The King, it said, had ordered that the Duke of Monmouth should die by the axe on Tower Hill on Wednesday morning, and had already signed the warrant. He now required Dr Ken, and his brother of Ely, Dr Turner, to go without delay to the Tower, to impart this news to the Duke and to do what they could, as divines, to prepare him for death. They were ordered also to go with him to the Hill on Wednesday morning, and to continue their ministrations to the last.

Nick related this, and Hal heard him in frigid silence. Nick Culley burst out in a swelling indignation.

'Hal, are we to suppose that James saw him, talked to him, and then ordered *this*?'

'He's within his rights, I suppose, but – '

'It's not decent. It's – '

'*Please!*' Nick Burnaby pushed himself suddenly back into the talk. 'May we leave this? I'm not concerned about the King at all, and I'm not concerned much about Monmouth, who's as guilty as a man can be. I'm concerned about my brother.'

'John?'

'Of course. Is he coming to this memorial service? It's also on Wednesday morning, and it's at St Dunstan-in-the-East. Monmouth will be on Tower Hill, only a few hundred yards away, and perhaps at about the same time in the morning.'

'Good God!'

'There'll be a stream of people all morning on their way to the Hill, and we'll be mixed up with them as we go to the church. When we're in the church, we shall hear all the noise of the crowd, and the gun they'll fire at the end. And how could John forget Monmouth, with all that going on? We shall all be thinking about Monmouth.'

'Instead of Richard?' Hal stared gloomily back at him. 'We'll have to try not to, but I'm afraid you're right about John.'

'It couldn't be worse. He mustn't go.'

'So far he isn't here to go, and that's what we'll have to hope for – that he's been delayed on the road and will come too late.'

But John was not too late. He came the next morning, with twenty-four hours to spare, and already, as he crossed London, he had heard the news. He walked into the Bell looking white and angry, perhaps sickened as well, and he spoke abruptly, without even a greeting to any of them.

'I've heard about it – about Monmouth,' he said. 'Will they really do it?'

'I'm afraid so.' Hal answered carefully, and stayed watchful. 'It's formally announced, and a warrant signed, and I hardly think the King will go back on it. Not this King.'

'This King!' The revulsion that had gripped him rang plainly in the tone of it. 'Isn't Monmouth his brother's son, his favourite son? And it doesn't matter?'

'John, you'll have to recognize that Monmouth is a rebel taken in arms. He'd even proclaimed himself King.'

'Ugh!'

It sounded as if John was in such an anger that he could no longer speak properly, and for a long moment Hal, too, was silent while he considered his eldest son. John was now twenty-four years old, slim and good-looking, and normally he had an easy pleasant voice and a charm of manner that could win him friends everywhere. Six years ago it had won him the favour of the Duke of Monmouth, to whom he had given in return a fresh and youthful loyalty; and it was now very plain that he had by no means got over this. The Duke's present strait had revived it in full force, and Hal eyed him warily. He knew very well that John, despite his charm and his good intentions, had never quite found the good judgement, or perhaps the stability, that could be seen in his brothers. He was well and happily married, and he had a young son of his own, but he was less mature than Nick, who was a year and a half younger. Harry, the youngest of the three, was perhaps the most confident.

'Tomorrow, isn't it?' said John suddenly. 'And what am I to do? Go to that church with you, right down by – '

'Of course you're not. You must stay here.'

'Here?' John looked wildly round the room. 'And alone? I'd go crazy.'

'Then take a walk instead. But upriver, not down.'

'Past Whitehall, do you mean? Our gracious lord the King?'

He was plainly in an impossible mood, and Hal told him tersely that he must face the unwelcome from time to time in life, and show a decent self-control. That, for a moment, silenced him, but he was probably seething inside. He was in obvious distress, and it might be too much for him unless, by some miracle, his thoughts could be diverted from Monmouth.

This took Hal to Westminster that evening, in search of Lord Mumford, who had his town house there. He was another who had a liking for John. When the Duke of Monmouth had been banished overseas by his father, and John had been left alone and desolate, Sir Charles Mumford – as he had been then – had put this right by taking him into his own service, which had turned out to be that of King Charles. It had become important, and in the end it had allowed Mumford to take John and his wife on a secret mission to Versailles, where they had been presented to King Louis – an experience which had certainly put Monmouth out of John's head for a while. It was not to be hoped that Lord Mumford would be able to do anything like that again, but he was still very much of the Court, very knowledgeable about what was going on, and if there was a possibility anywhere of anything that could divert John's thoughts, he was as likely as anyone to know about it.

He received Hal easily, and heard him with attention. Then he looked concerned.

'Difficult,' he said at length. 'Certainly you had to call John to this memorial service, and you could hardly have foreseen the rest of it.'

'I suppose I could have guessed that Monmouth would be taken.'

'But not this exact conjuncture of events. You'll have heard that James gave audience to Monmouth, and then signed the warrant?'

'I have indeed.'

'It's not civilized. However – ' The shrug of his shoulders was eloquent. 'It's John we must speak of, and he's certainly a problem.'

'You'll think him foolish, I'm afraid.'

'I'll just say sensitive. He was very young and impressionable when he took this liking to Monmouth, and I'd not like it if we now found him callous. I wonder if Churchill could help? He was very helpful to Harry, you'll remember?'

Hal did remember. Colonel Churchill had then been in the Duke of York's service, and he had chosen to help young Harry Burnaby to his commission in the Foot Guards. He had brought him to the notice of the Duke, who had given him his pair of colours. That had been five years ago, and the Duke of York was now King James, and Colonel Churchill was now Lord Churchill. But he was still in favour, and in the campaign against Monmouth he had been Feversham's second-in-command; which, at the moment, might not be pleasing to John.

'I'm not sure that it was pleasing to Churchill either,' retorted Mumford. 'As a soldier he's a hundred times better than Feversham, so why should be he placed second to him? Also, it seems that all through the battle Feversham was in bed, and stayed there. Churchill took command of the whole affair and won it handsomely, and the rewards for it are now going to Feversham. He's to have the Garter, it seems, so do you think Churchill can be pleased? He may have more sympathy with John than you'd expect.'

'But can he do anything?'

'I've a faint glimmer of a thought, but it's a long chance and I'd sooner not speak of it yet. So would you leave this with me for a while, and I'll have a word with him?'

'Mumford, it can't be left. The question, above all, is what to do with John tomorrow, till they've finished with Monmouth.'

'Oh, of course it is.' For a moment he stayed in thought, then he became decisive. 'That will be from about ten o'clock onwards, so will you send John to me, here, a little before nine?'

'I certainly will. Believe that I'm grateful.'

'You neea not be. I've a liking for John, and for that delectable wife of his too. Nine o'clock, please.'

Hal went back to the Bell, and one mention of the matter was enough for John, who had happy memories of Lord Mumford, particularly at Versailles. He said at once that he would call, and then he started grumbling that he had not the right clothes with him for such a call. Hal told him shortly to go in what he had, and be thankful he had not to go the other way.

Hal had to go the other way, to the memorial service. He went in a hired coach, with Nick Culley at his side, and Nicholas and Harry on the facing seat, and from the moment of starting they were in a steady stream of people, on foot, in carts, and even in coaches, all going east and all seeming to hurry, as if they must not be late. At St Dunstan's Church, even inside, there was a distracting noise of wheels and feet, and from further away the low steady drone of voices by the thousand. Yet not everyone was thinking of Monmouth. Some had remembered Richard Law, and the church was crowded when the service at last began. Hal did his best at it, and he was sure that others, too, were finding it hard to think only of this. Monmouth was probably in a coach by now, on his way; and a memory came of his thirtieth birthday, only six years ago, when there had been a masque and a banquet for him at Whitehall, and he had stood at his father's side to receive the guests. Hal had been among them, and John with him, and Monmouth had invited John into his own service.

He glanced to the side as they sat for the sermon, and from Nicholas, next to him, he had a wry grimace in return. Hal was in sympathy, and contrived a quick whisper.

'Don't think about Monmouth.'

'I'm not doing. Or not much.' It came back in the same tone, and Nicholas had not turned his head. 'I'm thinking of Ken – the Bishop. He and Ely are to be with him, and then they'll have to stand there and watch it done, a few feet away. That's worse than this.'

The Rector preached the sermon, and ordinarily it would have been thought a good one. He had known Richard Law for many a year, and had liked him, and he had composed this sermon with a proper knowledge of the man. But there were moments when his attention seemed to wander, and moments when his hearers looked up, or down, or round about, or anywhere but at the preacher; and he was little more than half-way through it when the dull boom of a gun broke in, reverberating through the church from one of the Tower batteries. He stopped short, with his knuckles whitening as he gripped the edge of the pulpit, and in the silence that followed there can be few in the church whose thoughts were of Richard Law; who had died peacefully.

An hour later, back in the Bell, Nick Culley called thirstily for wine, saying he hoped he would never again have to sit through such a morning.

'We did our best for old Richard,' he declared, 'and it wasn't our fault that it was impossible. Here's to him, and his memory!' He lifted his glass and drank it off in one. 'And I'll be eternally grateful to him for what he's left to us. All the same, I hope John's had a better morning. Where is he, by the way?'

They had to wait till they were almost into dinner before John returned, and he had a happy and excited look that Hal had seen once or twice before. It brought him to the alert at once.

'What's happened?' he asked.

'Oh – ' It sounded as if John were trying to be offhand about it. 'I went to Lord Mumford, and he talked for a while, and then Lord Churchill came.'

'To Mumford's?'

'Yes. And *he* talked for a while. Very pleasant. But then – ' John seemed to steady his breath. 'He took me to the Cockpit, and presented me to the Princess Anne.'

'Who?'

'The Princess of Denmark. She's gracious. A bewitching voice, she has. And it's hinted that I could perhaps – perhaps have a place in her household.'

'She said *what*?'

'She didn't. I mean it wasn't her. It was Lord Churchill.'

'But what?' Hal was by no means sure that he had heard this properly.

'He presented me to her, and spoke very kindly of me. But I think he's going to speak further to her, and ask a place for me. He didn't exactly promise, but – '

'In her household, at the Cockpit?'

'I think so. And I'm to be there again tomorrow, at ten o'clock, in case I'm wanted.'

Hal had no answer. Nothing of this was impossible, and nothing of it was likely. The Princess Anne was the King's younger daughter, twenty years of age, and married to Prince George of Denmark, a tall, blond, good-looking young man, who was said to be amiable and good natured, and to be interested in nothing but a quiet life. The late King Charles, who had arranged their marriage, had settled them in a house called the Cockpit, within the Palace precincts, north of the road on a site where the cockpit once had been, and here they were said to be living very happily together. Which did nothing to explain why she should have a place in her household for John Burnaby, or why Lord Churchill should suggest it and speak for it. It was a royal household.

But John did not seem awed by that. He had changed completely, and he was crisp and buoyant, plainly believing that his luck had turned at last, and that great things were in prospect for him. He said, after they had dined, that his wife had given him messages for Colonel Crosedale, who was her uncle, and for Mrs Crosedale, and he had better deal with these at once so that he might be free tomorrow for the Princess of Denmark. He went cheerfully off, taking Harry with him, and Nick Culley said that he had some shopping to do for his wife. He went off also, and then Nick said he would call at Ely House and ask after Dr Ken, who must have had a distressing morning. But as he was going he turned to look steadily at his father.

'Did you notice,' he said, 'that since John came in there hasn't been a word said of Monmouth, by any of us? It's a little odd.'

'This talk of the Cockpit is odd.'

'But it's like John. He has a way of falling on his feet, a special gift he has.'

'You think he'll get this place?'

'Yes, as he got the one with Monmouth. But this will be a better one.'

'It should be. It's the second household in England.'

'And one day, of course, it could be the first. Very good luck to John!'

Nick went on his affairs, leaving his startled father to think that this was an excellent appraisal of things, especially that last comment. The two princesses were the King's only legitimate children, and it was most unlikely that there would be any more. On his death, therefore, the Crown would pass to the Princess Mary, who was the Princess of Orange and lived at The Hague. But she, also, had no children, and no robust health. The Princess of Denmark was the next heir.

Hal considered this further, and then went again to see Lord Mumford, who was more likely than anyone to know what had happened. It could, of course, have been done at Mumford's suggestion.

But Lord Mumford disclaimed that, and he admitted to being surprised himself.

'It was Churchill's doing,' he said firmly, 'so let him have the credit for it. I'll admit it had occurred to me that Churchill is at the Cockpit a lot, and that something there might be suitable for John, but I didn't say so. I thought it wiser not to, so I just explained the problem and asked if he could help at all. Then the rest followed.'

'It's exceedingly good of him.'

'If he knew the Princess had need of another gentleman in attendance, he may have thought John just the man for it. John did it for Monmouth, he knows what's needed, and he has the style and manners for it. So perhaps this fits together.'

'I hope John fits also, if he gets this place.'

'I think Churchill will see he gets it.'

'Has he influence enough?'

'Plenty, and his wife has more. She's now the fond friend and confidante of the Princess, which is no doubt convenient.'

'I still find this odd.'

'That's not new, with Churchill. At times he's uncanny. He sees about three times as far into the future as anybody else, and more often than not he aims at purposes that the rest of us haven't even noticed. So stop asking questions, Burnaby. Just take what comes, and be thankful.'

Hal went thoughtfully back to the Bell, where he found that Tom Culley, who had been summoned like the others to the memorial service, had just arrived, a day too late for it, but not much upset by that. His ship had put into Gravesend that morning, where letters had been waiting, and since one of them was from the Secretary for the Admiralty, Mr Pepys, he had been able to get leave, not for two days, but for two whole weeks, and he was now impatient to see his mother and enjoy the comforts of his home again. His father, in high approval of this, was already saying that he and Tom must be away tomorrow morning. He had hardly said it when Nicholas came back from Ely House to say that Dr Ken was also insistent on taking the road the next morning to his stricken diocese. He was in no good shape for it, after his ordeal on Tower Hill, and Nicholas had more or less insisted on riding with him. Nick Culley, hearing of this, and liking the company of bishops, promptly said that he and Tom would join them, and give what help they could.

They departed accordingly, a little after breakfast, and an hour later John went off, a little nervously, to the Cockpit. Harry had already gone back to his regiment, and Hal was left to fill his morning as best he could until John returned at noon, looking happy and excited, to announce that he had been appointed almoner to the Princess of Denmark. He had kissed her hand on his appointment, and he had found her a very gracious lady whom he would be glad to serve. The place, he admitted, was a sinecure, since she had, in fact, no need of anyone to distribute alms for her, but he was not put out by that. To have no particular duties, he said, would be a positive advantage, since he would be free for anything that came, and small duties might lead to larger ones. For the moment he was well content; although, as he quickly added, the almoner had a salary of only two hundred pounds a year, and he would have to live for much of his time in Westminster. This thought seemed to please him.

It pleased Hal less, and not only because he foresaw that he would have to make John an allowance. It was more because John had a wife and small son, and did not seem to know whether they would stay at home or be with him in Westminster. Hal thought that to be separated for most of the year would not help their marriage; and that to move from the clean air and food of the country to Westminster might do no good to Doraty and could certainly do none to little Richard. But this, as he had to tell himself, was no longer for him to decide. John was twenty-four, Doraty only six months less, and they were entitled to decide it for themselves.

John rode away the next morning, impatient to be with Doraty and tell her of his good fortune. Hal, who had not quite finished in London, took a boat to Westminster, thinking that he must, if it was at all possible, speak a word of thanks to Lord Churchill for this help to John. He might perhaps be found at Whitehall Palace, for he was certainly in the King's service still, whatever he might be at the Cockpit.

Hal was fortunate. At Whitehall Gate he found Harry, very much on duty as officer of the Guard, and from him he learned that Lord Churchill was certainly in the Palace and might now be with the King. Hal went on, across the Great Court and into the Privy Gallery, and here again he was fortunate. Within five minutes Lord Churchill emerged from the ante-room and came striding briskly down the Gallery, a man now of thirty-five, lithe and handsome, and moving with uncommon grace and vigour. He was not in uniform, but in a suit of simple brown, not of the most expensive, and so plain that it could have made another man inconspicuous. His inscrutable deep-set eyes, something between grey and green, recognized Hal at once, and he came to a quick and courteous halt.

'Ah, Sir Harry! My service to you. It's some time since I saw you.'

'Our paths lie differently. But my service indeed to you, and my thanks also. You seem, this time, to have befriended my eldest son.'

'John?' There was a faint nod, and then he glanced at the sunlight in the tall windows. 'A pleasant morning. Shall we take the air?'

They walked down the Gallery together, and not till they were in the middle of the Great Court, where they could be heard by no one, did Lord Churchill have more to say.

'I hope I have been of service,' he said carefully, and then paused before he went on. 'Your son, I think, has the qualities that are needed in a royal household, and the Cockpit may be a proper place for him, his opportunity in life. But also – ' Again there was a careful pause. 'Looking to the future – the possible future – the Princess of Denmark may one day bear great responsibilities.'

'Certainly.'

'She would then have great need of gentlemen in her household whom she had learned to trust.'

'John?'

'I hope so. And, if so, I shall have done her a useful service. Which, to be honest, was my first concern. For in these days – '

The pause, this time, was sharp and deliberate. 'I neglect no chance to serve Her Highness.'

It was a loyal and proper sentiment which could safely be spoken. But the stress on it, and the strangely level tone of it, hinted at a further meaning. Hal understood at once, and knew as quickly that he must not speak of it.

'Excellent,' he said carefully. 'I hope John will do the same.'

'And not only John.' The reply came instantly, and the vivid eyes gave meaning to it. 'You yourself, Sir Harry, might consider it. For I wish you well.'

4 *The Summer of Fear*

Hal, taking it easily, reached his home on the Lancashire–Cheshire border a week later. His wife, who looked as if she had been impatient to talk to him, lost no time in asking what he thought of this appointment as almoner.

'John's been here the last three days,' she explained wryly, 'but I really can't get much sense from him. His head's too full of it. He and Doraty, by the way, are all but packed and ready to go.'

'So he's decided to take her with him?'

'It's much more likely that she decided. Of those two, she's the stronger, and when she can't push she can coax. She knows all about it.'

'I'll believe you. But what do you think of her hurrying off like this to live in Westminster? Young Richard too, I suppose?'

'Certainly. And her own mother doesn't much like it. As for me – ' Alison sounded careful. 'I suppose I don't like it either, but I can understand it. Life can seem very quiet here, especially when you're twenty-four and you've had a glimpse of a brighter life. I think that's the root of it. This place is dull.'

'Not everyone would think so. But what *do* the others think about his going as almoner?'

'They speak good wishes, of course, but I doubt if they're really interested. Their thoughts are elsewhere now – Monmouth and what was done to him, and what sort of a King we really have, and what his true plans are. That sort of thing – and who'll care much about an almoner?'

This came out very clearly the next morning, when the Rector called to see Hal; for Mr Allway was an ardent high churchman, who had accepted in full the doctrine that the King was the Lord's Anointed, divinely chosen, and therefore having from God an authority that could be neither diminished nor taken away by men. He had been preaching this for years past, and it had sounded well enough when loyalty could be to Church and King together, and to uphold the one was to uphold the other. But the King was now of the Church of Rome, and the loyalties were *not* the same. Mr Allway, whose sermons had committed him irrevocably to both of them, might soon have to choose between them; and he could renounce neither without eating his sermons.

He came quietly in, a man of forty-six, tall, slender, and sharp of face, with something of the scholar and recluse about him, as if he might sit long with his books and thoughts. He began by saying politely that they would all miss John when he had left for London. But then he turned hesitant.

'Could I,' he asked carefully, 'offer felicitations on this appointment as almoner?'

'Oh yes.' Hal understood at once the real meaning of the question. 'The Princess of Denmark is very staunchly protestant, and no more likely to desert the Church of England than you are yourself.'

'Ah!' Mr Allway nodded with satisfaction. 'An excellent household, if there is loyalty to both throne and Church.'

'Which we can no longer take for granted?'

'No.' The troubled look returned. 'How will affairs go?'

'There's nothing certain. Only some rumours, and some whispers at the Court.'

'Gossip?'

'Perhaps. But such gossip springs, in the main, from men who are close to the King and have heard him talk. So we heed it when there is nothing else.'

'Yes?'

'They will tell you at Whitehall that the King means to use this late rebellion to cow the dissenters, since the rebels were mostly dissenters. If they are now used with severity, or so it is argued, dissenters everywhere will learn the lesson, and be in no mood to resist the King, whatever he may do.'

'And what – will he do?'

'This is only talk, Rector. But the whisperers say that he may then turn upon the Church of England, since this, more than anything, bars the way for his own Church.'

'That?' It came softly, from a man tight-lipped and tense. 'Persecution?'

'We are not there yet, and we may not be. Whispers can be wrong.'

'It has happened before, forty years gone, and well do I remember it. Even as a child – '

'Rector, you have told me that before, and I can myself remember the soldiers in their breastplates, and the godly preaching ministers – '

'In their black coats and – '

'Do not dwell upon it. And do not look only upon the worst of things. I told you only by way of suggesting that you now might be wise, for a while, to cease your preaching of non-resistance and of divine authority in kings.'

'Sir! You ask me to be false, to renounce the Church's teaching?'

'I'm not asking you to renounce anything. I'm merely asking you to talk less of it, and not keep it so lively in your people's minds.'

'Have I no duty?'

'You've duties enough and to spare, and I'm only suggesting you give your mind to some of the others for a change. You won't run short of them.'

'But – '

'I'm being practical. The less you say just now about all this, the less embarrassing you'll find it later if a choice is forced upon us.'

'How can there be a choice when our duty is spelled out for us? You know what the scriptures say?'

'I've heard them till I'm weary of them. But if it's forced upon us between King and Church, that will be a choice, whatever the scriptures say.'

'It is *not* a choice. To the Church we shall give all the obedience we can, and to the King we shall give all the obedience that conscience allows. Where we cannot obey him, we shall be passive, not resisting anything he may do, even if it be to our hurt.'

'Passive obedience, as you call it?'

But at that point they were interrupted, and the Rector's heat was replaced by an air of cold courtesy. Mr Richard Gibson had come to the house, and the Rector did not like Mr Gibson, who hardly concealed his belief that the Rector was a fool. Mr Gibson was one of the Protector's old soldiers, who had given years of devoted service and had ended as a colonel after fighting at Worcester and Dunbar. He was therefore the last of men who could say that resistance to a King was sinful, and though, at the age of fifty-six, he had now mellowed and become more tolerant of details, he was still the same man. He was a thoughtful and militant protestant, with not a trace of high church notions in him, and in politics he was a Whig, who in the days of the Exclusion Bills had followed Lord Shaftesbury and been a member of the Green Ribbon Club. He had the courage and honesty and sense of duty that had been found in so many of the Protector's officers, but he could not be petty, and he had never allowed his disagreements with the Rector to lead him into discourtesy. He preferred plain words, spoken with ease and good humour in a way the Rector could not match.

To Hal he was an old friend. In the last reign, through the turbulent and dangerous years of the Pope-burnings, they had been in Parliament together, moderate royalist and ardent Whig, and they had come first to respect and then to like each other. Then John Burnaby had married Doraty Gibson, Richard's only daughter, and this had made a further link between them. In these present days Richard was no longer in Parliament, for King James had begun his reign by having a very royalist Parliament elected, and Gibson had been one of the many Whigs who had lost their seats. But he had retained his deep interest in Parliament and all its works, and he had welcomed the frequent and informative letters that Hal had sent to him.

He came into the room looking as if he would be put out by nothing, and for a fleeting moment, at the sight of his russet coat and riding boots, Hal had a memory of forty years ago, of the russet captains who had so stoutly borne the brunt of it for Parliament till the New Model had been raised and they had changed their coats for scarlet. There was something of it in Richard Gibson, and Mr Allway came quickly to his feet. He had no cause to love russet-coated captains.

'Forgive me,' he said stiffly. 'I'll take my leave. We must talk another day.'

He sounded none too pleased, but Hal knew of old that Allway and Gibson did not mix happily.

'By all means,' he answered. 'But remember, please, my suggestion.'

'Remember, please, the scriptures. The powers that be are ordained of God. Whosoever therefore resisteth – '

He left the quotation unfinished as he made a frigid bow to Gibson and then went at once to the door. Hal saw him away, and when he returned he found Gibson at the window watching the retreating Rector. He turned unhurriedly.

'And what,' he said placidly, 'is upsetting him this morning?'

'He came for news, and I gave him what I could. Then I suggested that he might now be wise to say less about passive obedience.'

'He isn't wise and he never will be. What *is* the news?'

He was quiet and attentive while Hal told him of affairs in London and the whispers that were to be heard in Whitehall. He seized in particular on the rumours of the King's intentions.

'Attack the dissenters, will he?' His voice was ominously quiet and steady. 'Being men, some of them, whom I knew. My old soldiers, and my brother officers. And the Church of England next, do you say? That may give him a closer look at adversity and the present shape of it.'

His sardonic glance through the window showed that he meant the Rector. There was a silence before he brought his eyes back to Hal.

'It's coming,' he said simply.

'What is?'

'What Allway won't face.' Gibson was slow and thoughtful now, using no word lightly. 'This King James has determination. And he's persistent. Grant him that. But his priests have so filled his head with what he ought to do that he hasn't a chink left in it for any sense. You'd think any man, attempting to turn a nation upside down, would go at it with care, always feeling his way, drawing back for a while when it looked too dangerous. But such moderation isn't in James. He'll see no point of view but his own, and he'll have as much tact as a charging bull. I don't know what effect he'll have on Allway, but for the rest of us – '

'Yes?'

'What do you do when a bull starts snorting at you? Talk of non-resistance, or reach for a pitchfork?'

Hal related this to his wife later in the day, and she showed some signs of amusement. Alison, at the age of forty-seven, had still a trick of lifting an eyebrow to show surprise or amusement, and in some way she could point the difference between the two. This time it was amusement.

'That's entirely Richard,' she said. 'Religion first and politics second, and I doubt if he thinks of much else. Did he tell you what he thinks of John and Doraty going off to live in West minster?'

'He didn't get as far as that. I shouldn't think he'd like it.'

'He doesn't. Nevertheless, he approves. He was telling me so the other day.' The eyebrow quivered for a moment. 'Conscience all the way, and careful thought. The Princess of Denmark is of the Church of England, and she may one day wear the crown.'

'She has an elder sister.'

'Who is wed to the Dutchman, and is ruled by him. So if she were Queen we'd have England dragged round Europe at the tail of the Dutch dog. I'm still quoting Richard, mind you.'

'It sounds like it. Go on.'

'Richard doesn't like it. He thinks of England, as well as of the Church, and for the saving of both he can only see the Princess Anne.'

'Who also has a foreign husband.'

'But harmless. He won't drag anyone anywhere, not even his wife.'

'Hmm!'

This was probably true. Prince George of Denmark was hardly noticed in London. He did not engage in politics, and seemed to have little interest in anything outside his bedroom and dining-room. There was even a tale of the late King Charles, in one of his Old Rowley moments, saying that he had tried him drunk and tried him sober, and found nothing in him. He and the Prince of Orange could hardly have been more different, and Hal nodded.

'Perhaps so,' he said. 'But I thought we were talking about Doraty going to Westminster?'

'So we are, but it's all mixed up with Richard's sense of duty.'

'What's his duty?'

'It's everybody's, not just his. We must all think very loyally of the Princess of Denmark, and take any chance there may be to offer her our service and humble duty.' Thus Richard. This, after fearing God, has become the whole duty of man. Do you see it now?'

'Not in the least.'

'Isn't this exactly what John is doing when he becomes her almoner? If we're to believe Richard he's now a sort of guiding light, showing the way to his elders – which includes you.'

'The devil it does!'

'You'll be hearing so from Richard. But the point is, he approves. And as for Doraty, she's John's wife, and if he must go to Westminster, she must go with him, to support and comfort him, whether she likes it or not. That's *her* duty, and Richard told her so.'

'What did she say?'

'She said very dutifully that she'd go. Then she told me the same, but rather differently. In fact she's all hot for going, but not precisely for Richard's reasons. Oh no.'

This became clearer the next day, when Doraty and John walked across from the Dower House to say their farewells. They were to start for Westminster the next morning, and Hal had by this time accepted the situation, but he did feel some disquiet for little Richard, who was only two years old and might be none the better for such a move. But then, and not for the first time, Doraty showed him that he had underrated her perceptions.

'You need not worry,' she told him firmly. 'I have *not* forgotten Richard, and I shall not forget him. Nor will John. He's going to be very well cared for.'

'Good.' He looked back at her, understanding that she had discerned his thought. 'By you?'

'When I can. And when I can't I'll make sure that someone else does, and properly.'

'I'm sure you will. But what will you be doing when you can't do it yourself?'

'I don't know yet. But I'll find something, somewhere.'

He could well believe that she would. He noticed again her slender figure, the clear sharp lines of her face, and the serenity of her hazel eyes, and he was sure that she would find something of what she wanted; whatever that might be.

'I'm not asking a lot.' she said slowly. 'But it's four years since we went to France with Lord Mumford, and then we had to come back almost at once to here. Think of it, Versailles to back here! Do you wonder I found it dull? And since then I've been here all the time, seeing the same few people all the time, people I've known since I was born, and now I want a change, even if it's only for a time.'

'I can understand it.'

'I hope so. It's been different for you, because you've been in

London for Parliament, but you should hear my father about it, now he's out of Parliament – nothing to do but read newsletters, he says. Do you know what he expects *me* to do, at Westminster?'

'Tell me.'

'Encourage all good protestants to wait on the Princess – as if I'll know whether they're good or not. Or care either, if only they're interesting.'

There was more in the same vein, as if she meant him to understand how she felt about this. But he learned afterwards that Alison had understood even better.

'My sympathies are with Doraty,' she told him, 'and specially about your having been in London for Parliament. I've had to stay here, and it's as short of new faces as Doraty says. So you know what we shall do when those two are gone?'

'No?'

'We shall just sit and wait for news of them. That's all there is to do here.'

She was right, and they were soon waiting not only for news of John, but for any news that might show what the King's intentions really were. But news was slow to come, and they were well into August before a letter from John told them that with the help of Colonel and Mrs Crosedale he had found a pleasant lodging at Westminster, in King Street, and had already entered on his duties at the Cockpit. These, he said, were much what he had learned when he had been a gentleman-in-waiting to Monmouth, taking messages, receiving callers, or doing anything else that might suddenly be needed. The Princess was gracious and not at all exacting, and he had hopes for the future. Doraty wrote in the same style to her father, adding that she had herself been received by the Princess, who had been very pleasant and very dull.

Then again they waited, and September was a week old when a newsletter told them that retribution had begun in the west. Lord Chief Justice Jeffreys had opened his commission of assize at Winchester, where the Lady Alice Lisle had been convicted of having harboured one Hickes, a rebel, and had been sentenced to be burned alive for treason. The clergy and gentlemen of the county had so protested that this had in the end been referred to the King, whose utmost mercy had been to commute the sentence to one of beheading; which had been carried out at once. The newsletter reported this guardedly and without comment, which did not lessen Hal's disquiet. He had some memories of Sir George Jeffreys.

The assize moved to Salisbury, where some fugitives had been captured, and Nick Culley, who lived nearby, wrote of the scandal and disgust that Jeffreys' behaviour in court had given to the local gentlemen. Then it was the turn of Dorchester, where the newsletters told of seventy-nine hanged and many more transported. The same tale came from Exeter, and again from Taunton, and here, among those convicted of treason, were a party of young girls, some of them only ten years old, who in their school had worked a banner for Monmouth. Then the assize was at Wells, and the newsletters reported ninety-seven condemned to death and nearly four hundred to transportation. But Nicholas, who had now returned to his work there, had more than that to say. He was a barrister, and his sense of outrage was plain in the letter he wrote to Hal.

The Lord Chief Justice has been here this past week, and his conduct throughout was vicious, and his savaging of prisoners was unbridled and indecent. He will flout the law in any way if he may but get a conviction quickly. That seems to be his only care, and he loses temper and the common decencies at anything which may hinder him and make him sit in court some minutes longer. There is talk everywhere about his behaviour, and mostly it is put down to drink and a malignant spleen, but the truth may be different. I learned from his chaplain that he has a stone in the bladder, and that the pain it gives him as it presses against the wall of the bladder is very great. It will be at its worst when he is sitting, and I can well believe it is past all bearing when he has to sit for hours in a coach, jolting and banging on the damnable roads of these parts. Small wonder that after such a journey he comes to the assize in a temper fit only for a devil. Then he must sit all day upon the bench, the pain everlasting, and all he can do for some small relief is to keep his bladder full, that there may be more room in it for the stone. For this he is for ever taking draughts of a weak punch, which, in the way of nature, gives him discomfort of another sort, so that he has frequently to go briefly out of court upon a necessary occasion. This, though wholly understandable, does not accord with dignity, and therefore does further hurt to his temper.

Hal read the letter with a mounting disquiet, and then sent it to Gibson. They met on Sunday, after service in the parish church, and Gibson handed the letter back to him.

'The dog follows his master,' he declared. 'By such men are we ruled.'

'You put this on the King?'

'Where else can I put it? Is not a judge the King's deputy?'

'The King may not know of this.'

'Then he ought to know. Does he not know what's in the newsletters?'

'How of this stone of Jeffreys?'

'It may be so. But if he's not fit for the work he should not have gone on circuit – or been allowed to.'

'Which puts it back on the King?'

'We shall know by what happens to Jeffreys. Will he be dismissed, or commended?'

The assize had still to go to Bristol, and then, as September ran out, the newsletters reported that the Lord Chief Justice had hastened to the King at Windsor. Two days later the *Gazette* announced that for his 'eminent and faithful services' he had been promoted to the great office of Lord Chancellor. Gibson made the obvious comment.

Then the look of things was changed. In mid-October a royal proclamation, dutifully read to them in church by the Rector, summoned the prorogued Parliament to meet again on November 9th, and Hal heard it with dismay. He had been looking forward to a Christmas at home with Alison, with the music and the mummers, the greenery, the ale and apples, and his house thrown open to his neighbours; and this would mean the London road again, in November, and then a Christmas in what would seem like exile.

'Perhaps,' said Gibson calmly. 'But perhaps not.'

'Why not?'

'I can think of only one reason why he should call you back, which is that he needs to ask for money. If he does, I hope you won't give it to him.'

'Why not?'

'Because if you refuse him he'll probably lose his temper and send you packing again, and quickly. You'd then be home for Christmas, and we'd welcome you twice over, for two reasons.'

'Being what?'

'We'd have your company, and he wouldn't have our money. I don't know which would please me the more.'

5 *The Bishop of London*

Parliament was to meet on Monday, November 9th, and Hal arrived the Friday before. He settled again into the Bell and sent a note to John and another to Nicholas, who had now finished at Wells and was in London again.

John was the first to call, and he came striding into the Bell with an air of brisk confidence, as if he had now a purpose in life. He apologized for not having Doraty with him, since she was busy with young Richard.

'Quite right,' said Hal. 'But how of yourself, and the Cockpit?'

'Oh – ' John sounded carefully nonchalant about it. 'First of all, of course, there's the Princess, and she's very easy and polite. I think she'd do anything she thought her duty, whatever it cost her, but I can't find much more in her. She isn't lively, and she eats too much. When she isn't eating she plays at cards, and she must find that expensive because she nearly always loses. She never reads a book, and I've never heard her talk of state affairs or of anything that's serious.'

'Religion?'

'She doesn't talk of it, though she's staunch enough – Church of England to the last rubric. But she can't bear being left by herself, so when she isn't playing cards she must have her women to gossip with while she nibbles at her sugared nuts.'

'But how of yourself? What are your duties?'

'Much what they were with Monmouth. Sometimes I escort her in her coach when she goes out, and I think she likes to have me to talk to, as a change from the women. It's none of it important, but it's interesting, and of course it could lead to something more.'

'How of her husband?'

'He's pleasant enough. But have you met him?' John laughed outright. 'He's like a big friendly dog who trots round all day looking for a bit more to eat. He's kind and affectionate, and I think it's a happy marriage, but no one could take him very seriously.'

'What of Lord Churchill? Is he seen at the Cockpit?'

'Oh yes, a lot, and he seems to be chief adviser to the Princess in almost everything. But that reminds me – the Princess told me to say to you that when you are in London she hopes to receive you at the Cockpit.'

'She knows I'm here?'

'I'd mentioned it to Lord Churchill, and that's what reminded me. But she did say it, so I suppose it's a command.'

'If she told you to tell me, it is. When should I go, do you think?'

'She said she'd be free tomorrow morning.'

'Then I must. But try to be at hand yourself, to take me to her.'

John went cheerfully away, and an hour later Nicholas came to greet his father. He brought a touch of formality to it, almost the style of Westminster Hall, and Hal, duly noting this, was aware once more of the difference between his sons. Nicholas, with his clear incisive mind and his insistence on sound reasoning, could no more have spent his days in attendance on a princess than John, with his up-and-down spirits, could have become a barrister. And Harry, the youngest of the three, was different again, sturdy and practical, obviously happy as a soldier.

Nicholas accepted a glass of wine, and then came, without waste of words, to what he had to say.

'My apologies for being a little late,' he said. 'I had an appointment to see the Bishop of London.'

'Still your diocesan work?'

'No. I've finished at Wells. Their Chancellor is back at work, so I must try to get taken into the chambers of someone of note. You know what I mean? You work for some leading Counsel, looking up cases for him, making notes for him, and so on, and then, little by little, he'll begin to give you work to do in court as his junior.'

'And whose chambers do you wish to enter?'

'Any of the leading men. But they get so many applicants that you need someone to speak for you. So I asked Dr Ken and he said he didn't know any Counsel here, but he'd give me a letter to his brother of London, as he put it – meaning the Bishop – who perhaps would know somebody. Which I thought very likely.'

Hal nodded. The Bishop of London was Henry Compton, and he was alone among the bishops in being of noble birth. He had at first been an officer in the Horse Guards, but had soon left the army and taken holy orders, and then, with the royal favour behind him, he had advanced rapidly. He was an almost militant protestant, and the late King Charles, to allay some public fears, had insisted on his being tutor to the Duke of York's two daughters. He had given both princesses a protestantism as staunch as his own, and he was believed to be still on the happiest of terms with both of them. As Bishop of London he was known for his dislike of popery and his friendly attitude to dissenters, and he was held in esteem by almost everyone of importance in the City; which would surely include some barristers. Hal saw the point at once.

'Of course,' he said. 'So what have you done?'

'Dr Ken wrote the letter, and as soon as I was here I took it to London House.'

'In Aldersgate Street?' Hal nodded, remembering the residence of the Bishops of London. 'And then?'

'He sent for me yesterday, and he gave a little time to me, asking about religion and the sort of friends I had, and whether I was likely to turn papist or not. But I remembered that he'd been tutor to the Princess of Denmark, so I told him that I had a brother in her service at the Cockpit – and that did it. It turned out that he still visits her there, so he knows John and seems to approve. He said I had no doubt the same good principles as my brother, and I didn't like to tell him that John hasn't any.'

'Nick!'

'But he hasn't. He isn't at the Cockpit on principles of any sort. He just likes that sort of life, and thinks he'll do well at it. But I didn't say so.'

'I hope not. But go on.'

'It couldn't have been better. Of course he does know some barristers, and he said he'd have a word with two or three of them and ask if there was a place in chambers anywhere. So I thanked him dutifully, and I thought I'd have to wait a month or so before I heard any more. But not a bit of it. He sent for me again this evening, and he has it half arranged for me already – with Henry Pollexfen. Do you know him?'

'I've heard of him.'

Hal answered a little doubtfully. Mr Pollexfen was known to

be of Whig sympathies, and he had perhaps been too near the Green Ribbon Club for Hal's liking. But Nick pushed this aside.

'I really don't mind whether he's a Whig or not. He's second to none as a Counsel, and I can't think of any set of chambers in which I could learn more. Also, I met him lately, when the assize was at Wells, and I like him.'

'Then what are the chances?'

'I'll know tomorrow. The Bishop tells me to call on Pollexfen in the morning, at his rooms in the Temple.'

'Then I'll wish you success, and I'll expect to hear from you. Leave that till the afternoon, though, because I must be at the Cockpit in the morning. That's through John, as you'll have guessed.'

King Street, in Westminster, cut through the precincts of the Palace of Whitehall. The Galleries, the Banqueting Hall and the royal apartments lay between the street and the river, but the Cockpit stood on the other side of the street, away from the centre of things. Hal, arriving at mid-morning, was at once taken in charge by John, who was looking very pleased and self-possessed. Then, in an ante-room, Lord Churchill gave him courteous welcome.

'I'm most pleased to see you again,' he said. 'Your son is settling very well here, and Her Highness is beginning to value him. But I think it may be useful that you should yourself be known to her, since she needs to know her friends.'

'I hope I may be thought one of them.'

'Any man is her friend – ' For a moment he paused, looking straight at Hal with eyes that seemed to cut through all pretences. ' – who will give allegiance to both the royal house and the protestant religion. Not to one only, but equally to both – as I am sure you do. Come, therefore, to Her Highness.'

She was in the inner room, sitting a little stiffly as if she had been waiting for them, and Lord Churchill perfectly blended dignity with courtesy as he made the formal presentation. Hal, making his deepest bow and then standing in silence, thought she looked more than her twenty years, perhaps because she was plumper than she need have been, with a round full face and soft white hands. It seemed a friendly face, and good natured, but he thought she might be slow in movement, and perhaps in mind as well; and when he met her eyes he had the same impression, friendly and well intentioned, but slow, perhaps to the point of obstinacy. Her father, he remembered, was also slow and obstinate, and could perhaps be called well intentioned.

'I am well pleased to see you in my house, sir.' She spoke quietly, and he noted at once the sweetness and pleasant ring of her voice. 'I am told that you think as I do, and that I may count upon your services.'

'I trust so, ma'am.'

'I thank you also that you have spared your son for my service. I value his attendance and yours, Sir Harry, and I shall hold you in most happy memory.'

She lapsed into silence, as if she had no more to say, or perhaps could think of no more, and then suddenly her round face softened into a smile, and she held out her hand. Hal bowed over it at once, knowing that this was dismissal, but of the most gracious. Lord Churchill coughed discreetly.

'Then, if you will give leave, ma'am, to Sir Harry and me?'

'Of course. I shall expect, Sir Harry, to see you again, when next you are here. But, my lord, I had hoped for a word – '

'Indeed yes. One moment only.'

Lord Churchill had a quick and reassuring smile as he answered her, and then he led Hal at once to the ante-room. He spoke in a quick whisper.

'She wants me, so I must go back to her. But all is well, and I'm sure you have pleased her. John will show you out, and no doubt happily.'

He went back within, and Hal was left alone, not much regretting the end of an audience which he had found formal and difficult. But the Princess, he thought, had been friendly, and it was not her fault if she was slow in thought. Old Rowley, with his wit and gracious words, had gone, and that had to be accepted.

He went slowly out of the room, and at the head of the stair he stopped. Below him, in the entrance hall, a footman had swung open the outer door, and John, a few feet away, was making an elegant bow to a man who had just come in, in full clerical black and lawn sleeves. Hal recognized at once the Bishop of London.

'Good day to you, my lord,' said John, and he sounded very much on duty, with his voice crisp and easy, yet unmistakably welcoming. 'Her Highness, I am sure, will be glad of your coming, and I will tell her at once. At this moment my own father is in audience with her – '

'Your father?' There was a faint note of surprise. 'Then you must not disturb him.'

'Oh, as to that – '

Hal, at the top of the stair, perhaps moved. The Bishop looked up, John stopped, and Hal, accepting this, went slowly down the stair. The Bishop seemed to know him.

'Ah, Sir Harry – ' He spoke at once, and he sounded crisp and cool. 'I have seen you once or twice before, in and out of Parliament, and this is fortunate. But of Her Highness – ' He turned quickly to John. 'Would you therefore inquire?'

That disposed of John, who made his bow and at once went up the stair, showing nothing of any disappointment he may have felt. The Bishop took a moment for thought, and then brought his eyes to Hal.

'It's an odd chance that we should meet here. I've now met two of your sons.'

'Nicholas, I believe, has cause to be grateful to you.'

'No.' He seemed to sweep that aside. 'Sir Harry, you will be here for Parliament, no doubt?'

'Yes, and not very willingly.'

'I sit in the Lords, so we are both in Parliament, and perhaps we could both wish we were not. The King, being what he is, will not fail to notice how each of us speaks and votes, and there are many ways in which the royal displeasure may be felt. You understand me?'

'I think so.'

'It would be hard not to, in these days.' It came grimly, and then the steady tone returned. 'Men comfort themselves by saying that the storm is not upon us yet, and therefore we need do nothing yet. I cannot find that comfort.'

'Why?'

'Because from friends I have at Court – where I have no longer any favour myself – I learn that when the King meets his Parliament he will ask for money for his enlarged army. He means, I'm told, to keep it – permanently.'

'Oh!'

'Exactly.' For a moment the Bishop was silent, watching him steadily. 'You will not much like a standing army, Sir Harry. Nor will some other gentlemen.'

They certainly would not. The Commonwealth had taught them what a standing army could mean, and King James in command might be even worse than the Lord Protector. Hal stood silent, as tight-lipped now as the Bishop, thinking that the time of trouble might indeed be upon him if he were asked to vote for a standing army.

'Also,' said the Bishop quietly, 'he has put in some papist officers, and I'm told he will next demand the repeal of the Test Act so that he may continue with them. The whole Test Act.'

His voice died away, and again he stood watching Hal, who thought this as bad as the standing army, or perhaps worse. It had been expected that the King might ask Parliament to agree to his keeping the officers he had hastily appointed in emergency, but a repeal of the Act would go far beyond that. It would open every office to papists, and Hal would guess how the King would use such freedom. His thoughts must have shown in his face, and the Bishop nodded.

'Yes,' he said firmly. 'If those are his demands – a standing army, and the Test Act set aside so that he may put in whom her will as officers – where then will be our liberties? And where our Church?'

'We can but guess.'

'And are there two guesses? Sir Harry, you know the truth as well as I do.'

'I suppose so.' Hal spoke unhappily, and knew that he must make some better answer. 'My lord, if these demands should come, I shall both speak and vote against them.'

'Well said. But by your leave, it is not enough.'

'Not – '

'No.' The tone was incisive. 'This new House of Commons has many members new to Parliament, knowing nothing of ways and procedures, or of what is practicable and what is not. Can opposition to royal demands, made from the throne in all his state and dignity, be left to such men?'

'No.' Hal answered reluctantly, seeing dimly where this was going.

'Of course it can't. If opposition is to succeed it must be planned and guided by men who know what they are doing. And that, Sir Harry, means you, and some few like you, who have the will and the experience – and the courage.'

Hal stood silent, thinking unhappily that this was true. But it went against all the loyalties he had lived in; and it could be the surest path to the royal displeasure. The Bishop of London stood a little more erect, and in some indefinable way he had changed. He had been a man, talking to another. He seemed now to be the Bishop.

'Sir Harry, this work is needed. For the nation and for the Church it is needed. As an Englishman I commend it to you for the one. As a Bishop I commit it to you for the other. May God uphold you in it!'

6 *The Occasional Conformist*

Hal went back to the Bell feeling that wine was needed after so disturbing a talk. The notion that it might no longer be possible to serve both Church and King was not new to him. He had himself pointed it out to Mr Allway. But he had not, so far, thought of it as applying so clearly to himself, and he had now learned that it did. The Bishop had been persuasive, and authoritative too.

But there was more to come. He was still sitting in the wine-room, sunk in his thoughts, when a man of his own age came in, looking firm and confident. He glanced round, saw Hal, and at once came across to him.

'Good day to you, Burnaby. May I have a word?'

His voice was clear and pleasant, and it brought Hal to his feet to return the greeting. He had recognized Sir Thomas Mallory, whom he had known for several years as a fellow member of Parliament. But Mallory was an extreme Whig, who had been intimate with Shaftesbury, had belonged to the Green Ribbon Club, and had spoken and voted for the Exclusion Bill. Richard Gibson, in his days as a member, had been warm in approval of Mallory. But Hal had been on the other side. He had tended to avoid such men, and all that had existed between him and Mallory was the rather formal courtesy that custom required between members. It now required that Mallory should be heard, and Hal waved him to a chair and called for more wine.

'Thank you.' Mallory settled himself, looked thoughtfully at Hal, and then came to it abruptly. 'Burnaby, have you heard anything about the King's Speech, and what he intends to ask for?'

'A little.' They were back with the same topic, and Hal answered warily. 'What tale have you heard?'

It turned out to be almost exactly what the Bishop had said, except that in Mallory's version the King was likely to ask also for the repeal of the Habeas Corpus Act; and Hal was sufficiently startled to forget his caution and say this was the only protection a subject had against imprisonment by mere decree of the King.

'Exactly,' said Mallory. 'And a repeal of the Test Act would be as bad, or even worse. As for his army, he has already added eight regiments of horse and twelve of foot, and I think you will like the thought of keeping them as little as I do.'

'But do not, please, suppose that I have turned Whig.'

'I do not suppose it, and I do not ask it.' Mallory's voice was clear and firm, but his tone was that of one who discusses with an equal, without trying to impose his views. 'What I do ask is that on this occasion you should join with me and some others – not all of them Whigs – in a concerted resistance. Is that reasonable?'

The question was quiet and courteous, but it was challenging, and for a long moment Hal was silent, not liking to be in concert with a Whig for even this. But it was very reasonable, and it was what the Bishop of London had asked of him – had done rather more than ask.

'If these demands are made,' he answered slowly, 'I must certainly stand against them.'

'But something concerted is needed, and I'm sure you'll see why. You know what our new members are like?'

He was again saying what the Bishop had said, but because he was a House of Commons man he was more precise about it. He could see the details better.

'We have courtiers in the House, quite a number of them,' he said. 'I mean men whose main hope is something for themselves, a place, a knighthood, or a grant of land, and in hope of getting it they'll do anything the King requires. If he makes these demands in his Speech, they'll certainly put down motions to give effect to them. And our problem isn't to argue against the Speech. It's to make sure that such motions come to nothing. How would you describe these new members?'

'Simple country gentlemen, deeply loyal, and full of good intentions – and they won't know what to do. They'll think it near treason to resist the King, but they loathe all thought of standing armies, and they cherish the Test Act. They'll be bewildered to know their duty.'

'An excellent word.' Mallory nodded approval. 'But they're too raw to the House, too new to procedures, to know that you don't always need to defeat a motion to bring it to nothing. You can talk it out, or halt it on procedure, or move friendly amendments that will make it unworkable. There are a dozen ways of doing it. But once these men understand that they may keep the Test Act and reject the standing army, while still not openly voting against the King – then what?'

He fell silent, waiting for an answer, and too wise to press for it. Hal took his time, and could find no flaw in this. It was perhaps deceptive, but it was within the customs of the House and it was the only practicable way. Men who could never bring themselves to vote openly against the King might grasp thankfully at this.

'Do you know Edmund Innes?'

Mallory's quiet voice broke in, and the change of topic was almost a relief. Edmund Innes was a successful banker who for several years, until the last election, had been one of the City members in the Commons. He was a quiet and moderate Whig who had supported the Exclusion Bills but not the Green Ribbon Club, and he had the name of an honest and upright man, courteous to everyone and liked by most. Only in one matter did Hal view him with a shade of doubt. Innes made no secret of it that he was by choice and upbringing a Baptist, but he had from time to time complied with the Test Act, receiving Communion in his parish church on a Sunday morning, and thus qualifying himself to sit in Parliament. But, like some others, he had done this only when it was needed, and in between he had been plainly and openly a Baptist. He was indeed one of the most influential of their laity, and he did not seem to share Hal's doubts about the propriety of this occasional conformity.

'He agrees that something must be done,' said Mallory, 'and he has asked some of us to his house tonight to see if we can settle on a course of action. I think a dozen or so will be there, not all of them Whigs. I'm glad to say that Meres will be one of them, because he may be useful.'

Hal nodded, seeing at once what was meant. Sir Thomas Meres, another moderate Whig, was known to be a staunch Anglican who would have no dealings with popery, but he was specially noted for his intimate knowledge of the rules and procedures of the House, and of its moods and feelings. He might be just the man to advise on this awkward problem.

'So will you come also?' Mallory's voice was earnest now. 'We need you. These men we must appeal to, the new members, will listen more readily to men like you than to us who are known as Whigs. So will you come?'

'I think perhaps I must.'

Hal answered reluctantly, and when Mallory had gone he stayed quietly in the wine-room, trying to reassure himself, seeing no other answer he could have given, and yet recognizing that he was now doing exactly what Richard Gibson would have done, and what he would himself, only a few weeks ago, have condemned as Whiggery. Yet he had not changed. The change was in affairs.

He was disturbed by the arrival of Nicholas, looking very pleased and buoyant, to report that he had made his call on Mr Pollexfen and had got what he wanted. He had been accepted as a pupil.

'He wasn't easy,' he said cheerfully. 'He wasn't taking me for granted at all, and he had a lot of questions to ask, but he said in the end he was satisfied. I can start on Monday.'

'Excellent. And on your side, are *you* satisfied?'

'Very. I like Pollexfen, and I'm sure I can work with him. And there couldn't be a better man to make a start with. If I don't get on now, it will be my own fault.'

'I don't think you need fear that.'

'I hope not. He's been helpful in another way too. He has a big set of chambers there, with a room or two to spare, so I can live there in the Temple, which will be a help. Cheaper too.'

'Again excellent.'

'I get the vacations clear. He says there are usually a few things to clear up when the Law term ends, but that's only a day or two, and then I can go off during vacation.'

'You seem to have had a successful morning.'

'Oh, I have. And I must thank the Bishop of London.'

'Ye-es.' Some thoughts returned of the Bishop. 'Yes, thank him.'

Mr Innes, as became a banker, had his house in Lombard Street, where the sign of the Scales showed above his counting-house. Above it he lived in elegance and comfort, and Hal was taken up the stair to a parlour that was bright with candles, and with sparkling glass on the glowing mahogany table. Mr Innes gave him wine and welcome, and asked if he knew the half-dozen men who were already there.

'You do? Excellent.' He nodded. 'I'm glad you are here, Sir

Harry, and that you, also, think this meeting necessary – Ah, Sir Thomas! Be welcome, sir.'

Sir Thomas Meres had just entered the room, quiet, slender, and scholarly, and Innes became the host again. Almost at once another man came in, then another and another, and there were fourteen of them round the table when Innes at last brought them to business.

'This,' he told them briefly, 'will be a matter of tactics, of rules and procedures, of persuading men who do not yet know their minds, and we should begin, I am sure, by hearing Sir Thomas Meres.'

He sat at the head of the table next to Meres, who spoke quietly and informally. He began by repeating what Mallory had said to Hal, that decision lay with some two hundred new Tory members, torn between a deep loyalty and an equally deep dislike of popery and standing armies. For the Habeas Corpus Act they would be less concerned, since some of them hardly knew what it was.

'These are the men to think of,' he said again, 'and what we must bear in mind at every moment is their veneration of the King. It is almost a religion with them, and if we offend against it we shall send every man of them to the King's defence, all matters such as standing armies notwithstanding. We must therefore speak of the King always with deep respect, whatever our feelings may be, and we must not seem hostile towards him, or unreasonable. If, for example, we should speak of the late rebellion in the west, we must in no way seem to condone it, or exclaim that any have been treated too harshly.'

'What!' From the back of the room a man spoke angrily, a Mr Windham who sat for Salisbury. 'It is a country now of gibbets, of corpses daubed with pitch, and stinking. It's a country of fear, and – '

'I dare say it is. I doubt you not at all. But it's these two hundred Tories we must think of, and their feelings about the King. We must *not* speak disrespect of him, or any open criticism. Or at least, not directly.' He paused, looking Mr Windham in the eye. 'You might, perhaps, say that you have seen in the west how the army is getting out of hand. Should it not, therefore, be reduced before it becomes a danger to him as well as to us? I don't think they'd call that disrespect.'

'But would they swallow it?'

'They dislike the army as much as we do, and if they're told they can vote against it for the King's own sake, they might take that at a gulp and not look for flaws in the argument. Likewise, if it be a matter of the Test Act he would have repealed, I do not think we can vote straight against him. We should do better to move, say, that a Humble Address be presented to His Majesty, begging that he may give such assurances as may quiet tender consciences. I'm not sure what that means, but the effect would be the same. He wouldn't give the assurances, and the Act would stay.'

'You sly old fox,' said Mallory. 'We'll do it like that.'

There was a murmur of agreement in the room. But then someone asked whether it would be enough merely to give a lead in the House. Inexperienced members might not understand it. Ought it not to be explained to them first? But once again Sir Thomas Meres had the answer ready. They would have to wait till Monday, and then, if the King's Speech was what they expected, they must press for a few days' delay before the House discussed it. A delay, he said, might be welcome to many an unhappy member, and was therefore likely to be carried, and it would give them time to persuade and teach an opposition.

There was general assent, blended with admiration of Meres' adroitness, and this brought them to the end of their business. The meeting broke up, and Hal was about to take leave when Edmund Innes surprisingly took him aside. He spoke in a hurried whisper.

'I had hoped for a word in private with you, Sir Harry. On quite another matter. So if you could perhaps stay a few minutes – '

'Certainly, if you wish.'

Hal stepped back, surprised and unable to guess what this occasional-conformist banker could wish to say to him. He stood by the fire while the others one by one took leave and went. Innes was pleasant and courteous with each of them, but when the last had gone he was looking grave as he came back to Hal.

'This touches my sister, Sir Harry, and her unfortunate son. You know of them?'

'No?' Hal was feeling bewildered now.

'You have not been told?' For a moment Innes was looking surprised. 'I have a sister, a little younger than myself, who lives in Bridgwater. A Mrs Allinson, though she's been widowed now some years. Her husband was a clothier there.'

'Yes?'

'A Baptist.' He was hesitant now, as if he were finding this difficult. 'They all were. He and Elizabeth – that's my sister – and their two children. A boy and a girl. I was myself bred a Baptist, as you'll perhaps know.'

'I've heard it.' Hal answered softly, with an uneasy feeling that tragedy was lurking in this tale. That mention of Bridgwater had been ominous, and dissenters.

'They all were.' Innes repeated the words as if a memory held him, and then he steadied his voice. 'And because of it they had some sympathy with the Duke of Monmouth when he made his venture there. At the least they wished him well, and they hardly made a secret of that. There were many such in Bridgwater.'

'Which is why the town suffered so.'

'Suffered indeed. They turned it to a slaughterhouse.' Again he had to steady his voice. 'But it's of Richard I'm trying to speak, my sister's boy. He was just twenty years old, young and eager, and it is not quite clear what he did that night.'

'Before the battle?'

'Yes. You will remember that the Duke was in Bridgwater throughout that Sunday, and that he led his men out for a night attack when dark had come. Richard, it seems, went after them, or with them, though he said to the end that he took no part with them, but wished only to learn what was happening on the moor. But you'll guess the rest. He was taken next morning as he tried to make his way home, and that was enough. Denials were of no use with that sort of assize. How could they be?'

'No. But what – '

'They hanged him, within sight of his mother's house, and his quarters were put on pikes, daubed with pitch, where his mother might see them if she went a-marketing. Can you guess what state she was in – his mother?'

'No.' The answer was short. 'It's beyond my wits, or any man's. A woman might know.'

'You say it well. Though one man, perhaps, came near to it. But you'll be asking why I tell you of this.' Again he stopped, as if he had now to seek for words. 'We, as Baptists, have no great cause to love the Church of England. But in the west country there was one who, in this strait, thought of us only as his fellow creatures, and fellow Christians. I mean your Bishop there, of Bath and Wells.'

'Ken?'

'Who else?' Innes came suddenly to a warmer tone. 'He would show compassion, though he could not obtain mercy, and as the judges rode out of Bridgwater the Bishop rode in. And Father in God he was. From his own purse he relieved the wants of many, especially the prisoners, and with his thoughts and prayers he gave hope to many who were in grief and anguish. One of these was my sister, and to her he showed also some good worldly sense. He saw at once that Elizabeth could not remain in Bridgwater, nor Judith either. They'd have gone near mad in that place.'

'Who is Judith?'

'Her daughter, my niece. Just two years older than her brother, and much attached to him. This was not a moment to ask where they might go, but the Bishop had them out of Bridgwater at once, sending them to his own house at Wells.'

'I had a son there, in the Bishop's service, but I had not heard of this.'

'Which is why I now tell you. This Bishop uses no state, and he rode into Bridgwater with no more than his body-servant and one attendant – being your son. It was he who escorted them, mother and daughter, to Wells and saw to their comforts there.'

'Nicholas? Then I think he did well.'

'Very well, and it did not end there. For the next day, he rode to Salisbury, where my sister had friends, asking if they would receive her, and three days later he took her there, she being with Judith in the Bishop's coach, and he riding with sword and pistols as their escort. It was a service greatly needed at that time, and his own thought, too, not the Bishop's, who had not yet returned to Wells.'

'He has told me nothing of this.'

'My sister would tell you that without him she could never have made that journey. She was in need of kindness then, and she is deeply grateful.' For a moment he looked steadily at Hal. 'She is my only sister, and I, too, am grateful. I have never met your son, but I wish to. But I am told that he has now left Wells?'

'He is in London.'

Hal explained it briefly, and Innes nodded a quick understanding of it.

'This is fortunate,' he said. 'I have known Pollexfen for many years, and think highly of him. But I wish to speak my thanks direct to your Nicholas. You would not object if I were to invite him here?'

'Indeed I should not.'

It was the only possible answer, but it hid some feelings of disquiet. Pollexfen was a Whig. Innes was another, and a dissenter too, and Hal wondered what sort of influence they would have on Nick. Their very worth and probity would make their influence stronger, and thoughts began to rise of Nick moving steadily, week by week, towards Whiggery; which was not Hal's wish for his son. He walked slowly back to the Bell, brooding on it, until the thought came shooting in that he was moving in precisely that direction himself. He had just been to a Whig meeting which had agreed on a Whig plan; and Richard Gibson would have told him he was learning sense at last. It was disconcerting, and it made him turn his thoughts to this tale of Nick escorting those women to Wells, and then to Salisbury. That, at least, was to his credit, and the more so because he had not tried to take the credit. He had said nothing, and he must be asked about it when the chance came.

It did not come immediately. This was Saturday, and Nick did not appear on the Sunday. He was no doubt busy with his own arrangements. Then Parliament met, and at once Hal had more to think about. King James, wrapped in the robes of state and a dignity he seemed always to be insisting on, told them in cold and hostile tones that he had decided to keep his extra regiments. In future, therefore, the cost of the army would be twice what it had been; and he expected Parliament to supply the money for this. He had appointed some officers who had not complied with the Test Act, and he had determined to keep them permanently, since they were men whose help he might at any time need. Which, as a member was heard to mutter afterwards, seemed to be his way of saying that he had broken the law and meant to go on breaking it.

The Commons returned to their own chamber, and at once the plan that had been made in Lombard Street was put into action. Persuasively, moderately, and in phrases of deep respect to the King, it was argued that discussion of so important a Speech should be postponed, that members might have time to consider it first; and this, to the consternation of the Court party, was carried. The new members were as glad of a delay as Sir Thomas Meres had predicted, and they responded quickly when they were approached by Hal and the others with suggestions that it might be worth while to talk this over and see if a way could be found. This, for Hal, led to his playing host at the Bell, on the Wednesday evening, to a dozen or so of worried men, who plainly found relief in speaking their troubles aloud, and learning that others had them too. Then he had no great problem in persuading them that a way did exist if they would only follow the lead of Meres and himself. He did not mention Mallory, the extreme Whig.

But later that evening Nick came again to the Bell, bringing with him Tom Culley, who had not been seen since the memorial service in July. He came breezily in, big and broad shouldered like his father, and explained that his ship was again at Gravesend, and that he had been having a few days' leave at his home. He was now on his way to rejoin, but he had stopped for a night with Nick. The pair of them stayed for supper at the Bell, and not till the meal had ended was Hal able to break into their talk and put a question of his own.

'Tom,' he said, 'I've heard nothing of your father and mother for weeks past. Tell me how they are, please, since you've just come from them.'

'Oh, my father talks politics all day. He's disgruntled. He doesn't like the set of the wind, and he's been saying he'll try for Parliament himself at the next election. He's taken to good works too, it seems, or at least to relieving the needy.' Tom's voice changed and he sounded less happy. 'Some folk from the west country have come lately to Salisbury and its parts, fleeing from what has been done, and I think, Nick, that it was your Bishop, your Dr Ken, who set him thinking that some notice should be taken of these people.'

'It might well be. If ever a man gave help and charity – '

'I don't know about the charity, but as for help – what about you?' Abruptly his tone changed again. 'What about the grieving widow you took to Salisbury, with the alluring daughter?'

'Tom! What are you talking about?'

'You.' Tom was laughing openly as he saw how Nicholas had jerked upright. 'From what I've learned, she allured entrancingly.'

'I don't know what you've been told, or who told you.'

'Don't you? But it seems you left her in Salisbury and rode out to see my father and mother.'

'Of course I did. They're only five miles out.'

'And you seem to have said enough about the daughter to set my father riding into Salisbury to have a look at her himself. He called on her mother, and that was when he started talking about relieving the necessities of the unfortunate. Just like Dr Ken. But he certainly seems impressed with the daughter. What's her name, by the way?'

'Judith.' Nicholas answered with a fine air of self-possession. 'But you're making much out of nothing, or your father is.'

'It's not quite nothing,' said Hal. 'I've heard something of it already, Nick.'

He waited for a moment, watching Nick carefully. This fitted the tale he had heard from Innes, but it certainly threw a different light on it, and one that he did not altogether welcome. But he could hardly say so now, while Tom was sitting there in amusement.

'I heard it the other day,' he said, 'when I was in talk with Edmund Innes, the banker. Do you know him?'

'I've heard of him.'

'It seems that this Mrs Allinson whom you took to Salisbury is his sister. Did you know that?'

'Judith said something of it.'

'Quite so. But what Innes said to me was that the service you rendered was very far from being nothing. He thinks it was a service greatly needed and well given. And because he is fond of his sister – and I suppose of his niece too – he adds his own gratitude to theirs.'

'He need not.'

'But he does, and he therefore asks that you shall call upon him in Lombard Street. He wishes a direct word with you.'

'Oh!'

'He's a man of influence, Nick. He's listened to in the City, and he might at some time be able to pull a string that would help you. So, courtesy apart, if he asks you to call, you'd be foolish not to.'

'You'd be downright mad,' said Tom heartily. 'If the niece is lovely, that's splendid, but if she has a rich and doting uncle too – '

'Don't talk like that. It wasn't funny at Bridgwater, and at Wells.'

'I don't suppose it was.' Tom looked calmly back at Nick. 'All the same, if something good comes out of it afterwards, you needn't throw it away. And this reminds me – where are you going for Christmas? Because my mother told me to tell you she'll make you welcome in her house if you care to go there.'

'At Salisbury? Now why – '

'She didn't say why. She just sent the invitation.'

'What have you in mind for it, Nick?' Hal spoke easily, thinking that this had gone far enough, and that Nick was showing signs of annoyance. 'Your mother will wish to see you, of course, but it's a long road for a short vacation.'

'You'll be taking it, I suppose?'

'I don't know that I shall. If Parliament is busy, it can sit through Christmas, and this year we're very busy. We're still six weeks from Christmas, so it may be a month or more before I know.'

But it was much less than that. The Commons met again the next morning, and, with most of the new members following the advice they had been given, it refused to consider money until it had discussed the King's disregard for the Test Act. The Humble Address, asking for assurances, was made and sent to the King, who quickly showed his displeasure in an angry and upbraiding speech to them. But the next day the attack began in the Lords, where some plain words were spoken about the new regiments and the papist officers, the plainest and most trenchant coming from the Bishop of London. The King's patience broke, and the next morning the Lord Chancellor spoke on his behalf the words of prorogation. The sittings ended abruptly; and for Hal, and all the others, there was nothing to do but go home.

7 *Judith*

Hal was home a few days later, sure that he had seen the last of this Parliament, and that it would be many a day before he need be in London again. In fact he was to be there within months, but not for Parliament or for politics of any kind. It was to be entirely because of Nicholas – and Judith Allinson.

It had become quite clear that Tom Culley's jesting tale had contained the truth, and that Nick was very much in earnest about this Judith. He was, indeed, no longer denying it, but he was saying as little about it as he could. Almost the only clear fact to emerge from his letters was that Judith's mother had never recovered from the shock of her son's dreadful death. She had become a semi-invalid, showing little interest in anyone and requiring constant care. There was no one to do this but Judith, and Nick had given this as his reason for not coming home at Christmas, but going instead to the Culleys' house near Salisbury. He had done the same in the short breaks at Easter and Whitsuntide, saying that otherwise he would not have seen Judith at all. It seemed reasonable, but his parents had not yet seen Judith, and they thought they should. Alison became terse about it.

'I'm not exactly objecting,' she told Hal. 'I can't very well object when I haven't seen her. She may be just the girl for him. But the fact remains that I haven't seen her, and it's high time I did.'

'We could, I suppose, invite ourselves to the Culleys for a visit. She's your sister.'

'I don't like doing it, Hal. We haven't been there for years, and to go just now would make it obvious that we were just looking at Judith. It would be embarrassing for everyone.'

'Ye-es.'

The discussion went no further, and matters were still in this unsatisfactory state when, in the middle of July, Nick wrote to say that he would be coming home in the summer vacation. He wished to see his parents. He would come as soon as the Law term ended, and he would stay till the end of August. He would have to leave them then, because in September he must go to Salisbury with Mr Innes. He would explain this when he was with them.

This, again, was not quite satisfactory. Alison said she would not agree to anything till she had seen Judith, and Hal said the same with an edge in his voice. He was in fact in no good humour. He had been put out of it a day or two earlier by the announcement that the King had appointed, under the Great Seal, a body of Commissioners for Ecclesiastical Affairs, to whom he had entrusted the entire government of the Church of England and its clergy. Hal read the details, and began to think that oppression of the Church and clergy would have been a better way of putting it. The Commission seemed to have almost unlimited powers. It could require or forbid almost anything, and to enforce its decrees it could deprive any parson of his benefice, and even declare him incapable of holding another for the rest of his life. It had been set up on the sole authority of the King, without any support in law that Hal could think of; and its President was to be Lord Chancellor Jeffreys, which was a fair indication of how it would behave. Hal had been appalled, and he had been in no way soothed by visits from the Rector and Richard Gibson, each saying what he might have been expected to say. He was still angry and disturbed, and this would not have been a good moment to ask him for a marriage contract or anything else.

But Nick, when he arrived early in August, made no request for a marriage contract. He admitted that he and Judith did not yet know each other well enough for that. For weeks at a time, as he pointed out, he had been stuck in London and she in Salisbury, and even on his visits they had been together only when she could get an hour or two away from her mother.

The admission made things easier, and he had two sympathetic listeners when he spoke of Edmund Innes. As far back as last November, he reminded Hal, he had been invited to the house in Lombard Street. He had called, and had been asked to call again, and was now a regular visitor there, having come to what he thought very good terms with Innes; which, he drily added, was fortunate, since Innes was not only Judith's uncle but seemed to think that he had now some further responsibilities to her.

'Though, mind you,' he said, 'I've not been going to him only for that reason. I really like him. He's a man I think very well of, even if they do call him an occasional conformist.'

'I'm glad you do. But what's this of going to Salisbury with him?'

'It's for Mrs Allinson – Judith's mother. She doesn't mend, and he's much concerned for her. He's been there once to see her, and now he says he'll go again in September, and this time, if he thinks her at all fit for a journey, he'll bring her back to London with him. Judith too, of course, and he'll have them for a winter in his own house, where she can be properly looked after and have the best physicians.'

'And you go with Mr Innes on this journey?'

'I thought I should. In these days he isn't much used to journeys, and this is going to be a difficult one. He'll have enough to do looking after his sister while I see to bags and ostlers and that sort of thing.'

It was still very reasonable, and nothing could be said against it. But, as Alison said a little later, it would suit Nick perfectly. His Judith would no longer be far away in Salisbury. She would be close at hand in London, in a house that he visited frequently, and she would have less to do for her mother. It was so happy an arrangement for Nick that Alison began to wonder if he had suggested it himself, or at least dropped the thought where Innes could pick it up and suppose it to be his own.

'I think he's wily enough for that,' she told Hal. 'He's always had a trick of doing his thinking carefully, and he won't have lost the habit because he's a lawyer. What will he do next, do you think?'

'Take his chance while he has it. Pay court to Judith through the winter.'

'And then ask for a marriage contract? Hal, we *must* see this Judith. It's becoming urgent, and if need be I shall have to tell Nick so.'

But there was no need to tell him. He came to the matter himself, and his way with it made Alison even more sure that he had done his thinking carefully.

'I'd like you to meet Judith,' he told his mother the next night. 'It would make things easier.'

'But how's it to be done? Do you think of asking her here?'

'How can I? It seems early for that. Besides, I can't yet ask her to take a journey with me alone.'

'You certainly can't.'

'I suppose – ' He looked at her carefully and then came out with it. 'I suppose you couldn't come to London for a few days in September?'

'London?'

'But why not?' He was speaking quickly now. 'It's before the winter. The roads should still be good, and the days could be pleasant. And how long is it since you were last in London? You must want to do some shopping.'

'Must I?'

'I'd have thought so. And you haven't seen John and young Richard for more than a year, or the Crosedales either.'

'Oh!'

She turned to Hal, and he knew at once that she had taken the bait. It had been well judged, and it was all quite true. She did wish to see John and Richard; and there was much to be said for buying some new clothes in London. Nick had certainly done his thinking.

'You've all the reasons for coming,' he said firmly, 'and you can tell them to anyone. It wouldn't look in the least as if you'd come to see Judith.'

She looked across at Hal, and he took only a moment for thought. Then, a little amused and not displeased, he nodded agreement, and the thing was settled there and then. Nick, who had it all ready, went on to explain that Judith could hardly be in London before the third week of September.

Hal and Alison travelled accordingly, and they were in London by September 15th, which was a Wednesday. From the Bell they sent word of their coming to John, and to Nick's rooms at the Temple. There was no response from Nick, but John appeared in the evening, looking pleased and cheerful. He had now been for more than a year in the service of the Princess of Denmark, and he seemed better for it, showing a happy confidence, as if he liked his work and had never even heard of the Duke of Monmouth. He apologized for being late, saying that he had been kept busy at the Cockpit.

'We've been at Windsor,' he explained. 'The King's been on a progress in the west country, round by Bristol and Bridgwater, and he had a look at Sedgemoor on the way. I don't think he had much of a welcome in those parts, and when he was back he said he was going to Windsor for a while. The Princess thought she ought to join him there for a day or two, so we went. That's to say she took me with her. We came back yesterday, and today we've had a stream of people at the Cockpit, paying respects on her return. That's what kept me.'

'Part of your work, John. But where's the King?'

'Still at Windsor, thank heaven! But he'll be back next week, or thereabouts. How long are you here for?'

'Not long. Just to see you all. Is Nick back yet?'

'I don't think so.'

'Trouble at Salisbury, perhaps, with Mrs Allinson.'

'That's what he was hoping for.'

'Hoping?'

'So that he'd have some time with his Judith. He talked of borrowing Uncle Culley's horses, and then riding with her on Salisbury Plain.'

'The devil he did!'

'He'll probably do it, too. I know you say I have a trick of making people like me, but I think Nick's getting pretty good at it. He'll get the horses.'

'Then we must wait till he's finished with them. How is Doraty?'

'Excellent. And she's another, by the way, who wants to see this Judith. She says Nick will be much better wed if Judith is the right one for him, but she'd like to have a look herself to make sure. She's quite protective about Nick.'

Nick came walking into the Bell the next evening. They had reached Lombard Street at the end of the afternoon, he said, and he had stayed for an early supper, and then gone to the Temple for a change of clothes.

'You look well,' said Alison. 'Are you tired?'

'Not a bit. We travelled too slowly for that.'

'And the others?'

'Mr Innes is glad to be back. He doesn't really like riding. Mrs Allinson is about as before, which means she droops. But she wasn't really any trouble. She didn't like coming, though.'

'Why not?'

'She wants to go back to Bridgwater, for memories, and of course she mustn't.'

'Indeed she mustn't. And Judith?'

'Exasperated. She's had three days in a coach with her mother.'

'Poor Judith!'

'It should be easier for her now. Mr Innes has given his sister a parlour of her own, as well as the best bedroom, and he has a waiting woman to care for her and see to her comforts. So it should mean less for Judith. But you'll wish to see her?'

'Of course.'

'Sunday, if you will. Mr Innes thinks his sister needs a day or two of quiet before she sees anyone, so he asks us all to go to dinner there on Sunday, after church.'

That was quickly accepted, and Hal and Alison went to Lombard Street accordingly. Innes gave them courteous welcome, but he had a careful eye on Alison, who stood intent for a moment and then eased into a smile. He obviously saw it, and he seemed easier for it.

'I'm glad indeed to meet you,' he said, 'and it's perhaps time I did, from – er – what my niece tells me. Where is she, I wonder?'

She came into the room at that moment, Nick with her, and then at once she stopped, standing quiet and composed as she waited to be presented. She was less tall than Hal had expected, but she was slim, seeming perfectly proportioned to her height, and she was sturdy and forceful, giving an unmistakable impression of strength and vitality. She was no classical beauty, but her face seemed to suit the rest of her, rather round, fresh and clear, with a slightly upturned nose, very white teeth and two vivid grey-blue eyes, and hair that was something between brown and gold. She stood well, looking lively and alert, and when she made her curtsey Hal noticed that she did it confidently, keeping a delicate balance that was always under control. He would have been surprised if it had not been.

She rose from her curtsey, very solemn and proper, and then she must have seen something in Alison that encouraged her. Her face changed, the solemnity left it, and a smile leaped into being that was dazzling in its light and warmth. Even Hal, standing apart, felt the effect of it, and Alison, much nearer, was at once smiling herself. She spoke approvingly.

'Thank you, Judith. I'm glad to see you. It's time we met.'

'It certainly is.' Judith sounded emphatic about it. 'You could say it's been all the wrong way, so far.'

'What has?'

'Oh – ' She glanced for a moment at Nick. 'All of it. But there was only my mother there, at Salisbury, and she didn't notice anything. She didn't always notice that Nick was even there, so we were left by ourselves, and I suppose we shouldn't have been.'

'It was a little early for it, certainly, but I can understand it.'

'Oh! I'm so glad.'

'I think, Judith, that in that west country, at that time, a great deal was being done that was very much more wrong than merely knowing each other a little quickly. So put it out of your mind. You should be looking forward now, not back.'

'I'm trying to.'

'It's the only way to forget.'

'Yes.' Judith's lips quivered for a moment. 'I've learnt that.'

'Then hold to it. Nick, you must help her to.' She glanced at him for an instant, and then came back to Judith. 'Don't let anyone persuade you not to, not even your mother. But how is she? Does she improve?'

'Not really. She's stronger, but she still won't look at the present. She's all in the past. I'd thought she'd heed my uncle, but I don't think she does.'

'I fail completely,' said Innes, 'and I'm near my wit's end. But is she ready to receive us?'

'As near as I could get her. Which isn't very far.'

'No.' He spoke gruffly, and then turned to Alison. 'I think you should meet my sister, if only briefly. Despite these troubles, she is Judith's mother still.'

Alison nodded in assent, and the others followed as he led to a smaller parlour at the back of the house, away from the street and quieter. It was warm and peaceful, with sunlight in the window and a fire burning brightly. Mrs Allinson, lying on a daybed, was in full black, broken only by a white lace collar and a little white cap, and with this, and her pale face and listless air, she seemed at first to be an old lady in the last years of life, which she certainly was not. Innes spoke clearly to her, telling her who the visitors were, and for a moment she made some effort to respond. But she seemed to be thinking of Nick, rather than of his parents.

'Yes,' she said slowly. 'He was very good to us, and the other man too, and we are most grateful. I ought to thank the other too, but he went away.'

'The Bishop,' said Nick quickly. 'Of Bath and Wells.'

'Was he? But he was kind. He was kind when the other men were being – oh, you know what they did. I can't say it.'

'Don't try to say it,' said Alison. 'You are here to rest now, and you may soon find a proper life again.'

'What do I want with life? And I shouldn't be here. It was in Bridgwater they did it, and I must be there. I'm being false to him coming here, and they tell me to forget. I can't even put flowers – '

'Elizabeth!'

Her brother's sharp interjection checked her, and for a moment she looked bewildered, as if she had lost her thought and could find no other. Then she found one near to it.

'I want to walk in the lanes again, where the summer flowers are. We used to walk there together. He had a dog.'

She burst suddenly into tears, forgetting all of them as the memory flooded into her and overwhelmed her, and at once Judith intervened. She ran to her mother's side, and with one imperious wave of the hand she as good as told the others to be out of the room. Innes took the hint at once, and led them back to the larger parlour, where he carefully shut the door.

'I'm sorry,' he said simply. 'I feared it would be so, though I had hoped for better. But that's the mood she's in, and she seems determined not to mend.'

'What do the physicians say?'

'Much that sounds learned and helps not at all. Nothing wrong with her except that she will not mend. She refuses to face her grief, this being the easier way. I think that's what it comes to, but it's hard on Judith.'

'Very,' said Alison. 'And Judith accepts it?'

'Yes, though I'm not sure that she should. In this matter I'm no longer sure what is right and what is wrong. Should she turn from whatever she may have hoped for in her own life?'

'I think – ' For an instant Alison glanced at Nick, who was standing stiff and tense. 'I think that if Judith can bring herself to give this service to her mother, she should do so only for a time, not for ever.'

The door opened before he could answer, and Judith came briskly in, even managing a smile for Alison. But she spoke first to her uncle.

'A little better,' she told him. 'I've given her four drams of the electuary the physician sent, and it should make her sleep. Mrs Warburton is with her now, and will call me at need.'

'Thank you.' He matched his tone to hers. 'Then let us now go to dinner.'

He plainly tried, through the meal, to keep the talk from Mrs Allinson, and in the main he succeeded, but not entirely. A gentle question from Alison brought immediate admission by Nick that he and Judith had indeed been riding on Salisbury Plain, using Nick Culley's horses. Judith, after a moment's hesitation, lifted her head and agreed.

'I had to get out,' she said slowly, 'and I had to talk. I can, to Nick.' Then she looked Alison straight in the eye. 'I'm not saying there was no more than that to it. Of course there was. But I had to get out.'

'I'm sure you had. And now that you're in London, Judith, I hope you'll be out quite often, and meet people.'

'She's starting tomorrow,' said Nick calmly. 'Doraty has invited us to dinner, and John is going to take her into Whitehall Palace for a walk round. She's never seen it.'

'Excellent. And a good moment, while the King is still at Windsor.'

Hal said little, thinking that it would be better left to Alison, but later, in the Bell, he asked what she really thought of all this, and of Judith.

'You were very easy with her,' he said. 'You seemed even to encourage her.'

'Ye-es. Do you disagree?'

'Not really. I couldn't help liking her. And that mother's impossible. Do you really think there's excuse enough for her behaviour?'

'I don't know. They quartered the boy after they'd hanged him, daubed his quarters with pitch and hung them within sight of her house – and I can't measure what that would do to a woman. So I'll say nothing. But I like Judith, and I think she and Nick might suit each other very well. So for the present, while Judith is tied up with her mother, I'm content to leave it alone and see what happens.'

'I doubt if Nick will leave it alone. He'll try to push it along, and from what I see of Judith I'd perhaps think him stupid if he didn't.'

'So she's conquered *you,* has she?' She laughed outright for a moment. 'I'll accept that, Hal. But I'm glad Doraty has invited them to dinner. She's no sort of fool, and she's just Judith's age, and able to look clearly at her. So I'll be interested to hear what she thinks.'

They learned that later in the week, when Doraty came to the Bell to see them, and it was at once clear that she approved.

'I like Judith,' she said. 'She's properly alive and awake, and she has a good clear mind and plenty of good sense. And certainly some notions about duty. I think Nick will do very well with her, and if he needs a little push – as I think he sometimes does – she'll give it to him, and in the right direction too. He's lucky, and she is too. Have you heard Harry about her?'

'I didn't know he'd met her.'

'He wasn't supposed to. Nick had told him to keep out of sight, because he didn't know how Judith would take to a red-coated soldier just now. But John took her to Whitehall on Monday to see the Palace, and when they went under the Gate the first man they saw was Harry – on duty with the Guard. Awkward!' Doraty began to laugh. 'Neither of them knew what to say, and then Judith said "Oh, are you the soldier brother?", and it turned out she's known all about him for weeks past – from Uncle Culley, of course.'

'Did she mind?'

'Not in the least. Of course his regiment wasn't there *after* the battle, and that's what counted. So she walked round the Palace between the two of them, and from what she said to me she didn't at all mind having scarlet and gold with her, and sentries saluting.'

'And what does Harry say of her?'

'He said that if Nick's fool enough to give her up, he'll have a try at her himself. And I'm not sure he didn't mean it.'

The days slipped by. Alison was busy with her shopping, and Nick was getting ready for the new law term. Judith was having some further trouble with her mother, who now complained that the smoky air of London made her cough and wheeze. John seemed to be always at the Cockpit, and Hal began to find less and less to do. Nobody he wished to talk to could be found. Lord Mumford had not been seen for weeks, and was said to be in France with his wife. Lord Churchill was at Windsor, where he was very much in the King's service, whatever he might be at the Cockpit. Even Sir Thomas Mallory was out of town, and was believed to be spending some quiet months on his country estate. The King was still at Windsor, and Hal thought this just as well.

He had read some weeks earlier that the Bishop of London was in trouble with the King over a sermon preached by a clergyman in his diocese. The King had thought it offensive to his own Church, and had ordered the Bishop to suspend the man from duty. The Bishop had answered that he had no power to suspend a man who had only set out the known doctrines of the Church, and the matter had seemed to end. Now, however, it was announced that the Bishop had been called before the newly appointed Ecclesiastical Commission and had himself been summarily suspended from all his episcopal rights and duties. Hal, remembering the Bishop, thought better of him than of the King.

He began to tire of London, and when the September days turned quiet and misty, with a touch of frost at night, he found in this a hint that it was time to start for home before October had its way. Alison agreed, and they settled their plans. Then, two days before they were to start, John had a word to say.

'You'll remember the last time you were at the Cockpit, to pay your duty to the Princess? She said she hoped to see you again, the next time you were in London, and she's remembered it.'

'Oh!' This was awkward, for he had no great wish for formalities at the Cockpit. 'If she said it I'll have to do it. But tomorrow is my only day, if I'm to keep to plan. Is that possible?'

'I expect so. She'll probably have mended by then.'

'Is she sick?'

'A good word for it. Her women are calling it the vapours, but I had it from one of them that it's really her stomach. Too many sugared nuts and cream.'

'You're very easy about it.'

'It's happened before, and she usually mends by next day. So if you come she'll probably see you. If she won't, I'll have to tell you so.'

Hal therefore presented himself at the Cockpit the next morning and his first thought, before he was through the door, was that he had found the wrong moment. The door was wide open, with a half-dozen lackeys standing stiffly beside it. John was in the centre of the hall, looking a little harassed, and on chairs by the wainscot two carefully dressed gentlemen were sitting in talk. They glanced superciliously at Hal, and did not trouble to get up. John took him to the other side, and spoke in a hurried whisper.

'It's the King. He came back from Windsor last night. He heard the Princess was not well, and this morning he walked across to see her, and no word that he was coming. Just two gentlemen with him. It's only a hundred yards, of course. He's with her now.'

'Then I'm out of place here. I'd best leave at once.'

'It might be as well. In another hour or so – '

Voices were heard at the top of the stair, a man speaking and another answering, and John took what seemed a single leap to his point of duty at the foot of it. The two gentlemen jumped to their feet and stood as erect as the lackeys. Hal, with some vague hope that he would not be noticed, pressed back against the wainscot as King James came slowly down the stairs, a man now of fifty-two, of little more than middle stature, strong and muscular, yet moving a little stiffly, with none of the lithe and easy grace that had added so much to his brother. Two steps behind him came the big blond Prince of Denmark.

At the foot of the stair the King stopped, giving a slight nod of acknowledgement as everyone bowed deeply. Then his dark eyes turned to Hal.

'Who's this?' he asked curtly.

He sounded none too pleased, and there was a moment of awkward silence till John roused himself and explained who this was. He did it gracefully, with all the poise and confidence he now had, and the King looked thoughful, as if he were searching his memory. Hal waited, knowing that it was not for him to speak.

'Burnaby?' The King spoke slowly, and he had turned again to Hal. 'I think I remember you. My brother had some talk with you one day when I was with him.'

The testiness had left him, but he had none of the graciousness that had come so easily to Charles. Nor did he look like Charles, though he had the same heavy eyebrows and the same prominent nose. His face looked long and lean, pale in complexion and hard in its lines. His lips were thin, and at the sides of the mouth they seemed to turn down, as if he were perpetually dissatisfied or displeased. His eyes were firm and steady, but Hal, looking into them, could see little of the sensitive understanding he had seen in Charles, and nothing at all of the impish humours that had made Old Rowley. But he bowed in assent.

'Sir, I remember it well. Some five years ago, I think it was.'

'Perhaps. I'll suppose that to my brother you were a loyal gentleman?'

'I hope so, sir. He commended me.'

'I should be glad if I could commend you also.'

'Sir?'

'You are less loyal, it seems, to me.' His tone had hardened, and a note of resentment was in it. 'Last year, in spite of the loving care in which I have been constant to my subjects, I had a disloyal Parliament, which took little heed of my clearest words.'

'Sir!' A gleam of light was coming unhappily to this. 'I do assure – '

'And *you*, Sir Harry, were one of those who spoke and voted against my wishes. You did not treat my brother so. Why, then, should I find in you a lesser sense of duty?'

'Sir, none wished to be disloyal, but there were considerations –'

'What had *you* to do with considerations? Are not the King's commands the duty of a gentleman? You knew what those commands were.'

If commands was the word, Hal had certainly known. They had been the establishment of a standing army and the repeal of the Test Act, but it would be hopeless, and perhaps dangerous, to argue about them now. He stood silent, feeling angry and mutinous, wondering what was coming, and then the King changed direction. His tone changed too, as if he were now trying to be persuasive.

'Sir Harry, this is, in the main, a matter of the Test Acts. Have you thought that to me those Acts are a matter of honour, my own honour as a gentleman? By those Acts I was put from the place of Lord High Admiral, even from my seat in the Council, and what is it, do you think, when the King's own brother is forbidden to serve the King? Is it anything but an insult, deliberate and wicked?' For a moment the resentment flared in his tone, and then he was persuasive again, or as near to it as he could be. 'Sir Harry, may I not properly ask of a loyal gentleman that he should help to remove that insult?'

'When those Acts were passed, sir, I was not in Parliament.'

'But you are now, and if I should call my Parliament to meet again, will you give to me your help and service in removing those Acts?'

'Sir, if it were that alone, I would do it most gladly. But the Church of England is by law established, and the Acts by which it is most established are the Test Acts. That it why so many of us think them needed.'

'So you refuse?' The harshness was suddenly in his tone again, and his heavy eyebrows seemed to thrust forward. 'Do you not know that I am the King, and that my arm is long? In my hands are honours, offices, commissions, places of many sorts, and all may be had by those who serve me faithfully. They could still be yours. No?' He was looking steadily at Hal. 'You stay stiff-necked, do you? Then on your own head be it.'

He went striding to the door, with ill temper showing in all the thrust and vigour of his walk. Then he stopped abruptly for a final word.

'Do not suppose that you will have your way, you and the others like you. I am the King, and I will be obeyed. If this Test is not repealed by Parliament, I will be rid of it in another way, as you will soon learn. Thereafter shall the undutiful learn their duty.'

In another instant, he was gone, striding angrily away, with his two gentlemen behind him.

8 *Royal Indulgence*

To Nick Burnaby, who had hoped for much, October was a month of disappointment. His parents had gone home, with his father saying angrily that after such treatment from the King he would never come to London again unless he had a pressing duty to do so. His brother John was depressed and angered by it also, and even the cheerful Harry was for the moment missing; he was in the eastern counties, on a recruiting march that would last for some weeks.

These, however, were lesser matters, and by themselves they would not for long have troubled Nick. What really mattered was that he no longer had Judith to cheer his evenings and his Sundays. Her mother had from the outset disliked the London air, laden with smoke from innumerable chimneys. This was not the clean smoke of wood but the fouler smoke of sea-coal, and it set her coughing. Then, with the coming of October, the nights grew cold enough to bring from the river a mist that thickened into fog by morning, and smoke and fog together were too much for Mrs Allinson. She became rapidly worse, and it was no longer merely a cough. Her breathing was hard and painful, and her state so alarmed her brother that he sent hastily for physicians. An unhappy Judith told Nick the result.

'We've had two physicians,' she said, 'and for once they agree. It's common, they say, among people who've a weakness of the lights and come to London from the country, and it gets worse as winter goes on.'

'What's the cure?'

'Take her away. There's nothing else, they say. Medicines won't help.'

'But – '

'Nick, I must.' She faced him firmly, though she was not hiding her distress and disappointment. 'They say they've seen too many die of this, and she won't live a month if she stays here. And I think they're right, if it's even a month. I'll have to take her home.'

'Judith!'

'Of course I shall. There's nothing else. It means Salisbury again, her own house and bed.'

The need was so plain that it could not be disputed, and Nick had to turn from that to loyally offering help; which meant that in the end he had once again to escort a coach and deal with inns and ostlers. He had to do it alone, for Edmund Innes had developed rheumatic pains and was in no fit state for riding.

Nick therefore lodged himself once again with his aunt, who gave him cheerful welcome and was sympathetic about the lonely winter that now seemed to face him. Sir Nicholas went a little further.

'Some people,' he said in his most buoyant tone, 'are born to plague the rest of us. It's something to do with the Garden of Eden. Bruising your head. Thorns and thistles. That sort of thing. and this woman's one of the thistles. That's why she won't die of this or anything else. She'll live to plague everyone. But I'll look after things here for you, and keep an eye on the pair of them.'

'I'll be glad of that.'

'It might be as well.' His tone changed suddenly. 'Things are getting difficult here, for dissenters.'

This, he explained, meant that some of the local Justices were now beginning to harass dissenters, for which they had only to enforce the existing laws more strictly than was usual. Already one or two dissenting ministers had been driven out of the town by use of the Five Mile Act, and now a few Justices were beginning to use the Conventicle Act against the dissenting laity. Some meeting-houses had been raided at time of Sunday service, and fines exacted from the congregations. This meant ten shillings for every offence after the first, and some of the poorer members, who could not possibly afford such a sum, had been forced to drop out of the congregations. Judith and her mother, of course, were dissenters.

'But I'll keep an eye on her,' he said firmly, 'and see she doesn't get into trouble.'

'It could mean that she couldn't go to any services at all.'

'Then she'd best turn Anglican and be done with it. She'll

have to do it sooner or later, because I don't see you turning dissenter.'

Nick had to be content with that. He went back to London and tried to give his mind to his law work for what remained of the term. London was quiet, the King seemed to be making no fresh move, and life went on as usual. But the newsletters reported a growing persecution of dissenters all over the country, and the King was doing nothing to stop it. John, whose duties took him often to Whitehall, said it was generally believed there that the King had in fact instigated it by some letters to the Lords Lieutenant of counties. Nick began to feel worried about Judith. She said little about it in her letters, but he knew that there had been some trouble.

He was in Salisbury again for Christmas, as soon as the Law term ended, and he found Mrs Allinson quite recovered from her coughing and painful breathing, but in no way recovered in mind. She was still living in her memories, and refusing to show interest in anything, except that she now seemed determined never to visit London again. She was clear enough about that, as Judith rather bitterly pointed out.

'I'm not surprised she doesn't like London,' she said, 'after the trouble it gave her. But if she can clear her mind on that, why can't she clear it on something that touches *me*?'

'Unless it is that she won't.'

'I'm trying not to think so. She nearly set her clothes on fire the other night by knocking her candle over, and I can't believe it was intentional. She *is* out of touch, and that means that I'm kept here. Oh yes, I am, Nick, and you know it. I can't just walk out and leave her. How could I?'

'Then you'd better be more careful with these Justices. You can't afford to provoke them while things are like this.'

He knew that Judith had already been fined twice after being caught at Sunday meetings. The money had hardly mattered, since Innes had seen to it that she was well supplied, but the Justices had also a power to search houses, which they might use if they thought she was an obstinate offender. Nick warned her earnestly against it, but the possibility was much in his mind when he was back in London. Mr Pollexfen, who was showing a friendly interest in all this, was also of opinion that Judith should be careful.

Soon, however, affairs in London began to take attention.

Early in February a tale spread that Parliament would be called into session in March, and John told Nick that this was probably true; the King, he said, had been heard to say positively that he hoped that by March he would be able to call a Parliament. The newsletters spread the tale round the country, and by the beginning of March members began to arrive in London to be in readiness. But not Hal Burnaby, who wrote that he had no wish to come at all, and would not stir a foot until there was a positive announcement.

Nick, going one evening to Lombard Street, found Innes having a last word with a departing guest. He turned out to be Sir Thomas Mallory, whom Nick had heard his father speak well of. He looked at Nick and asked if he was Sir Harry Burnaby's son; and it ended in his asking Nick to join him for wine and talk on Sunday evening at the King's Head, by Chancery Lane end. Nick accepted, in spite of the name the place had as a sink of Whiggery.

But after church that Sunday morning Nick went for dinner to John and Doraty, and John spoke of some more news he had gleaned at Whitehall.

'I had it from three different men,' he said, 'so I'm pretty sure it's true. You know a lot of Parliament men are in London now? Most of them are gentlemen of the old sort, so they come dutifully to Whitehall to make a bow and pay respect.'

'As Father would have done until – '

'Exactly, and that's the point, Nick. You know the treatment he had from the King? Well, these men are getting it now. It's become a system. As soon as one of these men comes to Court he's told that the King wishes to see him in the closet. Of course he's thunderstruck. He's never had such an honour in his life, never dreamed of it, and before he knows where he is he's with the King. They're alone, and the King's all sweet and gracious – as near as he can be – asking if his honest old friend will stand with him now in what touches his heart and honour.'

'Meaning the Test Act?'

'Meaning exactly that. And then it goes just as it did with Father. If the man doesn't promise immediately, the King turns sour and angry. There are hints of rewards, and then some threats.'

'And how do men answer?'

'I think the first few promised. I suppose they were too dazed and overwhelmed to do anything else. But word has got round by this time of what is happening, and now, if a man goes to the Court at all, he has his answers ready. I must say I respect such men. It must take courage to refuse the King to his face, when you're alone with him.'

'As Father did. Remember that, won't you? But I'm glad I'm not important enough.'

Sir Thomas Mallory put this into perspective when Nick went to the King's Head that evening. He was cool and pleasant, deeply interested in affairs, and possessed of a clarity of mind that Nick could appreciate. One thing led to another, and Nick was soon telling him this tale of how the King was treating members. Mallory looked thoughtful, and then nodded.

'It fits,' he said slowly. 'The King wants the Test Acts repealed, and because of that he has been trying all the winter to appear as a friend to the Church of England. Hence this persecution of dissenters. Now we have this closeting of members. It will press some men into supporting him, and it will let him judge how much support he now has. If it's enough, he'll call a Parliament. If not, he won't. I think that's it.'

It seemed a likely explanation, and Nick was inclined to accept it. The next day, however, he lost interest in this, and in all other talk of reasons why. Two letters came to him on the same day, one from Nick Culley and one from Judith. Nick Culley, in his big untidy hand, wrote that affairs had taken a sharp turn for the worse. He had prevailed on Judith not to attend any more meetings for the present, but the Justices had now taken to searching houses, as the Act allowed them to do if they had reason to think that a dissenters' meeting was being held within. One of these houses had been Judith's, though they could have had no serious belief that she, with her invalid mother, would have a conventicle in the house on Sunday morning. It had been hideously unpleasant for her, and it could be repeated at any time; and that was the reason for Nick Culley's letter. He thought that Edmund Innes should be told of this, so that he might have some other house ready if a move should become unavoidable.

The letter from Judith was almost as disturbing. She passed lightly over her own ordeal and wrote mainly about Nick Culley, who had been as impulsive and indignant as ever when he heard of the search. He had sought out the two Justices concerned and had spoken his mind to them in a style that they had perhaps not heard before. They had then told him that he had better look to himself, since a man so concerned for dissenters must be of disloyal sentiments, and no friend of the Church. Sir Nicholas, a devoted Anglican through all his days, had been so incensed that he had at once taken to befriending other dissenters, openly and noisily, and Judith feared that he had put himself into a dangerous position. She thought the Justices wily, as well as vindictive.

Innes took those letters seriously, but he stayed calm. The first need, he said, was to learn how affairs were developing, and what Judith thought of this notion of moving. This would be work for Nick, since they were now in the third week of March and near the end of the law term. Nick agreed, and lost no time. He was away on the Tuesday before Easter, and the last news he heard, just before he left, was that the King had again prorogued Parliament; which could only mean that his closeting of members had failed. It gave Nick something to think about as he rode the eighty miles to Salisbury.

He was soon in no doubt that those letters had not exaggerated the affair. On his first evening he heard Nick Culley speak gustily about it.

'Justices, if you please! It's a pretty name for them. Because I kept a friendly eye on Judith they tried to make out that I'm a dissenter too. The damned rogues asked me – *me,* mind you! – if I'd taken the Test.'

'What did you say?'

'I told them that quarter-sessions have the roll of names, and they could go and look at it. I've heard no more of *that.* Then they tried to make out I must be half a rebel, and I asked them what *they'd* done to help King Charles come home again – knowing that they hadn't done a thing between them. Then I told them they could go and ask what I was knighted for.'

'Which stopped them?'

'For the moment. But I've since heard they've been talking to the Constable here, trying to learn what visitors I had in the Monmouth time, and you'll see the drift of that. I complained to the Lord Lieutenant.'

'What did he say?'

'He looked unhappy, and said there were orders from the King that the law must be enforced. What do they mean by law these days?'

Judith was looking distressed when Nick went to her next morning. She had lost none of her courage, but she was less resilient than she had been, and she sounded once or twice as if she were getting near to breaking point.

'The neighbours have been kind,' she told him, 'but the Justices are horrible. We've had them in the house twice now, pretending we have a meeting here when they know quite well we haven't, and each time they've been shouting and storming at us, prodding and poking everywhere and throwing things on the floor. The house has looked a wreck when they've finished, and all the time I'm held tight by the soldiers.'

'You!'

'Why not? Trust them to paw me about, and in ways I haven't liked. I suppose I should be thankful it hasn't been worse, but I don't think I can take much more of it.'

'How of your mother?'

'Oh, as usual. She says it doesn't matter what happens. They may do as they please, and if they kill her she'll be glad. That makes it easier, of course, in a way. I can just think of myself.'

'You can't go on like this.'

'I know I can't. But what am I to do? If it goes on, I'll have to conform. I'll just have to.'

'Conform?'

'The Church of England. That would stop all this, of course. They wouldn't have an excuse then, and they'd have to say it was what they wanted.'

'I hope you will, one day, but not for this reason.'

'But I might have to. It depends, I suppose, on the next few weeks, and whether they keep at me or not.'

They discussed it further, and without getting further. The Justices could, if they wished, make life so intolerable for Judith that she would have to leave, but there was no way of knowing whether they would actually do it or would tire of her and turn to someone else. Only time could show, and Nick soon saw that it would be many a week before Judith would dare to attend a Baptist meeting again, even if there was one. It would be even longer before she would lose her fear of another visitation.

He stayed as long as he could, but a new law term was about to open, and he was in London again by April 4th, which was a Monday. He walked through the dark to Lombard Street, where Innes looked glad to see him.

'Unsatisfactory,' he said when he had heard the tale. 'Do you really think the Justices will now look elsewhere?'

'I've doubts of it. They might play cat and mouse – leave her for a month to gain hope, and then strike again.'

'Ye-es.' Innes nodded thoughtfully. 'But how of this Declaration?'

'What's that?'

'You haven't heard? It came to us this afternoon. They were crying it on the streets.'

He took up a printed pamphlet, with the ink still damp and smudgy from the press, and in silence handed it to Nick. It was headed with the royal arms, and below them it was styled *His Majestie's Gracious Declaration for Liberty of Conscience.* The first paragraph then said that the King had 'thought fit, by virtue of Our Royal Prerogative, to issue forth this Our Declaration of Indulgence'. Succeeding paragraphs declared that all penal laws in matters of religion were suspended forthwith, and that all people were given leave to meet as they pleased for whatever kind of worship they chose, any disturbance of a meeting being strictly forbidden. The Test Acts were set aside, and a formal pardon was given to anyone who might previously have offended against the penal laws.

'What do you think of it?' asked Innes.

'It's not lawful. This dispensing power doesn't exist. His prerogative doesn't extend to dispensing with any law he doesn't like.'

'I'll not doubt it, but that's not the point. Whether this is lawful or not, it's likely to have effect. He has probably power enough for the present to enforce it. So use your wits, please. What will it mean to Judith?'

What indeed? As soon as he thought of it Nick saw that this, and particularly the part that forbade all disturbance of meetings, might be exactly what Judith needed. It should check those Justices and give her the peace she had been denied. He said so, and Innes nodded.

'It should be the end of all her trouble,' he replied, 'and I'm deeply thankful. I little thought I should ever feel thankful to King James, but at this moment I do. And not, of course, for Judith only. There are thousands more who'll have ease from this Declaration, whether it be lawful or not, and I'm thankful.'

So was Nick, at that moment, with his thoughts entirely on Judith. But the law term opened, and Westminster Hall buzzed with talk about the Declaration. So did every inn and coffee house, and on a Sunday every churchyard too. It was impossible to escape from it, and little by little, as he heard the talk and took his part in it, Nick began to have misgivings, and then some downright second thoughts. The King, it seemed, was doing more than merely enforce his Declaration. He was himself showing favour to dissenters.

'The whole Court has changed,' said John, when Nick went to dine with him one Sunday. 'There's no respect paid now to any divine of the Church. A bishop may cool his heels for an hour and then be lucky if he gets an audience. But nothing's too good for a dissenter.'

'Are dissenters seen at Court?'

'They are now.' John gave a wry laugh. 'Word seems to have got round among the brethren – or the wealthier ones – that you can now go to Court, be received very graciously, and then beg a pardon for a minister who's clapped in jail, or a friend who's transported as a rebel. He's given quite a number of pardons lately, and there are tales of dissenters becoming mayors and aldermen, and even being put into the Commission of the Peace as Justices.'

'Is he standing on his head?'

'That puts it nicely. Until now he's hated the very sight of dissenters, and now he seems to be courting their favour and begging them to love him. You can work out for yourself what it means.'

It had been neatly worked out by Sir Thomas Mallory, when Nick next chanced to meet him. He spoke with a crisp assurance, as if he were sure of things.

'Our James has not a big mind,' he said, 'and it's not usually difficult to see beneath his schemes. What he wants is all power and favour to the papists, precious little for the Anglicans, and none at all for dissenters. That means that they'll both resist, and he isn't strong enough to attack both of them together. Even with his army he isn't, so it has to be one at a time, and all through the winter he's been trying to get the Anglicans to repeal the Test Act for him, and then they could do what they liked to dissenters. That failed, so now he's turned completely round and he's bidding for support of dissenters against Anglicans. Hence this Indulgence, and the other favours he's offering. He's bidding high, too, when he offers them complete relief.'

'Do you think he'll succeed?'

'I can only hope he won't. But dissenters have suffered greatly, and some are bound to leap at this and be thankful. They may be too dazed to ask whether they can really trust him, or what the end will be if they help him now against the Anglicans. For the moment they may be merely thankful.'

Judith was a dissenter who leapt at it and was thankful. In a letter that came a day or two later she poured out the news that the harassing had entirely stopped, and not only for her but for the whole of the Baptist congregation there. The two Justices who had mainly done it were hardly to be seen, and a third Justice had told her that she might now do as she pleased and had nothing more to fear. Sir Nicholas Culley, who had shown his defiance of the Justices by being friendly to every dissenter he met, was now being commended for his good sense and public spirit. It was all due to the King's Indulgence, and Judith's relief was obvious. Her Baptist minister, who had been chased away by the Five Mile Act, had now returned openly to his congregation, and meetings would start again next Sunday, without concealment or even a locked door. It was hardly to be believed, and Judith could now give her mind in peace to her mother, who was beginning at last to show a further improvement.

Nick had agreed with Sir Thomas Mallory that it would be a disaster if any large number of dissenters should be won to the King by the Indulgence. But this was not a large number of dissenters. It was Judith; and Nick, reading that letter, was as thankful as she was.

9 *The Whispered Doubt*

Judith was not the only dissenter who was thankful, and soon the *Gazette* was announcing, week after week, that addresses of thanks to the King for his Gracious Declaration had been received from guilds and corporations and other groups all over the country. The lists looked impressive till it was noticed that they came always from small and not very important groups. The majority of dissenters, and certainly the influential ones, were being more careful. They were going again to their Sunday meetings, but discreetly rather than openly, and few of them were accepting offices for which they were not qualified in law. Edmund Innes, who was still at heart a Baptist, put it clearly to Nick one evening.

'It's a matter of good sense,' he said. 'The King breaks the law when he offers these freedoms, and we break it ourselves if we even hold our meetings openly. But even a King may die, and if the crown were to pass to the Princess of Orange and her husband, what might we then expect if for years we had been breaking the law to support a papist King against our fellow protestants? What sort of laws would the Parliament of that day enact against us?'

He was certainly not speaking for himself alone, and it was soon clear that the great mass of dissenters were conducting themselves discreetly. They avoided all appearance of breaking the law, and they took what chances they had to show that they were now firmly with the Anglicans. The flow of addresses stopped, and it was said that some who had sent them now wished they had not. Nick found this believable, as long as he read it in newsletters. But when he learned that his own Judith was turning round it was another matter. This took him wholly by surprise.

It happened in the short Whitsuntide vacation, when he again spent his days with Judith. He found her looking calmer and happier, and he asked if she was still able to go freely to the Sunday meetings.

'They're quite free and open,' she retorted, 'and I've stopped going.'

'Why – ' He was baffled for a moment. 'What's wrong?'

'They're not worth going to. They've changed, or the minister has. What's a sermon for?'

'Expound the teachings, I suppose. And apply them.'

'And there's plenty to apply them to, just now. The parson's doing it at the parish church. He's preaching all the proper things about Jesuits and what will happen if the Test Act goes.'

'But your own man?'

'Yes, ours.' She sounded terse, and then, more quietly, she began to explain it. 'Something's happened to him. He can preach now at high noon if he likes, with the doors wide open, and not a Justice can touch him. But he must have promised something, or been warned, or we don't know what. All we do know is that he won't now say a word that could offend a papist, let alone the King. He's tact and politeness all the time, and if the Church of Rome is a little different from us, that's just an error of judgement. I won't spend time listening to that sort of thing, so I'm going to the parish church.'

'What!'

'Oh yes I am, and you needn't look surprised. Sir Nicholas suggested it. He said go and try it once, so I did. Do you know the sixth chapter of Ephesians, wickedness in high places? That's what he preached on, and he wasn't half-hearted about it. He was speaking what was in him, and I listened. It must have been in me too, because I went back next Sunday, and I've been every Sunday since. I like it, and I'm going to conform and join your Church.'

'Judith! Could you?'

'I've just said I could. Put something on Sir Nicholas, of course, because he's talked a good deal to me about this.'

'What does your mother say?'

'She doesn't show interest. Which for once is just as well.'

But Mrs Allinson was none the less much improved, as he quickly saw when he was taken to her. She was stronger, and in better health, and she had recovered enough in mind to give him some words of welcome; and between the one thing and the other he went back to London feeling buoyant and cheerful. Then, only two weeks later, a letter from Judith both pleased and astonished him. Sir Nicholas Culley, she told him, was a Justice of the Peace, an honour he had all but ceased to hope for. The Commission for those parts had been revised, the two persecuting Justices being taken out and Sir Nicholas and another put into their places; and Judith was in no doubt that this was a further move to please the dissenters and show that the King was their friend. Sir Nicholas stood high in their esteem because of his friendliness in their days of trouble, and they were now as pleased as he was.

Nick wrote at once a letter of congratulation. Nick Culley, in an exuberant answer, seemed specially pleased that it was an honour he would never have had if the King had realized who he was.

He hated the sight of me when he was Duke of York, and he isn't a man to forget such feelings. But he wouldn't make out the list himself. That would be done by some industrious mole at Whitehall, the sort they breed in Courts, who is always busy and never seen by anyone. Of course he wouldn't know of the older days. He'd just read the reports sent from here, and he'd jab his pen at me pretty quickly, and James, as like as not, would sign the thing without reading it. I'm in the Commission of Peace at last, and lawfully and properly, because this is something he can *do. It doesn't depend on his Indulgence or his Dispensing Power, so I'm properly a Justice, and perhaps before long they'll say I'm a good one. I do at least heed the law when I can.*

If Nick Culley was heeding the law, the King was not, and during that spring and summer he seemed determined to show the Church of England what it might now expect. He began by sending to the University of Cambridge a royal letter requiring that a degree be given to a Benedictine monk, which was so blatantly illegal that the Senate had to refuse. The King called in his Ecclesiastical Commission, and the Vice-Chancellor was summarily deprived of his office and his income. Then it was the turn of Oxford, where the Fellows of Magdalen were ordered to elect as their President a papist who had none of the qualifications required by their statutes, and was known to be of bad character too. They refused, and by the end of the year they had all been ejected and replaced by papists. In every county men read their newsletters with anger and resentment, and had forebodings of worse to come. The Anglicans were united, most of the dissenters were with them, and even the papists, except for some busy and foolish ones near the Court, were alarmed and dismayed, fearing that their present precarious freedom would be followed by something very different in another reign. But for the moment the King did nothing more, and little by little, as the days slipped by, a change of mood could be noticed in the nation. Men began to steady themselves, and then to say unwillingly that, bad as all this was, it might yet be endured for a few more years until – Here they fell silent. No one cared to say it aloud, but everyone knew what was meant. Sooner or later the King must die, and the Princess Mary was a protestant.

Edmund Innes, who was as mild and charitable a man as most, spoke of it to Nick one evening.

'Slowly but surely he's putting his papists into every place of power, and it will end, if he has time enough, with papists as our masters in everything. That's not to be endured, but how is it to be stopped? Few are ready for open war, which God forbid indeed! So men turn a little sideways now. They tell themselves they hope only for another reign, and they look past what they really hope for.'

Nick nodded slowly, for he, most certainly, did not want open war. He had been again to Judith in the summer vacation, and he had agreed with her that if her mother's improvement should continue till Christmas he would then ask his father to arrange a contract of marriage for them with Innes. He had every hope that this would come true, and he cared very little, at the moment, if a few more places went to papists, if only affairs would stay as they were, quiet and tranquil.

Then, at the beginning of November, a tale came out of Whitehall that the Queen, of all women, was with child, and the whole nation was aghast, consternation mingling with disbelief. It had long been accepted that the Queen, after some earlier failures, would have no more children. But if she were now to have a son, the next reign would not after all be protestant. And what then?

Nick, as disturbed as anyone, went in search of John, who was looking no happier than anyone else.

'I don't know whether it's true or not,' he answered briefly.

'All I can tell you is that the King seems to think it is. Nobody's ever seen him look so pleased.'

'What of the Queen?'

'She's cancelling engagements, and she's hung about with what they call sacred relics. So perhaps she believes it too. It'll be the devil if it *is* true.'

'But can it be? She hasn't had a child for years, and those all died. Can she start again now?'

'Why not?' said Doraty calmly.

'Why – ' Nick swung round to her, and he thought he could read amusement in her eyes. 'It's hardly to be expected. And the King, too, is getting on in life.'

'He's fifty-four, isn't he? Do you call that impossible?'

'I suppose not. But – '

'And the Queen is twenty-nine, which is very possible indeed. So why not?'

'It's surprising, after all these years.'

'Surprises of that sort do happen. Quite a number of women could tell you so.'

'Oh!'

Nick gave up an argument he was beginning to find unequal. He turned back to John.

'What else?' he asked. 'How does the Court take this?'

'Now that's interesting.' John became suddenly crisp and confident, as if this were fairly in his scope as a gleaner of gossip. 'You'll note that if this promised child is to be the heir the King needs, it will have to be a boy. A girl's no use. We've two princesses already, and another girl would just rank after them. But a boy would take precedence, and of course he'd be bred a papist.'

'True.'

'Everyone at Court is full of loyal congratulations, but that's only to be expected. It's Court manners to say what will please the King. But some people – papists – are taking it too far. They're saying, very confidently indeed, that the Queen will have a fine healthy boy, who will one day be King. They're talking already as if this is fixed and certain.'

'Oh, are they?'

'Nick, don't you see the point? Nobody can foresee whether a child will be a boy or a girl, and the obvious answer, if they can be sure as that, is that they *know* what's going to happen. In other words, there's a plot to pass off someone else's child – fine and healthy – as the Queen's, and call him the heir.'

'Men are saying *that*?'

'Whispering it, perhaps – when the King's out of hearing.'

'But, John – do you believe it?'

'I don't think I do. This confident talk is perhaps Court manners again, carried too far. And some of these papists are over-ready to believe in miracles, and it could be that. But either way it's exceedingly foolish. That answer's deadly, and it will soon be everywhere if we hear much more of the healthy boy. It will be believed, too, and perhaps in high places.'

'What places?'

'Any you please. But perhaps – ' John looked steadily back at him. 'Perhaps in the Cockpit. You don't think the Princess will like being cut from the succession, do you?'

That could only be guessed, for the Princess said nothing, and even John, who was daily in attendance on her, did not know what she thought. But the newsletters took the tale of the expected child everywhere, and soon it was being discussed and argued about, sadly or angrily, in every inn and tavern, every parsonage and manor house, from one end of the country to the other. Almost everyone heard it with dismay, very many with disbelief, and the tale that it was all a fraud found acceptance everywhere. Nick found the extent of this surprising, and he said so to Sir Thomas Mallory. He was soon put right.

'Not at all,' said Mallory tersely. 'It's very likely that a boy of some sort will be offered to us, and if we say he's heir to the crown we have only two choices left – a succession of popish Kings, which is wholly intolerable, or civil war for a second time, which would be very nearly as intolerable. To say he's *not* the heir avoids both choices, so is it surprising that men turn to it? They may or may not believe it in their hearts, but politically they *must* believe it. It's surely quite simple.'

'Hmm! And do you believe it?'

'Of course I do. I must.'

Nick let it drop, being once again more interested in his own affairs. It was already December, and Judith had agreed that in the vacation he should go to his home and ask his father to get in touch with Innes about a contract of marriage. He had little doubt that he would get it, but he could see some difficulty in bringing everyone together for the formal signing that was usual.

There might be delay in this, and there would then have to be a further interval between the signing and the marriage, and Nick now had his thoughts more upon this question of time than on anything else. He did not take much notice when it was announced in the *Gazette* that the King was revising the Lieutenancy list and the Commissions of the Peace, so that he might be represented only by gentlemen who would support his policies. Nick's concern was to get married.

He found slow riding on roads foul with mud, and did not win home till Christmas Eve. His mother gave him the welcome she always did, but his father was quiet and restrained, plainly out of humour over something; and this, when they had done with the Christmas festivities and were able to talk, turned out to be the political news, particularly that threatened revision of lists.

'And have you seen the new Sheriff list?' asked Hal gloomily. 'It's just out, and it's all but a new list. Men who've been in for years are dropped, and the new men seem to be either papists or turncoat dissenters. If he's going to treat the Lieutenancy and the Commission in the same way, what will that mean?'

There could be only one answer. The most important work of the Sheriffs was to control the county elections, under the general direction of the Lords Lieutenant and with the help and support of the Justices. Between them, if they showed enough bias, they could make it all but impossible for a man they disliked to be elected; and it looked, therefore, as if the King was preparing for a new Parliament, almost of his own choosing.

Hal continued in this gloomy mood until Nick began to speak of marriage and his wish for a contract. Then he became more cheerful, saying it was pleasant to turn to a matter on which the law had not yet been set aside. Nor did he show surprise.

'I've been expecting it,' he said, 'and if I'd been in your place I'd have lost patience sooner. That sick mother, I mean. But it's all right, Nick. I liked your Judith, and I'll certainly ask for a contract. That will be Innes, I suppose? Does he approve, do you know?'

'He's told me he does.'

'Then it should be easy. Where do we sign it, do you think? London?'

'I don't know whether Judith could leave her mother for it.'

'That's for Innes to decide. So I'll write to him.'

It was left at that, with Nick well content that it had gone so easily. He went off to see Richard Gibson, whom he had always liked, and told him all he could of Doraty and her sayings and doings. Gibson heard all that with full attention, but then, as usual with him, he turned to politics. He asked for all that Nick could tell him about the royal child and the whispered tale that it was perhaps not royal at all. Nick evaded that by telling him what Sir Thomas Mallory had said about a need to believe this tale, and Gibson nodded appreciatively. In his Parliament days he had worked with Mallory.

'He's quite right,' he said slowly. 'If we accept that child there will in the end be war. But did Mallory say what he thinks of this revising of lists?'

'No.'

'I don't understand it. It must, of course, be an attempt to pack a Parliament, but why? I don't think James is pressed for money, and in effect he's repealed the Test Acts by his Indulgence, so why a Parliament? Is it worth his while now to offend so many for no more than that?'

'I don't know. I hadn't thought of this.'

'Mallory has a very good understanding, so if you learn what he thinks I'll be grateful if you'll let me know. Especially if there should be some further move.'

'I certainly will.'

The further move came a day or two later, when a newsletter told them that the King had appointed a committee of Privy Councillors to regulate the municipal corporations. It consisted of Lord Chancellor Jeffreys and six papists.

'What a crew!' snapped Hal Burnaby in high anger. 'We can guess how they'll behave. It's the boroughs now, after the shires.'

The point was clear enough. The Sheriffs conducted elections only in the county. Boroughs conducted their own, with the mayor in charge. Votes were possessed only by the members of the closed circle called the corporation, and the qualifications for membership were always set out very exactly in the borough's charter, usually with a power reserved to the King of dismissing individual members at pleasure. So regulating the corporations would mean dismissing all who were likely to vote against the King's wishes, and replacing them by more obedient men. But it would rouse a bitter anger against the King in almost every borough in the land, and the question remained – why? Was a Parliament worth the anger?

Nick, remembering his promises to Gibson, lost little time, when he was back in London, in seeking out Sir Thomas Mallory and asking him how he saw the matter. Mallory, as usual, saw it clearly.

'We must suppose,' he said, 'that the King believes – or knows – that a boy is coming. He is determined that the boy shall be his heir and shall be bred a fervent papist. Grant that, and at once we see a difficulty. The King is fifty-four, and he cannot expect to live until the boy has come of age to take the powers of a King. It's likely that a regency will be needed, perhaps for many years, and how is a regency appointed?'

'Oh!' Nick had to think quickly. 'I don't think there's any provision for it, in law.'

'There isn't, and that's the difficulty. The Queen may *not* style herself Regent if the King should die. It's entirely for Parliament to enact that such and such persons shall be regents – and can you imagine any papist being named by any Parliament the present voters would elect?'

'They'd name protestants at once.'

'Most probably the Prince and Princess of Orange, by whom the boy would be placed with protestant tutors. By the time he came of age he'd be as strong a protestant as any, and the King's great hope would be defeated. That's his problem. He may have his heart's desire only from a Parliament, but certainly not from any Parliament that could be elected now. So he *must* change the voters' lists, and he won't care what offence he gives, or what anger he rouses, if he may but succeed. Do you see it now?'

Nick thought he did, and he wrote a letter about it to Gibson, who replied grimly that the road the King was taking looked more and more like the road to Armageddon, which might be nearer than he thought, and perhaps round the next corner. Sir Thomas Mallory agreed with Gibson, and pointed out that the committee to regulate corporations was already setting up local boards of regulators all over the kingdom. Hal wrote that such a board had already been appointed in his own area, and was getting no friendly reception from anyone. He added, with some amusement, that for the first time since he had known either of them, Richard Gibson was speaking highly of the Rector's sermons. This was because Mr Allway, now thoroughly alarmed, was energetically denouncing popery and all its ways and works, including boards of regulators, every time he entered his pulpit.

One matter was more cheerful. The negotiations for a marriage contract were now complete, and Innes had agreed with Hal that it could be best signed in London, and that the most convenient date would be about the end of April.

'Your parents will be coming here for the signing,' he told Nick, 'and that's about as early in the year as we can expect the roads to be in shape for them. Easter Sunday will be April 15th, and they'll probably leave home a day or two after that. So I'm suggesting the signing on the twenty-ninth. It's best on a Sunday, when men are free of their counting-houses.'

'Of course. But how of Judith?'

'That's the only difficulty. Who's to escort her? However, I hear that Sir Nicholas Culley is offering some friendly help, so I hope that we shall soon have all this arranged.' He gazed thoughtfully at Nick. 'I shall be more at ease when this is signed and the guests are safe in their homes again. We do not know, these days, how long London will stay quiet.'

'You think things will get worse?'

'The King's temper must be getting worse. He's set his heart on this remodelling of lists, and I do not think it is going well.'

It certainly was not. The regulators may have begun by thinking it would be easy, but they had reckoned without the temper of a stubborn and angry nation, all but united in its resistance. The Anglican clergy, for all their talk and sermons about non-resistance, were now openly leading the resistance, and Sunday after Sunday, with scarcely a voice missing, they were preaching to packed and excited congregations on the failings of popery and the evils of the King's policies. In this they had generous support from the dissenters, most of whose ministers were preaching as vigorously as the Anglicans. Even among the papists there were many who were now thoroughly alarmed, and were saying openly that they preferred the goodwill of their neighbours to that of a board of regulators.

From his father's letters Nick learned how things had gone in the borough which Hal had for the last nine years represented in Parliament. The charter required a corporation of sixty members and the regulators began by dismissing fifty-three of them as unreliable. They looked for papists willing to fill the vacant places, and found only seven. For the remaining forty-six they had to turn to dissenters, and forty-four of the chosen promptly declared that they would vote only for a known and trusted protestant who would pledge himself to uphold the Test Act. The regulators dismissed them, and appointed another forty-four, and the second lot were even worse than the first. One old veteran from Ireton's regiment, who now, to his own astonishment, found himself made an alderman overnight, told the regulators that he would vote for no man who would not first drink with him to the happy memory of the Lord Protector and of all the regicides as well. In a fury the regulators decided that they could find no more than a dozen good voters in the place, and that the only thing to do was to remodel the charter; which meant rescinding it and issuing another which would require a corporation of only twelve members. They wrote to Whitehall accordingly, and then moved on, leaving the dissenters still in office to deal with day-to-day affairs.

In due course a letter came from the Lord Chancellor requiring the surrender of the charter, and the dissenters, after consulting attorneys, refused. This made it a matter for the Court of King's Bench, to which the Lord Chancellor promptly sent it, and the dissenters, after consulting Sir Harry Burnaby, sent a brief to Mr Pollexfen. He accepted it, but told them that the court was so choked with such actions, coming from boroughs all over the country, that theirs would be a long time pending. They received this happily, knowing that until it was decided they would stay in office and be the voters in any election.

'For which give thanks,' said Sir Thomas Mallory. 'The dissenters have done wonderfully, better perhaps than we deserve. For the present they've saved the nation. But what will he do next, I wonder?'

'The King?'

'Of course. It's the same tale from everywhere, and it means that for at least the next year or two he won't get his Parliament and his regency. But all his hopes will fail unless he does get it. So what will he do next?'

Nick could find no answer. Edmund Innes found one, but he was brief about it, his thoughts being more on the marriage contract.

'The King?' he said shortly. 'He'll have to strike at the Church of England, and specially at its clergy. Their preaching has done more than anything else to rouse this spirit, and they've now such an influence, and they're held in such respect, that he can't make headway against them. If he can destroy that influence, he might have a chance. Otherwise he hasn't. So in one way or another I think he's bound to strike at them, and it may be something desperate, but don't ask me what. Now then – ' He changed his tone abruptly. 'I've had a letter from Sir Nicholas Culley.'

What it amounted to was that the arrangements were now complete, and were as good as Nick could wish for. Nick Culley would have Mary with him when he came to London for the signing, and Judith, of course, would travel with them. They would leave home immediately after Easter, which should give them nine or ten days in London before the signing. According to the letter, this was being done to allow Mary some extra time in London; but it would allow for Judith too, which set Nick wondering what the real thought had been.

'It's excellent,' he told Innes. 'But what of Judith's mother?'

'Also arranged for. Some good woman – of whom Lady Culley speaks highly – will live in the house for those few days and undertake the whole care of her. That seems satisfactory, and it may be good for her to learn that she *can* live without Judith.'

'I wish she could.'

'So do I. But I'm glad the Culleys are coming, since they have been good to both you and Judith. Is there anyone else you would invite from your side?'

'I don't think so.'

Yet two more there were to be. It was now the end of March, and at the beginning of the month Doraty had let it be known that she was expecting her second child. She had, of course, written to her parents about this, and her news had put them into some little flutter, since she was their only daughter. Nick's own mother was on friendly terms with Mrs Gibson, and they must have been putting their heads together. Or so Hal said, in a letter to Nick.

. . . their heads together. Richard came to me yesterday, and said that he and his wife would like to travel with your mother and me when we start for London after Easter. This, of course, is to let them see Doraty and be satisfied that all is well. That, at least for Mrs Gibson. Of Richard I am not sure, having a notion that what he really yearns for is the scent of politics again. If so, we'll hand him over to Mallory, and they may talk Whiggery to their hearts' content. What matters is that Richard and his wife will be at your signing ceremony if invitations may be had. Richard,

by the by, still approves of Mr Allway, who has now taken to preaching on texts from Revelation. It was 17, verse 3, last week – the woman on the scarlet beast – and Richard hummed with approval. He told me afterwards that a little more enlightenment, which he thinks will not be long in coming, may allow Allway to preach on 13, verse 10.

Innes read that letter carefully when Nick showed it to him. Then he reached for his Bible and found the text. He read it out aloud:

He that leadeth into captivity shall go into captivity: he that killeth with the sword must be killed with the sword. Here is the patience and the faith of the saints.

'Yes.' Innes spoke slowly, with his hand still on his Bible. 'They did call themselves the saints, in the Protector's day. So this is more than a text.' He lifted his head, to look steadily at Nick. 'He tells us his own faith, what *he* is ready for. And he won't be the only one.'

10 *Order in Council*

Easter passed quietly, and Edmund Innes had all the arrangements made, and all the invitations sent out, for the signing of the marriage contract, which was to be a fortnight later. He told Nick that one of the invitations had gone to Sir Thomas Mallory, whom he had chanced to meet, and who had expressed his interest and goodwill; though he had admitted also that he would like to meet Hal Burnaby again, and Richard Gibson, who would be present at the signing.

Nick Culley arrived on the Thursday of Easter week. He and Mary were to lodge at the Bell, but he took Judith at once to Lombard Street, where Nick found her in high spirits. Her mother, she said, had not liked being left with a Mrs Pemberton to look after her, but she was not likely to come to any harm and would have to put up with it. All had been quite, with no more harassing of dissenters, though she herself was now regularly at the parish church, where the sermons were still to her liking. The one thing that troubled her was that Nick Culley had been in some sort of trouble, and might at any moment cease to be a Justice of the Peace. Judith did not know quite what had happened, but it had something to do with the revising of lists.

That took Nick to the Bell, and his guess at what had happened proved to be right.

'Don't think I'm the only one,' said his uncle noisily. 'The Lord Lieutenant was the first. He was told he was to question all Justices in his county on how they'd vote and so on, and he answered that he wouldn't treat gentlemen like that. So he was turned out, and we were sent a man who'd do as he was told. He summoned the Justices, one at a time, and put the questions, and five out of six of us gave him answers he didn't like. So now he's scratching round for men to take our places, and he can't get them. The papists don't like it, and the dissenters give him worse answers than we did. So perhaps we'll be left in. The county must have Justices.'

'I've heard much the same from my father. Like you, he doesn't know whether he'll be put out or not.'

'We'll ask him when he comes.'

That, however, was not to be for another week, for Hal and his party had a longer journey and were taking it easily. They arrived with only two days to spare, on the Friday before the important Sunday, and in London they separated, the Gibsons going to Doraty in Westminster, and Hal and Alison to the Bell. Nick had been in Westminster Hall through the afternoon, but at the end of it he went to the Bell, hoping that his parents had now arrived, and in no long time he was telling them of the arrangements for Sunday.

'It's at Mr Innes' house, at three o'clock of the afternoon. There'll be yourselves, then John and Doraty, Harry, Mr and Mrs Gibson, Colonel and Mrs Crosedale, and Mr Pollexfen too, who has taken much interest. That's our side of it. On his own side Mr Innes has invited a dozen or so of his friends in the City, with their ladies. They're all of note, and he told me in that short way of his that it might be useful to me to be known to them.'

'That's good of him, Nick.'

'He *is* good. Oh, Sir Thomas Mallory is invited too, and he's another I've come to like.'

'Your friends seem a little Whiggish, these days.'

'That's not by design, and on Sunday I shan't ask if a man is a Whig or not.'

Nick left the Bell in mid-evening to take word of their arrival to Innes. He walked briskly, eager to see Judith again and give her the news, but at the corner of Chancery Lane he stopped. There were lanterns outside the King's Head inn, and in their light a hawker was holding up some printed sheets and bawling noisily. Nick moved closer, and in the man's shouting he distinguished something about a royal proclamation. Feelings of alarm flared at the words, and he hurried to buy a sheet. He stuffed it into his pocket, and stepped out for Lombard Street.

He kept it back while he told his tale to Judith. Then his first glance at it under the candles showed that it had the royal arms and was styled a *Gracious Declaration of Indulgence,* exactly as a sheet had been styled a year ago.

'Another?' said Innes sharply. 'But why, if you please? What does it say?'

The alarm in his voice was easy to understand. He had been saying for weeks past that the King, defeated everywhere in his attempts to change the voters' lists, must now strike at the Anglican clergy to destroy their influence. He must do it somehow, or lose all hope of a papist regency; and this, surely, must be his attempt. Nick began to read it, at first carefully, and then by merely glancing at it. He turned to Innes.

'I don't understand it,' he said. 'This isn't a new Declaration. Most of it is word for word as we had it last year. There's precious little here that's new.'

'Tell me about the little.'

'There's a new opening, which just says he's firm and constant and hasn't changed, and a new ending, which says he's resolved to call a Parliament in November. And that's all. The rest of it is the old one over again.'

'*That* won't hurt the clergy.'

'But what's his purpose? Why go to all this just to tell us he hasn't changed his mind? No one ever thought he had. It doesn't make sense.'

Neither of them could find an answer, and Nick learned the next morning that his fellow lawyers had done no better. Even Mr Pollexfen, who was as sagacious a Whig as most, could only say that it might come clear in time. John, coming with Doraty for dinner at the Bell, said that the talk at Whitehall could give no answer either. If there was a purpose at all, it was being kept uncommonly secret, and the puzzle remained.

It was put aside for an hour on Sunday afternoon while the contract of marriage was signed with proper solemnity. It was a happy afternoon, and Innes looked happier than anyone as he stood at the top of the stair to receive his guests. Nick Culley, in his most affable mood, came up with Mary on his arm. Richard Gibson looked pleasantly at ease as he came up with his wife. Doraty was escorted by John in a style that hinted of Versailles. Her uncle, Colonel Crosedale, came with his wife, and then Harry, with no one to escort. Mr Pollexfen looked as if he could represent the whole of the Bar and the law as well, and even Sir Thomas Mallory seemed for once to have thrown off politics. He was genial and smiling, and positively charming as he greeted Judith.

The attorney read out the contract, with some comments and explanations, and then it was signed by Hal and Innes as the principals; then by Nick and Judith, as proof that they knew of it and accepted it; and then, as witnesses, by a banker and two eminent merchants on the one side, and on the other by Sir Nicholas Culley, Mr Gibson, and Colonel Crosedale. The customary speeches followed, all tactfully short, and then came the wine, the sweets and savouries, the small talk, and the offering of good wishes. It was informal now, with the company breaking into little groups, each with its own talk, and Innes seized the chance to take Nick from group to group, making sure that he had a word with each of the eminent Londoners whom he might some day find it useful to know. This, in the end, brought them to a corner where Gibson and Mallory were standing apart, renewing their memories of each other. Their talk was what might have been expected.

'I get no further,' Mallory was saying. 'I keep hearing it said that he must now move against the Anglican clergy, but any sort of persecution would bring the nation even more behind them, and that's the exact opposite of what he wants. He needs to lessen the support they now have, not increase it.'

'But this new Declaration?'

'It alters nothing. But we'd better not suppose, on that account, that it hasn't any purpose. There could be more announcements, or more proclamations, and this new Declaration might then fit into place. It may be part of a pattern, but at present we don't know what. We can only keep our eyes open.'

Gibson nodded assent, as if on a political matter he would accept Mallory's experienced judgement. His own thoughts were perhaps those of the soldier who had quoted that text from Revelation, and what this could mean came out later in the week. Nick Culley and Mary, who had been in London for a fortnight, left for home on the Tuesday, taking Judith with them, and leaving Nick disconsolate, even though his parents and the Gibsons had agreed to stay some few days longer. On the Friday he had some spare time in the afternoon, and instead of returning at once to the Temple he called at John's house, which was only five minutes away, to see if there was anyone to talk to. He found Doraty by herself, also in a mood for talk, and she soon asked when he expected to be married; which was much in his own thoughts also.

'I've been hearing about it from my father,' he told her. 'He and Mr Innes think a betrothal should last six months.'

'I know.' She nodded sympathetically. '*We* had to wait six months, and it seemed a long time. It will mean October?'

'They say they'll agree to September, when it's easier for people to travel. I'm wondering if I can persuade them into August.'

'Don't expect *me* at a wedding in August.'

'Oh!' He had forgotten that her child was due in August.

'It doesn't matter. You can be wed without me. What I really wanted to ask was where will you live after you've got Judith?'

'I don't really know. It will have to be near the Temple, and near Westminster Hall.'

'That should mean you'll be close to us here in Westminster. Has my father said anything about that?'

'No. But why – '

'He's been talking with Sir Thomas Mallory a lot this week, and they think affairs grow so bad that there could be trouble at any time. Some sort of fighting is what they mean, and that was where my father started talking as a soldier. He said that if there's fighting at all, some of it will be here, because of Whitehall Palace, which both sides will wish to have. Then he told me that if things get any worse I mustn't risk being caught here in August. It mightn't be safe, and he wanted me to go home and be looked after there.'

'And will you?'

'Of course I won't. I shan't be able to take a two-hundred-mile journey just then, and I'm not going off in May to leave John by himself until about October. I didn't marry him for that. So I don't know what I shall do. I'm trying to think of something.'

'Perhaps you'd better.'

'And so had you.' Her voice was suddenly sharp. 'Nick, don't you see it? If this place is unsafe for me, ought you to bring Judith, in August, to live here?'

'Oh!' He stared blankly at her. 'But this is only a guess. It may not come to anything like that.'

'But we'd better have something in mind in case it does.'

They were not able to take it further. John came in, and he seemed disappointed that Gibson was not in the house.

'I came back specially to tell him,' he said. 'I'm afraid there's some news.'

'Oh?'

'Yes.' He was looking steadily at Nick. 'The King has signed an Order in Council that his new Declaration is to be read in all churches on two successive Sundays, during time of the service. Bishops are to send copies to their clergy, in readiness.'

For a long moment Nick stayed silent, and began to see the meaning of this. The Anglican clergy had for the past year been preaching against the Declaration, denouncing it Sunday after Sunday as unlawful and improper, a thing they could not in conscience accept. So what would be thought of them if they were now to halt their Sunday services while they read it, in full and as a royal proclamation, to their congregations?

'What happens if they don't read it?' he asked John.

'It isn't mentioned. But there's the Ecclesiastical Commission, which can deprive them of their livings.'

It all fitted. If they were now to read this Declaration, it would certainly be said of them that for all their talk of conscience they were, in the end, putting thought of glebe and parsonage first. Respect for them would drop, and their influence with it, and they might no longer be able to lead resistance to the King. It was exactly what Mallory and Innes had foreseen, and the purpose of the second Declaration was now clear. It sharpened memories of the first one, and it provided a convenient text that the clergy could be ordered to read.

'Do you think they'll read it?' said John.

'I don't know. They'll resent it bitterly, and they'll probably do a lot of arguing and consulting.'

'They're not given much time for that. The Order says it's to be read in London the last two Sundays of this month, the 20th and 27th. For the rest of the country it's the first two Sundays of June, the 3rd and the 10th.'

It was left to Richard Gibson, coming in a few minutes later, to sum this up for them, and to notice a further detail.

'The 3rd and 10th?' he said sharply. 'That's Whit Sunday and Trinity Sunday. A pretty choice of dates! Allway would call those days high festivals.'

'But what will he do?'

'Refuse at once, I should think. I'll say that for the man. He's at times a fool, but he does follow what he believes.'

'How of the other clergy?'

'It's hard. There's the Ecclesiastical Commission, and each

man will know that if he refuses he may soon be out of home and living, his wife and children with him. So we'd best think charitably. In the end, perhaps, they will look to their bishops.'

'For guidance?'

'Yes. If a bishop now shows his worth, if he refuses to distribute this Declaration and speaks firmly against it, I think his clergy will obey him. But if he is weak and fearful, and seems in two minds himself, this might be too much for a man alone in a country living, with no support or advice. Pray therefore for the bishops.'

'The bishops may look to their archbishop.'

'As they have a right to do.' Gibson nodded slowly. 'If Dr Sancroft were now to stir himself he could lead his bishops, and they could lead their clergy. So perhaps we must now all look to Lambeth to see what wind blows there. If it blows at all – '

'Yes?'

'There are passions in the nation that could fan it to a gale, and it could blow harder than this King has ever dreamed of. It could blow him from his throne.'

11 *The Water Gate*

Nick felt lonely in the week that followed. His parents had gone, the Gibsons had gone, and being formally betrothed to Judith did nothing to bring her back to him. She was at Salisbury, and she wrote that her mother had greatly disliked being left in the care of Mrs Pemberton, good as that care had been, and was already saying that she would accept no such arrangement again. There was no comfort in that. Nor was London a comforting place that week. The endless talk in the taverns and the coffee houses had made plain to everyone the importance of that Order to read the Declaration, and London was a tense and unhappy place as men waited for some sign of what the clergy would do. But the Bishop of London was still under suspension, and his clergy, left to themselves, showed no sign of knowing what they would do. Anxiety mounted, and men of every sort began to look to Lambeth, and the lonely figure of the Archbishop of Canterbury.

Lonely he certainly was, for he had no Archbishop of York to stand with him, that see being vacant. Three or four of the diocesan bishops, the most subersvient, were distributing the Declaration to their clergy, but the others seemed only to be watching Lambeth. Nothing came, doubts grew deeper, and men began to ask whether William Sancroft was the man to be Archbishop at such a moment. No one doubted his good intentions, but he was in his seventy-second year and was said to be in poor health. He was, moreover, on such bad terms with the King, after refusing to serve on the Ecclesiastical Commission, that he had been forbidden the Court altogether. He had responded by staying firmly on the other side of the river, and in the last two years he had hardly left Lambeth. He must therefore, it was now said, be wholly out of touch with everyone, and he could not now be the man to lead the Church against so determined a

King. Doubts grew deeper, and a belief spread that if the lesser clergy were to be saved at all they would have to save themselves.

Yet it was the dissenters who made the first move, and in some congregations the laity were ahead of the minister. Nick, calling at Lombard Street the next Monday evening, found Innes just slipping into his cloak, ready to go out.

'I go to a meeting,' he explained. 'I'm still counted among the Baptist congregation here, and some of us think our minister lags a little. He'll have to be told.'

'Told what?'

'What he can do. Directly, of course, he can't do anything. That's for the vicar, the Anglican. But he can speak to the vicar on our behalf, assuring him of our support and help, and beseeching him, in the name of God, that he in no wise read that Declaration. That's what he can do, and we hold this meeting to tell him so.'

His was not the only congregation to hold such a meeting in that day or two, and some ministers who had wavered were distinctly told what their congregations thought about it. But most of them had done their part already, and when the Anglican clergy of London met to discuss what they should do, they had before them the wishes and the generous promises of the dissenters. Even so, their debate was keen, but by Sunday it was known throughout the City that they had pledged themselves not to read the Declaration. Their sermons the next Sunday were mostly about this, and every congregation gave promises of support. But time was running on. The next Sunday would be the first of those set for the reading in London, and there was no word yet from the bishops, no hint of whether they would find the courage to lead their clergy in disobedience. The coffee houses talked of little else, and anxieties grew keener.

Letters began to come from the country, and even in family letters the family news for once took second place. A letter from Judith was in the style of many:

The people here speak of scarcely anything else, and ask daily whether the clergy will read it or no. Sir Nicholas Culley is said to be entering into an engagement with some other gentlemen that they will together pay a maintenance to their vicar should he be deprived for refusing to read, and I am told that some other parishes may do the like. All the dissenters here have said that they stand with the Anglicans in this, so high do feelings run.

The next post brought Nick a letter from his father:

Our bishop stands now in the contempt of everyone, having sent copies of this Declaration to his clergy, with his strict commands to read it. Our Mr Allway – I say this to his honour – will in no way bow to the wrath that faces him, and has just told us from his pulpit that he will in no wise read it or admit it to be lawful. This led to his being again complimented in the churchyard by Gibson; who added, perhaps by way of comfort, that the righteous find friends in adversity.

On the Friday evening, with only one day before the fateful Sunday, Nick went to supper with John. He stayed till near midnight, and when he walked back to the Temple the streets were all but empty, with only an occasional distant footfall to tell of another as belated as himself. Then, as he came near Temple Bar, the silence broke. Out of sight, in the dark, someone was bawling noisily. Lights appeared in windows, some heads were pushed out, here and there a door swung open, and he quickly guessed that once again a hawker was crying something of interest enough to bring men from their beds. Then he began to hear the voice: '*The petition of the bishops to the King. The archbishop and the bishops. This night at Whitehall . . . The humble petition* . . . ' Nick felt hurriedly for a penny.

In his room in the Temple he laid the sheet on the table and lighted both the candles. He read it standing, before he was even out of his cloak:

The humble petition of William, Archbishop of Canterbury, and divers of the suffragan Bishops now present with him, humbly sheweth:

That the great averseness they find in themselves to publishing in all their churches your Majesty's late Declaration for liberty of conscience proceedeth not from any want of duty . . . nor yet from any want of tenderness to Dissenters, but because that Declaration is founded on such a Dispensing Power as has often been declared illegal in Parliament, and . . . your Petitioners cannot in . . . conscience make themselves parties to it . . .

Your Petitioners therefore most humbly and earnestly beseech your Majesty . . . not to insist upon their distributing and reading your Majesty's said Declaration.

Seven signatures followed, of the Archbishop and six diocesan bishops, all in the stiff episcopal style, and Nick had to translate them into the names of men. Six of them were no more than names to him, but *Tho.Bath & Wells* was Dr Ken, whom he held in something more than esteem. For an instant memories held him, and then he turned again to the text, reading it for a second time, more carefully, and understanding it better. The Archbishop, in spite of age and infirmity, had surely risen to the occasion as befitted the Primate of All England, not prevaricating or making excuses, but boldly declaring the dispensing power to be illegal; too boldly, perhaps, or too bluntly, to please the King.

A candle spluttered, flinging a tiny splash against his hand, and his thought turned, asking some questions that this sheet did not answer. The petition must surely have been presented by now to the King. It could hardly have been printed before it was presented, and the hawker had been shouting something about 'this night at Whitehall'. It would have been proper for the bishops, after writing their petition, to present it to the King themselves. It had presumably been written at Lambeth; and Nick began to see them in the Archbishop's barge, running down the sunlit river to Whitehall in the splendour of the summer evening. It could well have been so, but there was nothing to tell him; and no hint of how they had been received, or of what the King had said to the petition. Its attack on the dispensing power went to the very root of things, and could have pricked him keenly.

Mr Pollexfen was cautious when Nick asked him about it the next morning. There was nothing illegal, he said, in presenting a petition to the King, and Kings had always received petitions politely, even if they had not liked them; and King James could hardly be expected to like this one, which told him bluntly that he had been acting unlawfully. He would not have liked it even in private, and it had not been kept private. It had been printed, and then cried through the streets of London; and Mr Pollexfen wondered who had sent it to a printer, and how, indeed, he had found a printer at that hour of the night. It would certainly make matters no easier.

Sunday came, and the London clergy kept to their agreement. In only four of a hundred churches was the Declaration read, and in those four, as soon as the reading started, the entire congregation got up and walked out, refusing to hear it. Nick abandoned for once the family traditions and went that morning with Edmund Innes to a Baptist meeting-house, where he heard a determined preacher commend the courage and conscience of the bishops, and then exhort his own congregation to be steadfast in their support, 'standing together lest we fall together, as our King assuredly intends'. It was heartening, and Nick learned later that he could have heard the like of it in a hundred other meeting-houses that Sunday morning.

He went to Westminster that afternoon, sure that John would have been to Whitehall in search of news. So it proved, but John was looking worried as he began to speak of it.

'There's not much news,' he said. 'The King's shut himself away. He's not appearing in the Galleries, and he's hardly seeing anybody. That's a sign of bad temper, so he must be more than usually angry.'

'Because this thing was printed?'

'He was in a temper before he even heard of that, on Friday when the bishops were with him.'

'What happened that night?'

'We don't really know. Six bishops arrived by water, in Canterbury's barge, something after ten o'clock at night. He hadn't expected them, but he agreed to see them, and we don't know very much after that. No one else went in with them. But there were one or two men in the ante-room and they heard his voice, raised pretty high. Something about a standard of rebellion, and then some more about trumpeters of sedition.'

'To the Archbishop?'

'No. Sancroft wasn't there. He's been forbidden Whitehall. This was the six suffragans, and they came out looking very unhappy. They got into their barge and went off back to Lambeth. And that's all that's known.'

'How about the printing of their petition?'

'Nothing's known, but I heard it called good Whiggery.'

'Why that?'

'It's made a private quarrel public, and therefore worse. It's King against Church now, and neither can give way. So there's more trouble coming.'

The Privy Council met on Friday, and then announced that it had taken note of a libel lately written and published against the King, and that the seven bishops who had signed it were to appear before the Council in two weeks' time, on Friday, June 8th. This would include the Archbishop, who had been the first to sign the petition, though he had not gone to Whitehall with it. London burst at once into a storm of talk and anger, most men saying that the Council would quickly send the bishops to the Ecclesiastical Commission to be deprived of their sees.

Sunday came, and again the Declaration was read in only four empty churches, and again, in all the others, crowded congregations hummed their approval of sermons on the reasons why. Then, on the Monday, Mr Pollexfen had a word for Nick, in whose affairs he now took a friendly interest. He sounded very calm, and very sure of himself.

'What do you intend during the vacation?' he asked. 'Salisbury, is it, and Miss Judith?'

'I hope so.'

Nick was in fact quite sure of it. The law term would end on the coming Friday, and the short vacation would be a most welcome break. He meant to be in Salisbury by the Saturday night.

'Ye-es.' Mr Pollexfen looked him in the eye. 'But some of us may need to be here for the 8th, or soon after it.'

That was the day the bishops were to appear before the Council, and it was exactly in the middle of the vacation. Nick thought of Judith, and had a sudden feeling of dismay.

'Why yes. But – '

'This affair of the bishops, of course. We must be ready for a brief or two.'

'Before the Commission?'

'Where are your wits? Didn't you notice that the announcement talked of libel? Do you think that's for the Commission?'

'Oh!'

'I'm glad you see it. If they were to be sent before the Commission they'd have been charged with disobedience, or something of the sort, which is what the Commission deals with. But a libel means King's Bench, where they can have counsel to speak for them, and from what I can learn, they're going to have every help the Bar can give them. I've never known such a feeling about a case.'

'Small wonder.'

'Certainly. But now – ' Mr Pollexfen's tone sharpened. 'We can't go with them before the Council. They must speak for themselves there, and all we can do is to advise them beforehand on what they should say or not say. I expect to be consulting with one or two others about that advice. Pemberton, I think, and Sawyer and Treby.' He had named three Counsel as eminent as himself. 'But of course it's after they're committed to King's Bench – if, indeed, they are – that we must go to work in earnest, and in that, Burnaby, you may wish to have some part.'

'I?'

'But yes. I do not, of course, mean that you should argue the case in court. You are a little too junior for that, and it is likely that three or four of us will do it jointly. But when we meet to discuss it, we shall need exact knowledge of what has been said in Parliament about the dispensing power, and what has been held in some earlier judgements. If you were to attend our meeting, ready to inform us precisely on all this, you would have earned at least a seat in the court.'

Nicholas stood staring at him, for once too surprised to speak. To sit with Counsel, in such a case, even if he did not speak – And then he remembered Judith. The 8th was in the middle of the vacation.

'I had thought of her.' Mr Pollexfen spoke crisply, and had plainly guessed his thoughts. 'I think, Burnaby, that we could spare you from the Hall this week. You have nothing to do except sit and listen, and you would have some ten days clear if you were to leave at once.'

Nicholas waited for no more, except to thank Mr Pollexfen and whichever good angel had put this thought into his head. Most certainly he would be back on the 8th, and most certainly he would then read the journals of Parliament and anything else that might be needed. But at the moment he would go to Salisbury.

He was away in an hour, on a road that was dry and firm in the sun, and he reached his uncle's house the next day, a week before he was expected. But nobody was put out by that. His aunt took this in her stride, and Sir Nicholas seemed delighted to have someone to talk to. This turned out, however, to mean the same topic. His newsletter had not arrived, perhaps because the post-boys were over-burdened with newsletters, and he had not yet heard that the bishops were to appear before the Council.

It was the same the next day with Judith. There was no getting away from it anywhere. She received him delightedly and took him to her mother, who was sufficiently recovered to talk with him for a while, and even to tell him that she was pleased at the betrothal. But within minutes after that Judith was telling him of the excitement in Salisbury, and of how the dissenters were as fervent as the Anglicans in their prayers for the seven bishops. On Whit Sunday he went with her to the parish church, and noted that the Declaration was not read, though this was the first of the Sundays set for the country reading. Instead he heard almost the sermon he had heard the week before in London. The style was more homely, and it sounded stronger for that.

He was back in London by noon of the 8th, and in the Temple he found Mr Pollexfen, ready for anything on that important day. He and others, he said, had advised the bishops that when they were before the Council – which would be at a special meeting at half-past six that evening – they should be brief in their answers, admitting as little as possible, and refusing altogether to answer anything that would incriminate them. The other news was that six more bishops, too late to sign the petition, had now given it signatures of approval; which, he added drily, might not improve the King's temper. Nick wondered whether that advice to refuse answers would improve it either. Mr Pollexfen, he remembered, was a Whig.

He went in the afternoon to Lombard Street to give the news of Judith and her mother, and Innes listened with due attention. Then he looked steadily at Nick, and blandly asked if he would like a sail on the river that evening.

It was the same topic yet again. It was known, he went on, that the bishops would again go to Whitehall by water, and many Londoners had thought it would be a pleasing gesture of support to wait off Lambeth in their own boats and then escort the barge down the river. Innes meant to be one of them, and Nick promptly accepted the invitation. After his dusty journey from Salisbury, an hour on the river might be very pleasant.

The sun was still hot, and the sky a rich blue, when they pushed away from the Tower stairs that evening, to let a mild south-east wind take them easily up the long westward reach to the Strand. Then, after the great bend, they had to beat up-wind, and now the river was busy, thronged with craft of every sort, all making their way to Lambeth. There were pleasure boats under sail, some under oars, and dirty workaday boats as well, whose crews had left their ferrying of coal and beer and candles and had come at the end of their day to give their own cheer to the bishops. At Lambeth the whole sunlit river was alive with boats, hove-to off the Palace stairs, and waiting, all waiting for the same thing.

'I'm glad we are here,' said Innes calmly. 'We are perhaps only just in time.'

He was looking to the east bank, where the Palace stairs were in the full light of the westering sun. At their foot a ten-oared barge was lying alongside, manned and ready, and the staging above was crowded with people, men and women together, who had come from the Palace to see the bishops go. They seemed to be of every rank, from servants in their working clothes to dignitaries of the Church, grave in their black and white. One or two of these set Innes peering keenly.

'Do I see lawn sleeves there?' he asked. 'Your eyes are younger.'

'Yes. Three at least. Bishops, I suppose?'

'Here like the rest of us, to support their brethren. Ah!'

His voice had risen, and from all round them there was a lap and splash of water as men, standing to look, set boats rocking dangerously. The crowd on the stage had parted, making a lane for the seven men who were beginning to descend the stairs. They stepped into the barge, one or two of them needing some help, and it pushed away. The ten oars lifted, hung poised for a moment, and then dipped together as the watermen found their steady stroke. The barge gathered way, and everywhere sails were trimmed and sheets hauled taut for the passage down and across to Whitehall. The rowing boats fell astern, and it was a flotilla of sailing boats that made the escort. White sails and rippling water seemed everywhere, and in the dancing sunlight the whole river seemed to gleam and sparkle as if this were some happy celebration. Only the bishops in their sombre garb, sitting composedly in the barge, gave a hint that it was not.

At Whitehall the privy stairs were as crowded as the Lambeth stairs had been, and with as varied a company; and these, too, parted to make a lane as the barge ran smoothly in, and the Archbishop, refusing all help, led the others up. A chamberlain stepped forward to meet him, bowed punctiliously, then turned about to lead the way. The watchers stood silent, but every man had uncovered, and here and there a woman had dropped to her knees, as if asking a blessing from the bishops. In single file they followed the chamberlain. They passed through an open door into the passage to the Stone Gallery, and the door swung to behind them. They had gone, and the time of waiting had begun.

It became tedious. Some of the boats left, but most of them

stayed, tacking to and fro across the river as they waited for the bishops to return. An hour passed and it was then half-past seven, with the sunlight slanting low across the water and no sign yet of the bishops. A red tinge of sunset was coming into the sky when Innes, as practical as ever, opened a hamper stored with bread, sliced cold beef, and a bottle or two of wine. That saw the next half-hour away, but the sun had sunk into the distant haze when their attention turned suddenly to the stairs again. The people, who had mostly drifted away, were coming back, and below them the barge had pushed clear and was moving out into the stream. It stopped and waited, hanging on the oars, while another barge came out of the Scotland dock and went to the stairs. It made fast, and the royal arms could be seen on its panels.

'What's this?' said Innes sharply. 'Why?'

He was not the only one to ask. Right across the river boats had altered course and were closing in to get a better view. On the wharf the people were hurriedly parting to make a lane, as they had done before, but down the lane came a half-dozen soldiers, marching stiffly with their muskets sloped. Behind them came an officer, marching as stiffly, with his drawn sword held before him. Then, after him, came the frail figure of the Archbishop, followed closely by the others. Slowly he led them down the stairs to the waiting barge, and the officer went with them, still with his sword shining in the sun. Above him the people pressed to the edge, bare-headed, and looking angry and turbulent. In the boat Innes was standing dangerously.

'Why?' he snapped. 'Are they under arrest?'

'They must be. But why as prisoners? Why not bail?'

'As a lawyer you should tell me.'

The barge pushed off, expertly handled by the royal watermen in their gold and scarlet jackets. It pulled clear of the stairs, and then turned down-stream in a wide half-circle, holding well out to take full advantage of the current. Everywhere the sailing boats turned also, and then, with the wind on the quarter and sheets paid out, they went with the barge, a close-packed escort on either beam, some of them dangerously close together. Innes turned suddenly to Nick.

'Where do they go, do you think?'

'The Tower? What else is there, below the bridge?'

'There's nothing else.' The answer came back angrily. 'Bishops, if you please! Sent to the Tower like criminals, and for no more than offering a petition to the King! Was there worse tyranny by his father?'

Nick let that pass. He did not yet know what charges had been brought and as a lawyer he would not form an opinion on nothing. He stayed silent, and soon they were round the bend of the river, tacking against a wind that was no longer with them. The barge pulled steadily on, and inexorably it began to draw ahead. The Tower came into view, and the last gleam of sun had left the river when the barge turned in another wide sweep to where a gate had opened in the long grey wall and the water-stairs showed black. It slackened speed, and the boats began to draw close again. There was an afterglow in the western sky, and the light was still golden, as Innes, watching intently, spoke for many.

'Traitors' Gate, if you please! For Christian bishops, and who'd believe it, if we hadn't seen it?'

12 *Trinity Sunday*

Nick went the next morning in search of Mr Pollexfen, who was as likely as anyone to know what had really happened. But this was the middle of the vacation, and Mr Pollexfen was not in the Temple. So Nick went in search of brother John instead, who might also know what had happened at Whitehall, and again he was disappointed. He was told at the Cockpit that the Princess Anne was at Bath, drinking the waters, and though she had not taken Mr Burnaby with her he was not at the Cockpit this morning. So Nick went next to John's house, where Doraty cheerfully explained matters. The Princess expected to be at Bath for some weeks, but she had been considerate. She had said that John must now stay in Westminster with his wife, and she would take Lord Churchill with her to Bath. But Doraty was still in excellent health and not in need of any help from John, who had therefore gone to Whitehall, hoping, like everyone else, to learn what had happened before the Council last night. He would no doubt come home for dinner, for which Nick had better stay. So Nick stayed, and John came in an hour later, looking none too happy at what he had learned. But he at least seemed sure of the facts.

The bishops had been asked whether the signatures on the petition were theirs, and at length, and under sharp pressure from the King, they had owned to this. Lord Chancellor Jeffreys had then told them that they would be prosecuted for a misdemeanour and must give recognizances to appear before the Court of King's Bench. It was at this point that things had gone wrong.

'They wouldn't give recognizances,' said John. 'They said that as bishops they were peers of the realm, and that it's a privilege of peers to give a simple promise instead of a written recognizance. Is that true?'

'It's usually allowed. But wouldn't they even promise to appear before the court?'

'Oh yes, but Jeffreys said it wasn't enough. They must give it in writing, and the King backed Jeffreys. But everyone says he's looking as black as thunder about it. He never expected this. But you know what he is. If they once started objecting to anything, he'd get into a temper and start threatening, and then he'd think he had to keep to it for the sake of his dignity. In the end he had to go on with it and send them to the Tower. It's all quite silly and quite unnecessary. Would it have mattered if he'd given way and accepted a spoken promise?'

'No. But would it have mattered if *they* had given way and signed the thing? It would have saved a great deal of trouble.'

'They seem to have been advised not to by their lawyers.'

'The devil they were!'

This was something new. But Mr Pollexfen, the next morning, was brisk about it, and forceful.

'Certainly it was necessary,' he said. 'For the King to sweep away that privilege of peers would have been a further exercise of the dispensing power, and it had to be resisted. In any case, they were in a mood to make martyrs of themselves, and they've done it very usefully.'

Nick wondered if that last comment held the clue to all this. Mr Pollexfen, as he again remembered, was a Whig. Few men would understand that the bishops had been refused bail only because of this punctilio about privilege. It would seem plain and certain that they had been sent to the Tower for petitioning the King, and the newsletters would be filled with this. The way of doing it – the barge and the sunlit river, the royal watermen, the fading light, the officer's sword, and Traitors' Gate at dusk – these were the very stuff of newsletters, and their accounts of it would set the whole country in a flame. Not even Lord Shaftesbury could have contrived more out of so little.

Then it was Sunday again, Trinity Sunday, when the Declaration should be read a second time in the country, and not a soul now thought it would be. Almost every sermon in London was about the bishops, the oppressions of the King, and the danger to the Church. Nick began to tire of it, and in the warm sunlight of the afternoon he decided to have some air on the river. He would call on Doraty and John.

A boat could usually be had at the Temple stairs, and he

turned down Temple Lane accordingly. Then, behind him in Fleet Street, he heard the frenzied bawling of a hawker, and he was in such a state of apprehension that even on a Sunday afternoon he could not leave the matter alone. He hurried up the lane, paid a penny for a small printed sheet, and read it there and then. In one short paragraph it said that that morning, in St James's Palace, the Queen had been delivered of a son, heir to the crown.

He stood in the sunlight, staring at it while a jumble of thoughts came at him together. There had been warning enough that this might happen, but the tales had been positive that a child was expected in the middle of July. It was now the 10th of June, a month early, which would be enough to set some men saying that this was indeed a fraud, timed at this moment to distract attention from the bishops in the Tower. But John might have picked up some further details at Whitehall, since he had not much else to do while the Princess was at Bath – and at once the thought came stabbing that she should *not* have been at Bath. She should have been at St James's Palace. She and her sister were the heirs to the throne, the one after the other, and if a birth was expected that would deprive them of that inheritance, then it was her obvious right to be present that she might satisfy herself that all was true and proper. Instead she was a hundred miles away, at Bath; unless, of course, she had been hurriedly summoned, which was just possible – and Nick went striding purposefully down the lane to find that boat. He must certainly see John, who would at least know where the Princess was.

But it was Doraty who received him at the house in Westminster, and when he asked where John might be she gave him a tart answer.

'On the western road. About twenty miles down it, I should think, and riding hell for leather. You'll guess where.'

'Bath, do you mean?'

'Where else? You'll know what news he takes?'

'So the Princess wasn't summoned?'

'She certainly wasn't. And I don't think anyone else was who should have been.'

'Doraty, what do you mean?'

'Oh – ' She sounded exasperated to the point of anger, and then she almost laughed. 'Sit down, Nick, and I'm sorry if I've been sharp. But I don't see much of John when the Princess is at the Cockpit, and I've been enjoying these last days, when I've had him nearly to myself. I was expecting another week or two of it, and now he goes tearing off like this at about a minute's notice – and I'm within a few weeks of my own time.'

'Can you manage?'

'I'll have to. John did just think of it, for a moment. He said Penny Crosedale would see to me, and I expect she will. I'll have to get a message to her.'

'I'll go. At once, if you wish.'

'It's not to a minute – or an hour, for that matter. And I suppose I oughtn't to blame John. He was really upset.'

'About the birth? Or was there something more?'

'More!' She echoed it angrily, then calmed herself and spoke quitely. 'We went to the Whitehall chapel this morning, because I didn't want to go all the way to the Abbey, and when he came out the Palace seemed odd. There was nobody of importance anywhere, but there was a crowd of lesser folk, and they were all talking and chattering. They'd heard the news, of course, and it didn't take John a minute to learn it too. That was bad enough, if it put the Princess out of line, but he'd caught a whisper of something else, and he found me a chair in the Gallery while he went from one to another, asking and making sure.'

'Nobody had expected it, I suppose, a month early?'

'They certainly hadn't, and even the Queen hadn't. That seems pretty certain, because one of the things he learned was that last night she sat up till midnight, playing cards. Then she didn't feel well, and she was whisked off to St James's, where they were running round like mad, getting ready for her. There were messengers flying about everywhere, summoning people.'

'Quite right, I suppose.'

'No, it wasn't right, and that's what's upset John. You know this tale that the Queen couldn't really be with child of her own? John says that he now believes it, and that the whole nation will believe it before the week's out. He says that a lot of Privy Councillors and so on have to be present for a royal birth, so that they can make oath afterwards that it was all true and proper, and this time there wasn't a single person present whose word will mean anything. The whole lot, he says, were either papists or near papists, who'd either welcome a fraud or swear to anything to please the King. So what can that mean, he asks, except that there *was* a fraud, and honest men couldn't be invited because they'd have learned the truth?'

'Doraty!'

'I'm telling you what John told me. And this, of course, is why he's gone riding post to Bath to tell the Princess. More than anyone, of course, *she* should have been there.'

'Could she have been, if it came as a surprise?'

'Her uncles could have been, and they were both left in their houses.'

'Clarendon and Rochester?'

Nick had seen the point. The Earls of Clarendon and Rochester were the brothers of Anne Hyde, the King's first wife; and if the Princess could not be present, her two uncles were the obvious men to be summoned in her place. Nor would this have been difficult, for both had houses near by. They could have been called in minutes, and Nicholas could think of no reason why they should not have been – no good reason.

'John says,' said Doraty, 'there can be only one meaning to it. So I suppose he *had* to ride. The Princess can't be left to learn this from a newsletter.'

'And you won't know when he's coming back?'

'When the Princess lets him. And if it's not too long I'll be all right.'

'I'll warn Mrs Crosedale all the same. I'd better go at once.'

The Crosedales lived in Primrose Lane, which led from King Street to the river, and on this summer afternoon they were sitting in the trim little garden behind the house. Nick was made politely welcome, and Penelope was quick in her response to his tale.

'I'll look to Doraty,' she said firmly. 'Leave her to me, and I'll perhaps go this evening for a word with her. There's no immediate trouble?'

'Not in that way.'

'But plenty in other ways?' Colonel Crosedale came suddenly into the talk, looking grave and thoughtful. 'A Prince is born, and the news sends John to Bath. But what more have you heard?'

'Only what John told Doraty.'

He recounted it, and the Colonel took it quietly, and then nodded.

'More or less what I've heard,' he said. 'But over the years, in my duties, I have seen a good deal of the King, and I do not believe he is such a liar and a cheat. But I have not known a man more dense of understanding. He sees his own views only, and in all his life he's never had the least glimmer of how anything looks to anyone else. That's probably what happened this time. He'd think of all the people he personally wished to have there, and he wouldn't have a thought for the Princess and her uncles and all the others he should have called. I don't pretend that this makes matters better, because the nation doesn't know about it. And we have now an angry nation.'

'Then what do you expect?'

'Trouble. I shall have to remember that I'm a soldier.'

It came uncompromisingly, with no attempt to evade it, and for a moment Nick was in a chilled silence. Colonel Crosedale wore the King's uniform. Richard Gibson, his brother-in-law, might yet command a regiment again, or at least a troop; and they might meet. Nick liked both of them.

'When do you think to be married? August, is it?'

The pleasant voice came again, sounding quite unperturbed, and Nick had to recall his thoughts hastily. This was what concerned him.

'Yes – if I may bring Judith here. Will it be safe?'

'Perhaps not.' The answer was immediate, and again with no attempt to evade. 'If trouble does come, I'll no doubt be ordered away with my regiment to wherever the danger point is, and I agree with Richard that once we're gone the London rabble may well come swarming here to seize the Palace. That's what I fear, and I won't have Penny left alone to it, so I've bought a small house for her, twenty miles upriver. She'll be safe enough there, and she's asked Doraty to go there with her. So that's arranged.'

'Yes.' Nick's thoughts were still with Judith, and whether he could bring her to Westminster. 'So you think there *will* be trouble?'

'I don't know.' Crosedale spoke quietly and with slow deliberation. 'But this boy born today means a papist succession, and that by itself could set men feeling for their swords. But if they accept also this tale that it's to be a succession imposed by fraud, there'll be no measuring their anger. It won't be a matter then of feeling for their swords. The swords will be on the grindstone.'

13 The Warming Pan

Nick soon learned what every Whig, and many another too, was saying about the royal child, and it was a more precise tale than he had expected. He learned it, fittingly enough, from Sir Thomas Mallory, whom he chanced to meet the next day. Sir Thomas was not troubled by doubts. He insisted on taking Nick to the King's Head for dinner, and he came to the matter at once. It was, after all, the only topic in London that week.

'It's plain enough,' he said crisply, 'and it has all come about exactly as the papists so knowledgeably predicted. You are quite right, of course, about the Hyde brothers. Unquestionably they should have been called. So should the Dutch ambassador, on behalf of the Princess Mary. You could add also the Archbishop.'

'But he's in the Tower.'

'Who sent him there, and why? Was it, perhaps, to get him out of the way for this? He could at least have been brought from the Tower for a few hours, and he most certainly should have been. The Church of England was most vitally affected. But these are minor matters. Have you heard this tale of a warming pan?'

'A *what*?'

'A warming pan. The tale's spreading fast, though I can't learn where it comes from.'

He went on to tell it. Whatever had been done at St James's, he said, had been done in the conditions usual for a royal birth. A large room had been cleared of all furniture except a few chairs round the walls and the heavily curtained bed in the centre. The curtains were hung rather further from the bed than was usual, to make what was almost an inner room round the bed. Those who were invited to be present were therefore present in the sense that they were in the room, but no one went through the curtains except Mrs Wilkins, the midwife, and her two assistants. Eventually Mrs Wilkins had come through the curtains carrying an obviously new-born child, which she had briefly shown to the company before taking it back within. But one of her assistants had come out a little before this. She had left the main room, and had soon returned carrying a warming pan, which she had taken through the curtains. That had seemed reasonable, and no one had taken much heed of it; but the tale now told was that the warming pan had contained, not coals, but the child, which had been born a very little earlier to someone else, carried to Mrs Wilkins in the pan, and then produced as the child of the Queen.

'This makes sense of the whole affair,' said Mallory. 'With it, everything falls into place, and without it there's nonsense.'

'But aren't new-born children delicate? Can they be carried about in warming pans?'

'I haven't tried it. But why not, with a small child and a big pan? There could be a blanket in the pan, I suppose?'

'But – '

'Burnaby, we must not look for flaws in this, or we shall find we have accepted a succession that isn't to be thought of. Be thankful, please, for the warming pan, and don't raise difficulties.'

That was certainly Whiggery, clearly and succinctly stated, and Nick could see no point in arguing against what might well be a very linchpin of Whiggery for years to come. He turned Sir Thomas from it by asking how the Green Ribbon Club had conducted its affairs in this King's Head tavern, and Sir Thomas responded willingly. Memories woke and a light came into his eyes as he told of the crowded wine-room, deafening with talk, reeking with the vapours of tobacco, and dominated by the tiny figure of Lord Shaftesbury, frail, bright-eyed, and commanding. Then he told of the balconies that had fronted the street, and of the speeches that had been made and the charades that had been acted on them for the jostling spellbound crowds below. He told how the members, himself among them, had gone down from the balconies to lead the crowds with drums and torches in vast processions through the streets of London; and finally, warming to it now, he told of the great Pope burnings, when once a year, on November 17th, the accession day of Elizabeth, the Club had roused all London with a vast and expensive pageant and a ceremonial burning of the Pope in effigy at Temple Bar. Sir Thomas spoke of all this with zest, but a tinge of regret was in it too, as if these had been the brave old days, and he had found life thinner for their passing.

'It was all Shaftesbury,' he said quietly. 'He was the life and the breath behind us all. He gave something to us, and never, I think, did so great an enterprise fail by so little. And never was a failure more to be regretted. It was by a dozen votes in Parliament that we failed, no more. And for want of them in those days we now have bishops in the Tower, and we talk of warming pans.'

He fell silent, and Nick slowly nodded. The Exclusion Bills, one after another, had sought to exclude the Duke of York from the succession, and if any one of them had become law the Princess of Orange would have inherited in his stead; a very protestant Queen with a very protestant husband. There would have been no fears then for Church and liberty.

The silence lengthened as Sir Thomas sat brooding. Then a note of purpose came into his voice, as if he were leading to something.

'The Club has gone,' he said. 'We can never have it again, for there is no Shaftesbury, and it *was* Shaftesbury. But what else is there? Something is surely needed, even if it be but a loose association, but not even that can I find. Do you know of anything?'

'No.'

'Then how is it now in the Temple? We had many lawyers in the Club, young ones in particular. But what now?'

'Some are Whigs, of course. Others begin to say that if something is not done, and quickly, there will be an end altogether to the law.'

'There will indeed. But of an association?'

'I don't know of anything.'

'They perhaps wait for a lead, which I can perhaps give, since I have experience. Say, please, to any who may be interested, that they may at all times inquire for me here, at the King's Head.'

He evidently meant to have a Whig association, and if its views were not at first extreme they were likely, under his determined guidance, to drift that way. So Nick left it alone. He mentioned it to some Whigs of his acquaintance in the Temple, and then he turned to other things. He was busy now for Mr Pollexfen, studying the Commons' journals for anything that could be used in legal arguments for the bishops, and in the evenings he had letters to write, more of them than he wished; to Judith, telling her about everything, and to his father, telling him of John's journey to Bath and the urgent reasons for it. Most of this he wrote again for Nick Culley, who would be as eager as his own father for reliable news.

Then it was Friday, when the law term opened and the bishops were to come before the King's Bench and ask for release from the Tower. Nick, remembering a promise from Mr Pollexfen, asked no permission when he quietly took a seat behind defending Counsel. He glanced round, and saw in the front seats more peers of the realm than he had known in the Hall before. Mr Pollexfen quickly whispered that the peers were as angry as anyone, and were here to make their gesture by offering bail if it should be needed.

But it was not. Sir Robert Wright, the Chief Justice, did what the King had probably required of him. He ruled that the bishops could properly be committed on such a charge, and he ordered that the trial should be resumed in two weeks' time, June 29th. Then he glanced cautiously at the waiting peers and said that from men of such high consideration he would not require bail; simple recognizances would be enough. Mr Pollexfen, for the bishops, answered that they would give the recognizances. He could perhaps have added, though he did not, that their protest about privilege had done its work and could be forgotten. They had been sent to the Tower, the nation had been roused to anger, and Whiggery was for the moment satisfied. It had a warming pan to turn to now and to put to use.

The bishops departed, temporarily free. The court turned to its next case, and Westminster Hall was in its routine again. But towards the end of the afternoon it was learned that the Princess of Denmark had returned from Bath, and that was enough to send Nick to Westminster that evening in search of John, who had perhaps returned with her. He had, and both he and Doraty were looking very pleased and cheerful. Nick, who had seen no cheerful faces lately, promptly asked why.

'Oh – ' John looked even more pleased with himself. 'It was a good thought to go off to Bath last Sunday. I used a fresh horse every ten miles or so if I could get it, and I didn't heed the expense, so I was there by six in the morning, and feeling half dead. But that didn't matter. I was first with the news, and I had Lord Churchill out of bed for it.'

'How did he take *that*?'

'You can't upset that man. He listened, and he asked some questions – just the right ones – and then he roused the Princess.'

'And was she pleased?'

'She was pleased with *me* for showing what she called such zeal, but not with the news. You couldn't expect her to be.'

'But what happened?'

'I don't know. I went to bed. But she has a proper mind, and I think she wanted to write a dutiful letter to her father about how pleased she was he had a son. Churchill had to talk her out of it.'

'It sounds correct enough.'

'Nick, you're being stupid. It wasn't just the news of the birth I'd gone to Bath with. It was the other part too, all papists there, and no good protestants, not even – '

'Oh, I see.'

'That was what mattered, and that was why she was so pleased with me, after Churchill had explained it to her. If she hadn't known it soon enough she *would* have written. She'd have had to, and then, when doubts turned up, she'd have had to make the best she could of going back on it. Very awkward.'

'I'm glad she was pleased with you.'

'Pleased!' For a moment John seemed breathless with excitement. 'She sent for me that evening, after Churchill had told her how well I'd done for her, and she clearly told me that if she should ever rise in the world, I should rise with her.'

That could only mean if she should one day inherit the crown; which would not be possible if the King had an accepted son. Nick saw the point at once.

'Go on,' he said. 'Did she write to her father?'

'I think they argued most of the day about it, Churchill all against it, and she not knowing what to do. She doubted, but after all there *was* a child. It existed, and she didn't see how it could be explained away.'

'But – '

'Listen. On Monday night she was still undecided, and that was just as well, because on Tuesday Lord Mumford turned up – also after some hard riding.'

'A day late, all the same.'

'No, he wasn't. It was this warming pan tale that brought him, and he was first to the Princess with it. So he was about as welcome as I'd been. It explained everything, and it did away with the difficulty. Just what was needed.'

'And does the Princess believe it?'

'Of course she does. What else can she do? What's left to her, or to any of us, if it isn't true?'

'I see.'

Nick could see it very clearly. The child brought through the curtains by Mrs Wilkins meant a papist succession, and the warming pan made it a protestant one. It was as simple as that. Some would believe it in heart and truth, some because belief in it might now seem a duty to Church and State; and those who were in doubt would be chary of speaking their doubts aloud.

The days went by, and a letter came from his father, mainly to thank him for his own long letter of news. But it mentioned something else:

I have, in return, a piece of news for you about Mr Gibson, who, from the fact (which he does not believe) that the Queen was a month early, draws the conclusion that his Doraty may be a month early too, and that it may therefore be prudent for her mother to be with her earlier than had been planned. His wife, who wishes to be with Doraty, has agreed very happily with this, and you may expect therefore to have the two of them in London about the middle of July, though I much suspect that Richard's true purpose has not much to do with Doraty. His sense of duty has never weakened, and in these present days he thinks he should no longer be living, as he puts it, like a cabbage in the country, but should be in London, ready to take his part in whatever may come. He is likely to have time on his hands, since he can hardly do much himself for Doraty, and you may see a little more of him than you will think convenient, but in the main I think he will consort with Sir Thomas Mallory. Those two are as alike in Whiggery as pease in a pod.

The days had been running on, and it was now the last week in June. The bishops were to come to trial on Friday, and the most eminent Counsel at the Bar had joined to conduct the defence. On the Wednesday Nick went for supper with Harry, usually so carefree and detached; but even Harry was now talking politics. He was insistent with questions about the bishops, and then he told of high feelings in his regiment about the putting of papists into the army. This, he said, was no longer the mere putting of a few officers into existing regiments. Whole new regiments were now being raised in Ireland and brought to England, every officer and man in them a papist. In his own regiment, he added, there was such an anger at this that both officers and private men were now saying openly that they would sooner fight Irish papists than English Whigs.

It was past ten o'clock, with dusk deep upon the town, when Nick walked back to the Temple. He found it quiet, and he met no one as he walked to his stair. He went into the dark archway and then stopped short, startled to see a man on the lowest step, blocking his way. He stood back, momentarily alarmed, and the man spoke eagerly, in a remembered voice.

'Nick!'

'Who? Lory?'

'I've not seen you since Wells.'

It was Lory Leclere, whom Nick had waved away in the first light of a summer morning, three long years ago. There had been nothing since then but some vague tales that he had been seen in Amsterdam, and at The Hague.

'Lory! I thought you were in Holland.'

'I was. But now I'm sent here.'

'Sent?' Thoughts occurred of Whiggery and of the Prince of Orange. 'You'd best come in, and we'll talk.'

'That's what I'm here for. But it will soon be more than talk.'

14 *King's Bench*

Lory looked a little older, and there were moments when he seemed to hesitate before he spoke, as if he had learned to guard what he said, but it was the same Lory, with the lean face, the wiry figure and the sharp and restless eyes. In place of the riding clothes and the bright green sash he now had a suit of sober grey, with black stockings and plain unbuckled shoes, and he could have been a clerk to a merchant or an attorney. But with Nick he made no pretences, and he did not even wait for the obvious question.

'I'm in the service of the Prince of Orange,' he said when they were at ease in Nick's quiet room. 'I got safe to Holland after Wells, and I've been there ever since, except for two visits to London. Now I'm on my third, and that's what I mean by sent.'

'You take this service earnestly?'

'Should I not?' He was suddenly sharp. 'You, in London, should know what the times are like, and for me there's more in it than that. I'm of the west country, remember, out of Bridgwater.'

'Oh!' Memories of the assizes flared suddenly. 'But you need not tell me. I was in Wells, in the killing days, and then riding elsewhere – which you, at least, were spared. You were at The Hague.'

'Or I'd have gone mad.' The answer snapped back, and Lory had to steady himself before he went on. 'But my father was in Bridgwater, and my mother, and after a little time, when it was safer, letters began to come – and it was a good thing I wasn't there to see it. They were hanging men in Bridgwater on any pretext, men I knew, some of them.'

'Did you know Richard Allinson?'

'John Allinson's son? The clothier?' Lory seemed to be searching his memory. 'But he died, didn't he, John Allinson?'

'So did Richard.'

'But I didn't really know them. My father was in the linen trade and had dealings with the clothier, so I knew who they were, but that was about all. How do you know them?'

'Because he had a daughter, whom I'm to wed in some three months' time.'

'What!'

It had to be explained, and Lory seemed pleased, and said so. But then he returned to his point.

'So you do know what it was like in Bridgwater and the west, and then you ask me why I'm earnest in the Orange service. Do you need to? I'm like others from the west country. I've a score to pay with James Stuart, and that means Orange, the only man now with force enough to throw him out, him and his papist crew. He should never have been King at all. He should have been excluded ten years ago. We knew, even then, what he'd do. Shaftesbury told us, and he died half-mad in Amsterdam. Now it's an end to our religion, and our laws and liberties as well, unless we do with force what we could have done ten years ago with votes. And force means Orange.'

By Nick's cool standards Lory was ranting now. It had all come boiling out of him, his Whig upbringing, the Calvinism of his Huguenot forbears, and his burning anger at what had followed Sedgemoor; and Nick eyed him warily. Such feelings as these, blending with his quickness of mind and his restless energy, could make him dangerous, and if zeal should override caution he could put his friends in danger too. He would be better if he cooled a little.

'Yes.' Nick nodded calmly. 'But, Lory, what does this mean? Are you here to make a plot?'

'No.' The answer was prompt, and then it seemed as if Lory had taken the hint. 'Nick, if I'd come for that, I'd not embroil *you* in it. I'm too much in your debt for that. You got me away, and without you I'd no doubt have hanged with the others. I'm here to ask your help again, but it isn't dangerous help.'

'What then?'

'I'm here to gain intelligence of the London Whigs, who they are, what they do, and what they might do. No more than that, and it sounds easy. But I've two weeks at most before I must return, and since I'm to report to Orange, I must have it sure and certain. He's not easily satisfied.'

'You report to the Prince himself?'

'In this I do.' For a moment Lory hesitated. 'I don't mean, of course, that I'm in his confidence. Obviously I'm not. I'm too junior for that, and anyway he keeps his confidence for his Dutchmen. He just makes use of Englishmen.'

'And you serve him on those terms?'

'I must.' Again there was that slight hesitation. 'I don't say I like Orange. He isn't lovable. He's cold and silent. He's hard, and he might be selfish. But he has some great qualities too, a will that won't break, and courage in abundance. He's thoughtful and far seeing, and, of course, he's protestant, a Lutheran. In most things he's the very opposite of Monmouth, and just the man to succeed where Monmouth failed. I served the one and regretted it. Now I'll serve the other and not regret it.'

'But, more precisely, why does he send you here?'

'I've told you I'm not in his confidence. But if he were to come here, he could bring only enough of an army to protect him in the first few weeks. He'd not have ships for more, and he'd have to depend on a great rising through the country to tip the balance. So he needs to know what the chances are, and specially in London, which could be all important in such a rising. I'm one of those sent to learn the temper of the London Whigs.'

'Others are sent too?'

'Oh yes, though I don't know who they are. But I'm not to concern myself with men in high places. It's the ordinary Londoner, the man in the shop and the counting-house, that I'm to enquire about, how far he's roused for action, whether he has preparations made, and whether he has leaders who'll hearten him and tell him what to do. That's what I'm to learn, but I don't even know who the City Whigs are these days, and I can hardly be surprised if they're hiding their heads. But do *you* know them? Can you tell me of one who'd talk to me, if you'll assure him that I'm not a spy of James? How of this London brother of Mrs Allinson?'

'No.' Nick answered tersely, quite sure that he must not have Innes brought into this. 'Talk to Sir Thomas Mallory.'

'I've heard that name. Wasn't he one of the old Green Ribbon Club?'

'He certainly was.'

Nick gave it a second thought, and still found Mallory the obvious man. He was itching to organize precisely what was wanted, and he would no doubt be delighted to be in touch, even indirectly, with the Prince of Orange. He and Lory were probably as one in their Whiggery, and he was certainly the man for Lory. He could be inquired for at the King's Head opposite.

He was easily found when they went there at noon the next day, and he was all attention when he was told who Lory was and what he did. But Nick did not linger. He kept himself to assurances that Lory was no spy of the government, and then he left them to it, declaring that he was too busy to stay; which was more or less true. The bishops were to come to trial the next morning, and there was to be a last meeting of Counsel in Mr Pollexfen's chambers that afternoon, which meant Nick taking the notes and having ready any papers that might be wanted. In the event it was simple, for they were all in agreement, but it took his afternoon.

He was at Westminster Hall the next morning, sitting behind his seniors with nothing to do but be ready with papers, yet feeling highly privileged to be there at all on such an occasion. He had expected that the Hall would be filled to its utmost limits, as it was, and that the foremost seats would be taken by an array of peers, as they were. But he had hardly expected the thousands who were standing in the streets outside the Hall, unable to get in; and most certainly he had not expected the scores of boats that were on the river, all filled with people and keeping as near to the Hall as they could get. The trial seemed to have roused all London, and all Westminster too.

The leading Counsel took their seats, the jury was sworn, and in a few more minutes the Archbishop and his six suffragans were facing the four judges of the King's Bench. The Clerk read the indictment, which charged them with having written and published in the county of Middlesex a false, malicious, and seditious libel. Then the Attorney General, Sir Thomas Powis, rose, looking neither happy nor confident, to open his case, and quickly ran into trouble against a defence that was ready to object to anything and to pounce on the slightest weakness in argument. In the end it took him and the Solicitor General the whole of a tedious morning to establish only that the bishops had written a petition and shown it to the King. But showing it to the King was, in law, publication, and the real trial could now begin.

It developed during the afternoon. The petition had plainly said that the dispensing power was unlawful, and the Attorney

General now chose to argue that this was untrue, that the power was lawful and the petition therefore false. This put the dispensing power into the centre of the case, and for three long hours, that sultry afternoon, Mr Pollexfen and Sir Francis Pemberton argued against it, insisting that the power was illegal, was known to be illegal, and had repeatedly been declared to be illegal. They used all the precedents that had been so carefully prepared for them, and they were so precise and thorough that the Attorney General, when his time came to reply, was found to be without an argument. The Solicitor General, who followed him, was so hard put to it that he abandoned the dispensing power altogether and brazenly declared that nobody had a right to petition the King, and that it was on this ground that the bishops should be convicted.

It was evening, and the light was fading in the Hall, when the four judges began their summing up, and the Lord Chief Justice, who began it, looked a frightened man. He kept glancing at the assembled peers, as if, in another reign, he might be impeached before them, and he looked, as somebody said afterwards, as if they all had halters in their pockets. He spoke with great caution, evading the dispensing power altogether, and leaving the jury to decide whether the petition was a libel or not. Two more judges said much the same. Only Sir John Powell was forthright, declaring boldly that the dispensing power was illegal, and, if continued, would mean the end of rule by Parliament. He looked straight at the jury and told them he must leave that to their consciences. There was a rustle in the Hall as he ended, as if men could no longer sit still, and then a deep hum of approval.

Candles had been brought when the Lord Chief Justice finally sent the jury to consider their verdict; and then, to the relief of everyone, he made it plain that he had no intention of sitting there through the night, waiting for them. He adjourned the court till ten o'clock the next morning, and the whole vast crowd went pushing out of the Hall, desperate to get from its heat into the fresh cool air of the summer night. Nick was amongst the last to leave, and when he emerged, breathing deeply and thankfully, he saw a man coming towards him, vague at first in the dark. It turned out to be his brother John.

'Ha!' said John. 'I've been waiting for a word with you, after sweating in there all day, wishing I was somewhere else.'

'Then why stay?'

'Because the Princess is half-fevered over this affair, and she sent me to watch it for her. She doesn't approve of this for bishops, specially for Dr Ken. He's her favourite preacher.'

'So he should be.'

'Nick, be a little helpful, will you? I can't just go back to her and say the jury's out. She'll be near mad with waiting, and she'll be full of questions about what's going to happen and what verdict is likely. What am I to say to her?'

'It's all guessing. You can never tell what a jury will do. But Pollexfen's a wise old owl, and Pemberton's another, and they both think there's a chance. It isn't more than that, though.'

'Then I'd better get back and tell her so, or she'll be thinking I've run. I may see you tomorrow. I expect I'll be here again.'

John went hurrying away, and Nick began to walk slowly back to the Temple, too sunk in thought to notice that he was tired. It had not occurred to him that even the Princess could not avoid the common anxiety about the bishops, but between this and being left at Bath while a child was born, perhaps from a warming pan, she must now feel bitter towards her father, and might soon feel worse. No one could suppose her to be a Whig, but she might soon be forced into courses not very far from Whiggery. So might those about her, Lord Churchill, Lord Mumford, and John as well, all of whom might see an inexorable future dictating what they must do.

Temple Bar was quiet, with no more than a throng of apprentices standing round, but the King's Head had its windows lighted, its door wide open, and a lantern above to show the groups of men who were standing in talk outside. It was plainly busy, and Nick stopped in his walk, wondering what was going on inside. There was no longer a Green Ribbon Club, but the inn, with its associations, would be a natural meeting place for Whigs, and never more so than tonight, when men were strained and restless and might well come from their homes for talk with others. Sir Thomas Mallory, or someone like him, might think that this was the moment.

Nick crossed the street, deciding that he would look inside and see for himself; and the first thing he saw was a great bunch of evergreen hanging by the door, as it would have done at Christmas. For a moment he stared in surprise, and then he understood. Whiggery was indeed showing itself in the King's Head.

To his left was the long wine-room, and through its open door he could see that it was filled with men, and hazy with the smoke of candles and tobacco. He pushed in, threading his way slowly to the wine counter, and almost every man he passed had green ribbon pinned to his coat. He bought a glass of wine, and gave thought to this. One could not call for green ribbon in an inn, as one could for wine, and expect it to be there. Someone must have gone earlier in the day to a mercer, bought the ribbon, cut it up, and put it ready. He looked round again, wondering if Sir Thomas Mallory was here, but he could recognize no one except a young lawyer or two from the Temple. At the end of the room a door led, as he knew, to a smaller room which might be used by any who wished to talk in quiet, away from the crowd. Its door was ajar, and he made his way slowly to it, then pushed it a little further open.

It was certainly a quiet room. A score of men were there, all silent, all intent on Sir Thomas Mallory, who was standing against the hearth, speaking quietly to them. His tone was smooth and easy, but it was not that of a man who argues and disputes. There was authority in it, as of one who explains and then gives orders; and his favour of green was three times the size of anyone else's.

Nick slipped quietly away, thinking that the wheel of time was turning. Perhaps in Shaftesbury's day this room had known such meetings.

15 The Flooding Tide

Nick was back in Westminster Hall by nine the next morning, and it was none too soon. The crowds were even greater than before, and the streets in Westminster were thick with people. Already it was hot, and he thought the best of it would be had by those in the scores of boats that were lying off the stairs or beating about in the stream. But his own place was in Westminster Hall, and there he had to wait, air or no air, for the opening of the court at ten.

Fortunately it was prompt, for everyone was as impatient as he, and all were early rather than late. The jury came trooping in, and every one of the hundreds in the Hall stared intently at them trying to read something in their tired and haggard faces. The last rustle of sound seemed to leave the Hall as the Clerk of the Crown flung his question at them. The foreman came to his feet, looking pale after his sleepless night, and in the throbbing silence they could hear him draw his breath. *Not guilty*.

For another instant the silence lasted, as if it had gripped and numbed them all; and then Lord Halifax, heedless of decorum, jumped to his feet and waved his hat. That broke the spell, and at once the whole vast multitude followed him, leaping up, waving hats, stamping their feet, and then cheering. Startled judges recoiled, ushers thumped with their staves, and no one even noticed. The shouting and the cheering went on, swelling into a din that went ringing far outside the Hall to the crowds in the streets. It could have only one meaning, and at once, all the way to Whitehall Gate and almost to Charing Cross, answering cheers came back, loud and exultant. Even the river was in uproar as the men in the boats joined in, some of them even pulling out pistols and discharging them into the air. The noise spread on, one street passing it to another, till the whole City of London, all the way to the Tower, was in uproar, all work forgotten, everyone in the streets. Then, from the river, came the thunder of guns, as the crowded ships in the Pool took the sailors' way of giving vent to feelings. Even this did not complete it, for at Westminster Abbey the bells burst into a swelling roar of triumph which carried to the City, where in church after church it was taken up. In belfry after belfry the ringers hurried to their ropes, waiting for no orders, and soon the pealing of bells was everywhere, joining with the guns and the cheers in a pandemonium that made speech impossible.

Westminster Hall was emptying. There could be no thought of hearing another case, and no one even took notice as the judges left the bench. Everyone was struggling to get out, to join in the rejoicing or to crowd round the bishops' coaches as they went away. When Nick at last left the Hall the coaches had gone and the door was clear, though in the street the crowd was as thick as ever. He stood for a moment, savouring the summer morning, and wondering what he should do. John had no doubt already hurried to the Cockpit with the news, and Nick began to think of Edmund Innes, who would be as glad as anyone of a first-hand tale. He hesitated, and then Lory Leclere came suddenly at him, his lean face crinkling with delight.

'Nick,' he burst out, 'what a day this is! God be thanked that I'm here to see it.'

'But aren't you imprudent to be here, in Westminster?'

'Who'd notice *me* in a crowd like this? I've been in the Hall this morning, and good it was to see the place again. Better still to hear the verdict, and now – hark at them! Do you hear those guns?' He listened ecstatically, with his head thrown back, and then he changed his tone. 'Nick, I've been waiting for you. I knew you must come out some time. I want you to dine with me. I don't know when we'll meet again, so let's dine while we can.'

'You're going back to Holland?'

'Could there be a tale greater than this to take to Orange?'

'He'll know of it. His ambassador – '

'Of course he will. But it's what happens in the streets and taverns that I'm to report about. So I must give the day to noticing and then I've a berth bespoke in a ship to Amsterdam, from the Pool on the night tide. Now let's walk through this.'

They walked unhurriedly. At Whitehall there was a great press of people round the Palace, and an unusually strong guard at the Gate, but they learned from bystanders that the King was not there. He had ridden out at nine o'clock with a strong escort. So they walked on, and before they were at Charing Cross the noise in the streets was making talk difficult. Soon it was impossible as they came to the churches and the bells, and they had all but reached the Tower before they could speak at ease again. The firing of guns had stopped, and instead the ships were gay with flags and pennants. The bells, too, were stopping, and at first they thought that the ringers had had enough, and wished now to join the rejoicing in the streets. But then, as they walked slowly back to Temple Bar, they saw that at church after church people were thronging in for hurriedly arranged services of thanksgiving. Not every Londoner was thinking of inns and taverns.

But the taverns were full enough, and at Temple Bar the King's Head looked as if not another man could be squeezed into it. In the warm sunlight every window was open, and they could see the crowd of men inside, and even the green favours that most of them were now wearing in the light of day. Whiggery was lifting its head in the sun.

'Here,' said Lory, 'we dine. And where else, this day of days?'

'You're certainly a Whig.'

'And you, my friend, are on the way to becoming one. Come inside – if we can.'

They pushed in somehow, and in the big wine-room, before even their glasses were filled, the drawer handed a favour of green to Nick. Lory had already pulled his own from his pocket, and now he firmly pinned Nick's into place.

'If you are in Rome,' he said tersely, 'do as the Romans do. And this is Rome – or will be, before the year is out. Good fortune to us all!'

He lifted his glass happily; and then Sir Thomas Mallory came pushing through the crowd to join them.

'There is a tide in the affairs of men,' he quoted. 'Pray God we have the wit to take it, for here's the flood indeed. But Leclere, I'm glad you've come in, because I've had three or four men asking for you, all with messages they want you to take to Orange. I've told them to return at two o'clock. And Burnaby, I'm much in your debt for bringing Leclere to me. He's been of great help, and I think he may now be able to make Orange a report that wil hasten the day. Which reminds me – ' He turned again to Lory. 'I wonder if we were right to give out these ribbons of green? Should they, perhaps, have been of orange?'

'Oh, I see.' Lory nodded. 'Yet the green remembers the Club, which – '

'Exactly. The past and the future, and it was perhaps too early to make the change. Orange should move first.'

'Will he, do you think, after this? Will all this decide him?'

'He's a man of sense. He'll see the flood, and he'll know that he, too, must take it when it serves. But now let's dine. We could have no happier day for it.'

They dined well, and all that hindered Nick's enjoyment was that the talk was unceasingly of politics, of the King and the Prince of Orange, and what each might do. Nick remembered Innes, whom he had meant to visit that morning, and John, who had hurried from the Hall to the Princess, and he thought it was perhaps convenient that men with messages would be seeking Lory at two o'clock.

He made that his excuse when they had ended dinner, telling Lory quite truthfully that he hoped they would meet again in peace before the year was out. Then he walked quietly through the warm sunlight to Lombard Street, where he found the counting-house empty and locked. But Innes welcomed him into the parlour above, and explained that he had been off the Hall in his boat all yesterday and again this morning, and had found on his return that his clerks had gone into the streets. In view of his own absence he thought he could hardly blame them, and he added that it mattered little, since business seemed to be at a standstill anyway.

Nick gave him a precise account of what had happened in the Hall, and it set him looking very thoughtful.

'Things become impossible,' he said gravely. 'The court has as good as declared this dispensing power to be illegal, so now the King must either defy the highest court in the land, or abandon his whole policy – which I do not think he will do. So it looks as if we shall soon have to choose between King and Law, as well as between King and Church, and we can guess how men will choose, ninety-nine out of a hundred of them. I don't like the prospect.'

It was not cheerful talk, and Nick was for once glad to get away from Innes. He walked down to the river and took a boat to

Whitehall stairs, hoping that John might be at home. At least the river was pleasant.

John was not at the house, but Colonel and Mrs Crosedale were there, she in deep talk with Doraty about possible emergencies. The Colonel, left more or less to himself, was willing for some talk also, and his first request was for a first-hand account of how it had gone in Westminster Hall. Then he looked cheerful.

'Yes.' He stretched himself comfortably. 'The King, I may tell you, is *not* pleased. We're in camp just now on Hounslow Heath. I suppose you know he has most of the army mustered there?'

'There's been talk enough in London about it.'

'I expect so. The muster, I suppose, was meant to frighten Londoners, to show them that the army's close at hand and they'd better not give trouble. If so, it's another of his plans gone wrong.'

'Oh?'

'Yes.' Crosedale sounded even more cheerful. 'We don't let the soldiers come into London, but we can't stop Londoners coming to Hounslow, and they come in hundreds. Curiosity, I suppose, to see what soldiers are really like. But on a summer evening it isn't long before they're talking with soldiers, and in no time after that they're drinking beer with soldiers, and they get along very well together. Each finds that the other is more like himself than he'd expected. I'm speaking, of course, of our English regiments, not of these teagues who keep arriving.'

'Teagues?'

'A teague, my dear Nick, is simply an Irishman. I think it's an Irish word for him, and it's certainly the soldiers' word. The King is recruiting whole regiments of them, and that's something we don't like at all.'

'Are they dangerous?'

'Not yet. They've never been from home before, and they don't speak our language, and they don't properly know where they are. They're also completely raw, and their officers are about as untrained as they are. They're far too lost and bewildered to be a danger to anyone, and the only effect they've had so far is to annoy our English soldiers and the Londoners about equally. Between that and the beer, we should now have some trouble to get our soldiers to fight the Londoners. They'd more willingly fight the teagues. But did I say we had the King at the camp this morning? He inspected a regiment or two, and then a messenger came pounding in, horse all lathered, with a note telling him the verdict, and you should have seen his face.'

'Hadn't he expected it?'

'I don't know what he'd expected. But he didn't keep the news to himself. He let it out, and it went down the line till it reached the private men. And just as he was getting on his horse to leave us he heard them cheering, whole regiments of them. He asked what it was, and some fool told him it was nothing, just soldiers glad the bishops were acquitted. Do you know the way he sticks his lip out when he's in a temper? "Do you call that nothing," he said. "The worse for them." He just growled it, and for all I know he's still growling it.'

'Then what's going to happen?'

'Don't we all ask that? But I'll have to leave you, Nick!' He changed his tone abruptly. 'It's time I was getting back. I'm not quite sure of discipline tonight. So if I leave you, will you see Penny safe home?'

The Colonel went off, and Nick stayed for a longer time than he had intended. Doraty wanted news and talk, and Penny Crosedale was in no hurry, and between them they kept him for the rest of the afternoon and then for supper. It was past nine o'clock, and after sunset, when he at last persuaded Penny that the streets might be riotous tonight, and that she had best be home before it was full dark. Reluctantly she agreed, and in the growing dusk she set out with him on the short walk to her house in Primrose Lane. They reached it safely, and then he took quick leave and began to walk back alone to the Temple. He turned into King Street, and at once, by the Palace of Whitehall, he could see tongues of flame leaping into the sky, with showers of sparks and billows of drifting smoke. He could not see quite where it was, for his view was cut by the two great arches that here spanned the road, but it was plainly a bonfire, and he thought it must be by Whitehall Gate. Then, as he watched, he saw the bright flashes of firecrackers in the smoke, and he heard shouts and cheers, blending with the noise of the crackers.

He quickened his pace, wondering who had impudence enough for fireworks and a bonfire so close to the King. He passed through the first of the arches, so-called King Street Gate, and then the street was running through the precincts of the Palace, the main buildings to one side and some lesser ones, including the Cockpit, to the other. In front of him was the second arch, the

Holbein Gate, which carried a covered passage across the street, and through it he could see the glare of the fire and the flashing of squibs that someone was throwing about. He passed under the arch, and then, to his right, was the Banqueting House of sinister memory, silent now and dark, except where the red flickers of flame were reflecting from its windows. Immediately beyond it was Whitehall Gate, the main entry to the Palace, and the fire was in the middle of the street, exactly opposite the Gate. It was a monster of a fire, for which load after load of faggots must have been brought, which surely meant design. Already a noisy hooting crowd was round the fire, adding to the din with the squibs and crackers someone had provided. Scores of others were hurrying up the street towards it, attracted by the glare and the noise; and the fire was telling everyone, including the King, that Whiggery was up again.

By the wall of the Banqueting House a few men were standing together, watchful, but seeming to take no part in what was going on, and Nick guessed that these were the Whigs who were guiding and controlling it. He eyed them warily, remembering tales of men who, in times of excitement, had been mistaken for papists and handled roughly, and then, on a quick thought, he felt in his pockets for the favour of green he had worn at dinner. He pinned it on to his coat, and went boldly forward, to find them all in his path as soon as they saw his green. They received him without question as a fellow Whig, asking him what orders he had for the night, and then they would not let him go till they had produced some bottles of wine for a toast to the seven bishops. He drank this sincerely.

He went on, and at Charing Cross he found fireworks again and another bonfire, though a lesser one, and another in the Strand by the maypole. Then he was in sight of Temple Bar, and already he could see, beyond it, the red glare of yet another fire. He drew close, and he heard a steady thump of drums, followed by wild cheering that went on and on. He quickened his step, guessing that here, under the windows of the King's Head, the Whigs would be making their greatest effort, and he pushed past Temple Bar into a crowd so dense that he had difficulty in moving at all. The space before the fire was being kept clear, and in it a cart was standing, painted a vivid red, and carrying a tall and high-backed chair which looked as if it had been gilded. It held the effigy of a man, again a thing roughly done, perhaps with rags and canvas, but on what passed for its head it had what could pass for a tiara, in crystal and strips of brass. This, with a cope of damask on the shoulders of the effigy, was enough to set anyone thinking of the Pope.

The men with the drums, who must have been leading the cart in procession through the streets, came forward to lift the figure from its throne and hold it for all to see. The crowd gasped and seethed, breaking into a roar of triumph as the crowned and vestured thing was hurled into the fire. For a few short minutes it flared and smoked, and then, with a great flash of light and a deafening bang, it exploded. The smoke went billowing, while a shower of sparks and bits of flaming rag came falling dangerously on everyone. Nick pressed back against the Temple wall, and glanced towards the King's Head opposite, which was dark and quiet, diverting nobody's attention. But an upper window was open, and in it, by the glare of the fire, he could see a man standing still and quiet, watching the scene below. He looked like Sir Thomas Mallory.

From the side of the fire a man jumped into the cart, gesturing for silence as if he would address the crowd, and Nick left him to it. He could guess what sort of a speech it would be, and he slipped away into the quiet of the Temple, knowing that this had been a Pope burning. It could not, indeed, compare with those of Shaftesbury's days, which had been enormous and elaborate affairs, mounted after weeks of work. This, by comparison, had been a poor untidy thing, done with whatever could be had at a day's notice, but a Pope burning it had been, and it held the same vicious insult to the Church of which the King was so fervent a member. Therein lay the danger; for between this and the acquittal of the bishops, the King would surely strike back, somehow, at someone, and no one could feel safe. Nick brooded on it, and the belief hardened in him, and grew sharper, that it had all become intolerable, and that the only way to avert an outright civil war was intervention by the Prince of Orange. He alone could do it without being accused of treason, and he alone with force enough to give him a chance of being heeded. He was a silent and ungracious man, and few would like him; but affairs were now so rushing to disaster that he must surely be invited soon.

Though Nick did not know it, the invitation had already gone, and by the same tide that was at that moment carrying Lory

Leclere down the silent river on his way to Amsterdam. In another ship, disguised as a common sailor, was William Herbert, who had been Rear-Admiral of England and Master of the Robes until he had been closeted by the King and dismissed for answering as a protestant. He carried a letter to the Prince of Orange, signed by seven of the highest and most influential men in England. They pledged their fortunes and their lives to his service, if he would but come to them quickly, and in arms.

16 Signs of Storm

A day or two later Nick went to see if all was well with Doraty, and he found Penny Crosedale with her.

'Do you think of buying a house?' Penny asked him suddenly. 'You're to be wed this summer, I'm told, so I suppose you'll need a house. Have you thought where it's to be?'

'I'd thought perhaps here, in Westminster. I must be near the Hall, and it's pleasant here, and – '

'Exactly. But do you know that for the moment it's easy?'

She went on to explain it. The belief that Westminster might become soon unsafe was now held by many. It was why her own husband had bought a house up the river for her. He, indeed, was keeping his house in Westminster too, because his duties required him to live there, but others had no such need. Often they had no duties at all, but merely frequented the Court in a hope of getting favours and places, and these men had nothing to stay for. They wished merely to sell their houses, and then go elsewhere till the times should change. For the same reasons, few now wished to buy, and prices had therefore fallen. Houses were cheap in Westminster, and this could therefore be the moment, if Nick chose to buy.

He took this seriously, thinking it a useful suggestion, but he still thought he could not bring Judith to live in a place that others were leaving. He said so, and Penny Crosedale at once agreed with him.

'No, I don't think you should,' she answered. 'But if you wait till everything is safe, there may be a rush for houses here, and prices will be up again. If you were to buy one now, and then leave it empty for a few months, you might still save money. But that's for you to decide. I'm not trying to push you into anything.'

He thought that a good suggestion, and it was one he had the means to carry out, for he had carefully preserved intact his legacy from Richard Law. So he wrote a careful letter to Judith, and added that they would talk this over as soon as he could be with her. That, he hoped, would now be soon. July was already a week old, and the law term would end with the month for the summer vacation.

Richard Gibson and his wife arrived the next week, and Mrs Gibson settled down at once to take Doraty in hand. Richard, being more or less told to keep out of it, was soon spending much of his time with Sir Thomas Mallory, and was no doubt offering his earnest help in anything that was hatching. But he was in an amiable mood, and a few days later he invited Nick to dine with him at the Angel in King Street, which was conveniently near Westminster Hall.

They met accordingly, and Richard was soon expressing his high approval of Mallory's attempt to band the Whigs together again. He thought the improvised Pope-burning, crude as it had been, would do much to revive old memories. But he had been told by Mallory of Lory Leclere, and he was saying as they began their meal that Lory's report of what he had seen in London might well speed the decision by the Prince of Orange.

'To come here, do you mean?'

'Of course.' The answer was firm and prompt. 'Sooner or later Orange must come, for he needs our help against France as much as we need his against James. And will there be another moment when half the nation or more will rise in his support?'

'Only half? I'd have thought it more. Who'll support James?'

'Only a handful. But have you heard what our rector says he'll do, the high-flying Allway?'

'Non-resistance?'

'So he's said for years past, but we're now learning what it really means.' Richard was showing one of his rare moments of amusement. 'To resist the Lord's Anointed, you'll remember, is a sin, with a row of texts to prove it.'

'I remember them all.'

'As do I. So he isn't going to commit that sin. Oh no. But if the rest of us, sinners like you and me, choose to commit it for him – if we ride out and resist – well and good. He isn't going to preach us out of it. We must follow our own consciences, and if there's a sin, it won't be his, and we can go to hell instead of him. That's how I understand him.'

'It sounds confused.'

'He *is* confused. I've been saying that for years. But he won't be alone in this. There'll be high-flyers by the hundred, parsons and squires and lesser men, who'll do the same. For very shame, after all their high words, they can't fight against King James. But they won't fight *for* him either. They'll give only passive obedience. They'll sit at home while the rest of us make home safe for them, and when we come riding back – those of us who do – they'll give us a mug of ale and set the church bells ringing. That's how I see it. That's a high-flyer.'

Nick nodded, and thought that this was probably true. Allway, indeed, was a man of conscience, and his motives would be higher than Richard's sardonic tone had suggested, but this, none the less, was what he would probably do. He was likely to be finding it a hard choice.

'What of yourself?' said Richard quietly. 'How will you serve? You are not, I take it, a high-flyer?'

'Oh!'

Nick sat upright in a chill of dismay. This was something he had never thought of. He had asked only how he and Judith might be affected if other men took to fighting. It had not occurred to him that he might himself be expected to march with a sword, or ride in a troop of horse. But one moment of thought made it seem all too likely. He had no better argument for escaping it than had anyone else. He did not think his father would hold back if neighbours were riding out. Nick Culley certainly would not. Harry, as a soldier, would be in it from the beginning, and John would be bound in honour to stay with the Princess and take whatever part might be needed in her defence. Nick could guess what would be thought of him if he alone were to insist on peace, comfort, and safety; and he would probably think it of himself.

'I was hoping,' he said unhappily, 'to be wed this summer.'

'I know.' Richard's tone softened, as if he understood this well. 'I'm not saying that you should not.'

'But – '

'If you may be wed quickly, say in August, then in God's name do. I saw enough last time of those who did not. War plays tricks on men. It brings what we do not expect, and some who stayed their wedding for safer days never came to it at all.'

'But – why August?'

'Because it should still be safe then. Even September, perhaps, though that runs it fine. After that, not till January, at the soonest.'

'How do you come to that?'

'By considering the facts. If Orange comes at all he must bring troops with him, some thousands of them to take the brunt of it while we raise and muster men. That means a hundred or more of ships for them, and more ships for horses and stores. Then warships to escort the whole. It's a great preparation, and if he starts at this moment he'll be hard put to it to be ready in October. He must not be much later than that, or he may meet November gales. Think of an armament that size, caught in what November can bring. So between the two we come to late October as the likely time, the time when you should *not* have a wedding planned. Put it well before that time, or well after.'

It was something more for Nick to think about, and the letter he had sent to Judith now seemed out of date. There were so many things to discuss with her, and all that seemed to matter was to be with her and begin to talk, but he had still a week to go before the term would end, and he was too busy to be able to ask for time away. Most of the cases were of borough charters, which the King was trying to recall and remodel.

Then the answering letter came from Judith, and it put a further excitement into his thoughts. She had more to say than he had expected, and not much of it was about the house in Westminster. On that she simply told him that he was on the spot and must do as he thought best. Most of what she had to say concerned her mother.

I fear I have been most undutiful, and most ill mannered too, but I could not help it. She has been going on as before, saying that she will not be left again with Mrs Pemberton, and yet refusing to try it with anyone else, even though some other suitable women could well be found. I have already found half a dozen, and she has said no to all of them, and this time I must own to getting out of temper. Perhaps I lost it altogether, for I told her plainly what I truly thought of her and her behaviour. I told her I should not stay a spinster all my life for no better reason than that she would like it better that I should stay with her and keep her house than that someone else should. I said, too, that I should now agree with you on a day for being wed, and then keep to it, since I would have no more of being put off and off and off. All of which, as you may well suppose, caused a most unhappy day, I not knowing what I had provoked. Yet this morning, to my great surprise, I learned that all is much better than I had dreamed of. She told me very prettily that she now agrees that I should not be asked to wait any longer, and that for herself she can manage very well – as, indeed, she can. She will, however, have no woman as housekeeper. She says she will have the management of her own house, and she can do very well with a girl or two to work as she bids – as I am sure she can.

Nick read it with delight, seeing this obstacle removed at last. But there were still five days before he could go, and he fretted while he waited. He did, however, have a word with Colonel Crosedale, who was now and then riding over from Hounslow to have an hour with Penny. Crosedale agreed that October was the likely month, and he said he had orders to have his regiment ready for anything. He would have it ready by October, but he did not know what its temper would be. The private men, like the officers, were becoming increasingly angry at the number of Irishmen who were arriving at Hounslow. They did not like the Irish, and were much more willing to fight against them than to fight with them.

Then, two nights before Nick was to leave for Salisbury, he found a letter pushed under his door in the Temple. It did not seem to have come from the Post Office, and when he broke the seal he found it was from Lory, a single sheet, with nothing to show where it had come from.

This is to tell you that I am safe returned to my proper place, being well received here. The news I brought, and my tales of what I saw, were well received also. I therefore hope, and have good cause to believe, that I shall soon be with you again, and have friends with me.

Some still come and go, and I have therefore a chance to send this to you by a safe hand. Do not, pray, be at the risk of sending me an answer.

Lory

The meaning was easy to guess – and Lory would be coming soon, with friends. It could hardly be plainer, and Nick took the letter with him when he went the next day to the King's Head for dinner with Richard, a last meeting before Nick left London. He passed the letter across the dinner table, and Richard read it impassively, but with a sharp intake of breath.

'God be praised!' he said as he handed it back. 'Orange is coming. He's making ready.'

'It sounds like it.'

'It can mean nothing less. And if I were you, I'd burn it.'

'So much? There's nothing to show – '

'Burn it. Would anyone doubt, if you were caught with that, that you're in treasonable contact with someone? Put it in the fire, now, while I watch you.'

Nick obeyed, feeling suddenly frightened. Richard was right, and Nick, lawyer though he was, had failed to see what a prosecuting counsel could do with that letter. He came back to the table feeling a little unsteady, and through the rest of the meal Richard talked tactfully of John and Doraty, of Mr Allway and the prospects for the harvest, and anything else they could be easy about.

But affairs came at them again. After their dinner they went out into Fleet Street, and they were standing there in talk, before going their separate ways, when they heard the thump and bang of drums and a shrill wail of pipes. Richard spun round as if he were startled, breaking off in the middle of a sentence and then taking a few quick paces to get a view past Temple Bar. Nick went with him, and at once he saw a regiment of soldiers on the march, brilliant in scarlet, and headed by their pipes and drums. Richard stepped back against a door.

'Teagues?' he said incredulously. 'In London?'

'I don't – '

'Irish.' The answer snapped back angrily. 'Those are Irish pipes. I heard them when I served there under Oliver, and it's not a sound to forget. Look at their marching.'

He sounded as if he did not approve of it, and a few moments later, when the drums went banging past, even Nick knew why. This was not what he had seen before from any soldiers, let alone from Colonel Crosedale's Foot Guards. Men seemed to be rolling as they marched, swaying about and limping, as if they were not used to shoes. Some were not in step, and some were scraping heels on the ground, rather than lifting them clear. Instead of keeping their eyes to the front, they were turning their heads to stare at the shops, the houses, and the passers-by. Muskets were at every angle of slope and pointing in every direction. Hats were at the front of the head, the back of the head, or anywhere on the head, according to each man's fancy. The fine new uniforms were splashed with mud, most of it old and dry, and buttons had mostly been undone for comfort. On top of all this, there was an air of bewilderment about the men, as if they had seen nothing like London before, and did not know where they were going or why. Nick looked at open mouths and staring eyes, and found himself feeling sorry for them. He said so, and Richard dealt promptly with that.

'You'd be a deal more sorry for them if they were to meet just a quarter company from a seasoned regiment. They'd not last three minutes. They're no more than bogtrotters, with their heads turned by talk of pay and food. They're untaught and untrained, and to add to it they haven't any English, so they don't even know what's been said around them. Did you notice their officers trying to keep order?'

'No.'

'Nor did I. So the officers are as untrained as they are, and I've heard Crosedale say as much of the teagues at Hounslow.'

'But this isn't Hounslow.' Nick stood watching as the last of the Irish took their unsteady way into the City. 'Why here?'

'Why indeed? It's the sort of King we have, who can think only of threats and force. He'll show us his fine new soldiers, and he hopes to frighten London – *that* way.' He glanced for a moment at the receding regiment, then turned angrily back to Nick. 'If there's a Londoner left who isn't a Whig, this will make him one. The King's our recruiting officer.'

17 *Lillibullero, Bullen-a-la*

Sir Nicholas Culley, deeply disturbed by all he had heard from London, seized on Nick as soon as he arrived, and demanded the latest news. This meant the talk about October and the Prince of Orange, and Sir Nicholas sat with his fingers twitching and his lip quivering as if his thoughts were in turmoil.

'Who'd have dreamed,' he said slowly, 'that I could ever hear a tale like this, and then hope for it? But that's what we're driven to now, however loyal we are. What do *you* think of it?'

'I wasn't hoping for it. I was hoping to get wed.'

He explained the difficulties, and Sir Nicholas seemed to put his own worries aside while he considered them. Then he spoke gruffly.

'Yes,' he said. 'Gibson's right. So hurry it along and wed the girl. I can remember one or two myself who never got wed because they put it off.'

'But what then? Can I take her to Westminster, as things look?'

'I suppose not. Leave that till you're safe past October.'

'That could mean Christmas. So what till then?'

'You'll have to stay here with her, and drop your law work for a while. She'll be safe enough in this forgotten place.'

'But Gibson hinted that if trouble comes I should take some part in it, in a troop of horse perhaps, or something of the sort, and I suppose he's right. Can I, if it comes, just bury myself in some safe place till it's over?'

'No.' It sounded gruffer than before. 'I hadn't thought of that, but you wouldn't like it later. But if Orange comes, you won't be the only one who'll have to leave his wife. Not by a long way, and it will mostly be the young ones. It always is, in a war.'

That sounded more true than pleasant, and Nick had it very much in mind when he went to Judith the next morning. He found her in high spirits, and she said with no hesitation that she was willing to be married as soon as it was possible; but it would not be possible next week.

'I must give some thought to things,' she said firmly. 'My mother wants some changes in the house before she's left in it – store cupboards, and an extra window in the kitchen, that sort of thing. It's quite reasonable, and I'm getting men to do it, but it will take a week or two. Then I must find two girls to her liking, and agree on a wage for them. All in all, it will be two or three weeks before I can leave her.'

'Make it September, then. That should be just in time.'

'But where? And how do we get people together for it?'

This, once they began to look at it, seemed a serious problem. Innes, who was giving the dowry, would certainly expect to be present. So would Nick's parents, and perhaps the Gibsons, probably the Culleys, and others too, and it soon began to look like the betrothal all over again, with London as the only possible place. They agreed unhappily that their present time together would have to be cut short. Nick must return to London and learn what Innes thought of this, and whether he would play the host to a wedding. He must then make his best speed to the north and see if he could persuade his parents to come to it. He should also, if time allowed, try to buy a house in Westminster, even if it had to be left empty.

Innes, when Nick asked him about it, was both cautious and encouraging. The signs were bad, he said. Reports were persistent that the Dutch were busily fitting out ships and recruiting seamen, many of them English. In return, King James had ordered eight more warships to be made ready, and press gangs had been out on the waterfront, beating up for seamen. There were tales, too, of more Irish soldiers being brought to England. None the less London was still quiet and safe, and unless things got very quickly worse a wedding should be possible in September. He agreed that there was now much to be said for having it quickly, and he would do his part; but the sooner it was arranged, the better.

Nick agreed fervently, but he could not leave for the north without getting the latest news of Doraty. He went at once, and Richard Gibson took him into the parlour and told him that Doraty had been delivered of a daughter only a few hours ago. All was well, it seemed, with both of them, and Richard drily added that John had now calmed enough to be sent back to the

Cockpit and told to stay there. Then he reached for his hat and suggested the Angel and a bottle of wine.

They settled, and Richard gave full approval when he was told of the plan of an early wedding. Most certainly he and his wife would wish to be at it.

'It's fortunate that we're here,' he said. 'We must stay a week or two anyway, and we can stay a little longer at need. So get you off home, and bring back word of what your father will do.'

'I must inquire for a house here first, and I don't know who wishes to sell. I'll call on Mrs Crosedale and ask her.'

'No.' The word was sharp. 'Don't trouble her with that just now. She's upset.' Richard seemed to pick his words carefully. 'Her husband is suspended from duty, and he no longer commands his Foot Guards.'

'What!'

'It's a matter of those teagues who keep coming over, the sort you and I saw in London the other week. I told you their officers weren't trained, and perhaps the King saw that too. At all events, he's now putting parties of teagues into good English regiments to be trained by the English officers and sergeants. Crosedale was sent such a batch, and he refused to have them.'

'Was he right?'

'Very right. He's proud of his regiment, and he wasn't going to have it spoiled and his men turned mutinous by that sort of thing, especially as he can get as many English recruits as he wants. He said so, and this is what followed. He's told he must now face court martial.'

'It's wicked.'

'I've told you before that if a man isn't a Whig the King will make him one. Crosedale has had more than thirty years in the army, and it's to end like this. He must be mad.'

He meant King James, and for a long moment he sat in a hard silence. Then he became easier.

'It's not surprising that Penny Crosedale is upset, and that's why you should not trouble her now about houses. But leave it to me. I'll see her in a day or two, and by the time you're back I'll have it all ready for you, who wishes to sell, and at what price, and so on.'

Nick accepted the offer at once, and he went off to pack his valise yet again, anxious to gain even a few hours. He was away the same afternoon, and he did the journey in four days. Yet when he was able, the next day, to have a quiet hour with his father, the talk did not go quite as he expected. He began by telling of the belief in London that the Prince of Orange would come, and his father merely nodded, as if there need be no dispute about this. Then Nick gave Gibson's argument that October was the likely month, and again there was only a nod of agreement. Nick began to think this odd, but he went steadily on, telling of his talks with everybody, and finally asking if his father and mother could by any means come to London in September for a wedding. To this he had no immediate answer. His father sat still and silent, as if he were going round it in his mind. Then he spoke slowly and deliberately.

'Nick, you have put it very clearly, and I agree that you have now good reason to be married as soon as possible. I'll wish you all speed in it, and all happiness. None the less, I can't go to London this side of Christmas. I must stay here.'

There was sympathy in his tone, but a firmness too, as if this was a decision already taken, which could in no way be altered. Nick looked back in surprise, not yet understanding it.

'No?' he said briefly, and made it into a question.

'No.' It came like an echo, confirming the decision, and then there was a pause. 'Nick, if the Prince of Orange comes at all, he will surely be expecting help when he gets here. Perhaps he's been promised it.'

'Yes?' An inkling began to come of what this might mean.

'If he should land, say, in the north of England, it would be unfortunate if he should find nothing prepared, no one knowing what to do or where to do it. He'll have been promised more than that.'

'Yes.'

There was no need to ask more. It was as plain now as it was likely to be. Something was being prepared in the north, and in deep secrecy. It could not have gone very far yet. There could have been no raising of troops and mustering of men. But quietly and secretly an organization was being got ready, perhaps only a few score gentlemen who had promised each to be in a particular place doing a particular work when the moment came; and his father must be one of them. Nick sat silent, seeing it quite plainly, and knowing that he must not ask for more. These were life and death matters, where secrets must be kept and questions not asked.

'If you can arrange to be married in September, Nick, I give you leave to do it. I'll be sorry indeed not to be there, but I can't at present go to London.'

'No.'

It stayed at that. Whether he could bring himself to be married with his mother and father not there, he did not yet know, or what Judith would say to it, or Innes, but for the moment there was no more to be said. He stayed a few days longer, and then he set out again for London, and perhaps for Salisbury. But while he waited for his horse his father took him quietly aside.

'Some messages,' he said easily. 'You already know what you're to say to Doraty, and of course to John, on our behalf. Next, to Innes, my compliments and my regret that I cannot see him just at present.'

'Certainly.'

'Then Colonel Crosedale. My full sympathy, please, and my belief that he's been treated scandalously.'

'Indeed yes.'

'Finally, Richard Gibson, and for him there's rather more. Say it to him, please, when you are private, no one else within hearing.'

'I'll try to.'

'Make sure of it, please. Then say to him that he should not now tarry in London longer than he must. Say that employment waits for him here which he may think a duty. I think he'll understand.'

'Ye-es.'

'It's convenient that you may take that message, Nick, for I should not have liked to put it in a letter.'

It was the first week of September when Nick reached London, feeling that he had spent a deal of time in travelling, and had come to little profit by it. What mattered now was to complete as quickly as possible what he had to do, so that he might still have some days with Judith before the law term opened in October, and he therefore went to see Innes that same evening. He explained, without going into exact reasons, that his father could not at present come to London, and Innes looked sympathetic, but perhaps not displeased.

'It may be as well,' he said, 'though I'm sorry you should be put from it yet again. But the town is far from quiet, and it gets worse.'

'Is there more trouble?'

'None in particular. It's rather that tumult is growing, and we don't know what it will boil into. Each night now we have the rabble out, parading through the streets and singing. It's almost like Shaftesbury's days, and I don't doubt they're guided by Whigs. They have a new song, too, which seems to make them worse. It's some Irish gibberish about one teague talking to another, and the words don't make sense, but it has a rousing tune and it seems to put heart into them and inflame them for anything. That's dangerous in these days.'

He continued in the same vein, and he was clearly of the opinion that Judith should be now kept safe in Salisbury. An early wedding seemed impossible, and Nick walked sadly back to the Temple, wondering if there was any more that he could do. Then, as he came to the top of Ludgate Hill, he heard a crash and bang of drums, a steady tramp of feet, and voices by the hundred singing a stirring tune. He waited while they went noisily past him, the drums, some flutes and hautboys, and then the men, Wapping men perhaps, five or six hundred of them, marching eight abreast and bawling out their song. He stayed by the wall as they went swinging past, held all together by that lilting tune, and he did his best to hear the words. But these seemed to be gibberish, as Innes had said. He could not put them together, and he could make out only a refrain that seemed to follow every verse: *Lero, lero, lillibullero, lero, lero, bullen-a-la.* The men had it pat, whatever it might mean, and it came thumping at him, heavily accented and helped by a crash and roll of drums. Innes had been right. The song, with its rousing tune, had gripped these men, and it was working them into a mood of exaltation, which could indeed be dangerous.

He made no attempt to keep pace with them. He was too tired for that after his days of riding, and he followed at half their speed as they marched down Ludgate Hill, shoulders squared, arms swinging, and heads held high, kept together by the tune and the banging drums. When he reached the Temple they were out of sight along the Strand, and he left them to it, thinking that it was now time for bed. But the tune would not quite leave him. It had got inside him, and in some quiet corner of his mind it was dancing away as it pleased, in spite of him, and by some life and power of its own. *Lero, lero, lillibullero* – he could not stop the thing. It went on and on, and even when he was in bed, had blown out his candle and was in the dark, it was still beating away inside him, quieter now but still there: *Lero, lero, lilli-bullero, lero, lero, bullen-a-la.* It was with him till he fell asleep.

He took things easily the next morning, but when he sought a boat to take him to Westminster he had some trouble in finding one. All down the river, he was told, the press gangs had been taking up men for the Navy, and all the younger watermen had either been impressed or had gone into hiding to avoid it. But two of the elders took him to Westminster, and he quickly learned that all was well with Doraty and her infant daughter. John was in the house, and explained that the Princess was in Tunbridge for the waters, and had considerately let him stay with Doraty. The King, he added, was at Windsor.

'And perhaps that's just as well,' he went on, 'with a thousand or so of rabble outside his gate each night. Have you heard this song they've taken up – "Lillibullero"? It's becoming a sort of Whig anthem, and they're singing it by Whitehall Gate each night, just to let him know they don't like him and his teagues. I suppose they don't understand that he isn't there.'

'Does the song mean anything? And where did they get it?'

'Tom Wharton wrote it, I'm told, and *he's* an out-and-out Whig. But the tune, if you please, comes from Westminster Abbey, from the organist there, Purcell. He called it a quickstep, but someone must have seen that it would just fit Wharton's doggerel. Now some City Whigs have given money to have it printed, and they're handing copies out all over London, free. They've seen what it could do for them. Or so Richard says.'

'He's probably right. But I want a word with him. Where is he?'

'In the Angel, I should think. He's often there of a morning.'

He was there that morning, sitting comfortably in the wine-room, and he was genial and hospitable when Nick joined him. He asked for news of home, and Nick took the chance at once to deliver his father's message. Richard listened quietly, and then nodded.

'Employment and duty, does he say?' He nodded a second time. 'That's easy to understand, and I'll go home at once – or as soon as I can persuade my wife to it. Doraty is all but herself again, and I think she can well be left.'

'What if there's trouble in Westminster? Can John stay with her?'

'No. He's taken this service with the Princess of Denmark, and now he must stand to it. But Doraty and the children may at need go up the river, to Penelope Crosedale's house. She's invited them there. Crosedale, by the way, will be free to escort them. He's now dismissed from the army by court martial.'

'I'm sorry indeed. Is that the end for him?'

'Under James it is. If we come to Queen Mary he might have his command again. It would be among much she'd have to put right. Now what of yourself? Do you still seek to buy a house here?'

'If I can.'

'You certainly can. Here's a note of several.' He passed a folded sheet across to Nick. 'Some men are now so wishful to see their families settled elsewhere that they'd take almost what you choose to offer. You won't find it difficult. But what is it after that? Salisbury again?'

'I hope so. I've time yet for some days with Judith.'

'Then God be with you.' He paused, and looked earnestly at Nick. 'If I thought less well of you I'd bid you stay safe with her in Salisbury till all is done. As it is, and because I think better of you, I commend you to have your days with her, then leave her. Come back here and give some service, as the rest of us will do.'

'I'll try. Though I don't know what it will be.'

'Something may appear and require you, and when it does you may be much surprised. That's common in war. It takes men in ways they do not expect.'

18 *The Protestant Wind*

Salisbury seemed to be in a different world when Nick arrived there two days later. After London it was calm and peaceful. Newsletters, indeed, were being eagerly read, and everyone was asking whether the Prince of Orange would really come; and they were near enough to the west country to have a hope, which they did not always speak aloud, that he would remember the savageries that had followed Sedgemoor, three years ago. But that was all, and the town was quiet and orderly. No one marched through the streets, no one sang 'Lillibullero', and no one asked if he should now join a troop of horse or an association to defend a street. There would be no troops of horse to join, for the writers of newsletters had been to the Pool of London to talk to the sea captains, and had been told that if the Prince of Orange got a wind at all, he would have to go where it took him, which would probably be to the north-west. He might, said the captains, land anywhere from Yarmouth to Edinburgh, the coast of Yorkshire being perhaps the most likely, and Salisbury was content with that. If war should come, they would not this time be in its path, and they would think what to do when they saw how things were shaping.

Sir Nicholas Culley was not finding it so easy. He was by this time sure that for one reason and another he must give support to the Prince of Orange. He was as restless as ever, and he had a vague notion that when the moment came he should at once ride the length of England to give his sword and service to the Prince. His wife, who had never been short of a clear good sense, had told him that at the age of sixty-two he would do nothing of the sort. He would stay quietly at home, give what local help he could, and be thankful that the trouble was not upon his doorstep. Since he had lately been complaining of feeling his age he had no good defence against this, but his acquiescence had been only grudging, and he broke out again as soon as he heard from Nick that Hal Burnaby was likely to be caught in something. If Hal could serve, he said, so could he, and he had better ride at once to Hal to share it with him. This brought the retort from Mary that Hal was not sixty-two, but only fifty-one, and that eleven years could make a deal of difference. That set enough going to last the rest of the evening.

Judith had been having an argument also, and it was the first thing that Nick heard about the next morning. Judith was plainly troubled.

'It's a Mr Moore,' she said briefly. 'Out of Bridgwater. He's in the cloth trade there, and he and his wife were neighbours. My mother was friendly.'

'Yes?'

'He's been to London for his trade, and on his way back he turned aside to call here. He and his wife would like my mother to make a visit to them. Several weeks of it.'

'When?'

'Next month, perhaps. Of course it's just what Mother wants. She's been saying for a year past that she should be back in Bridgwater.'

'Do you approve?'

'I can't think of anything that would be worse for her. She'll just wallow in it, turn it into a sort of pilgrimage, Richard all the time. And before she's been a month there she'll be saying she must have a house there and stay where she always used to be, with Richard.'

'If she's set on that, I think you'll have to let her. She might be happier so, and you can't spend your whole life like this.'

'I'm not going to, and I think you're right. If she's determined to go, I can't stop her, and I shouldn't have a right to. But I'm not going with her, and that's what matters. This isn't going to lie on me.'

'Why, what – '

'Nick, do get it clear.' She was facing him tensely now. 'What happens if I take her to Bridgwater and then she frets herself into something near collapse again? I mightn't even be able to get her back here. She wouldn't want to come, and she'd make every sort of difficulty. I could be stuck there for ever with her – till you grew tired of waiting for me, and I won't chance *that*. We've been put off long enough, you and I, and this could be past bearing.'

'Then what will you do?'

'I won't do anything, and I've said so. I told Mr Moore that if he and his wife want her in Bridgwater, they'll have to see to it. They'll have to get her there, and if need be care for her there.'

'Do you think she'll need much care?'

'I don't think she'll be bedridden. But it's more than likely that she'll insist on having a house there, and all the work I've done to make this one ready will have to be done again. But not by me. I've done it once, and I'm not going to do it a second time. I'm thinking of a house in Westminster now, not one at Bridgwater.'

'How did Mr Moore take that?'

'Better than I expected. He said he understood. But whether he and his wife will continue the invitation now they know what it might mean, I don't know. If they don't, I shall get the blame.'

She was plainly unhappy about it, and he had sense enough not to argue. He told her that as like as not no more would be heard of this invitation, and then he talked of the house he had agreed to buy in Westminster, and of what they might do with it when they had it. He tried to keep to what was happy and about themselves, and he said nothing of the thoughts that kept shooting into his mind of the Prince of Orange and what might be needed if he came. He knew what hung on this, for himself and Judith and for countless others, and he could not bear to speak of it.

He returned to London at the end of the month, wondering how much interest he could now have in Westminster Hall and cases about borough charters. He went that evening to Lombard Street, and the first news that Innes gave him was that the King had suddenly become conciliatory, as if a light had now broken upon him. He had begun with a proclamation which solemnly declared that he would in future protect the Church of England and uphold the Act of Uniformity, and in particular would no longer insist that papists might sit in Parliament.

'That was on Monday,' said Innes. 'On Thursday he announced that he will put back into office all the Justices he lately put out. And yesterday we were told that suspension is to be removed from the Bishop of London. He's to have his powers again.'

'But why all this? Does the King give a reason?'

'He will make great sacrifices for the sake of concord.'

'Oh?'

'Exactly. He has perhaps woken up to it that he now needs friends and has quarrelled with too many of them.'

That seemed to be the general opinion. John was positive about it on Sunday afternoon.

'Seen the light?' he retorted. 'That puts it prettily. But it was a despatch from The Hague that did it, from his ambassador there.'

'What did it say?'

'He hasn't told anyone. But one or two men saw him read it, and they say he looked as if he'd been hit with a club. Then he stuffed it in his pocket, and he won't let anyone see it. But now he's in his angry mood. Sullen. He was even heard muttering that he'll have to make concessions – and he's been saying for years that kings should never make concessions. That's what killed his father, or so he says.'

'Then let's hope he'll make more concessions.'

'There's a belief at Court that he will. They say it's now occurred to him that his ungrateful subjects may all turn against him altogether.'

'That wouldn't surprise me.'

The King did make more concessions, and they went further than anyone would have predicted. The hated Ecclesiastical Commission was dismissed. The Lord Chancellor was sent to Guildhall to restore the forfeited charter to the City of London. All over the country charters were restored to boroughs, and protestants were put back as Lords Lieutenant. At Oxford the intrudent papists were turned out of Magdalen, and the protestant Fellows put back. But by all these blandishments the nation was unmoved. The reasons for them seemed all too plain, and men were quickly saying that if thoughts of the Prince of Orange could persuade the King into some attempt at good government, then the sooner the Prince was here in person the better. Impatience for his coming grew keener, trade seemed at a standstill, and the coffee houses buzzed with talk and rumour, inseparably mixed. Two hundred horses had been taken from the hackney coachmen of London. The Dutch had fifty-seven warships ready, and three-hundred transports. Wagons were being seized from farms for the use of regiments, and all horses and cattle were to be driven twenty miles from any place where the Dutch might try to land. This would certainly be in the north, and orders had gone to the Lords Lieutenant there to fire the beacons and call out the militia at the first sign of them. The talk went on and on; and in the Palace of Whitehall, with all pomp and solemnity, a child was christened James Francis Edward, with the Pope, acting through his Nuncio, as godfather, and the Queen Dowager as godmother. Outside Whitehall Gate men in hundreds were rattling drums, waving warming pans, and putting all their fervour into a full-throated chorus that could be heard in the royal chapel: *Lero, lero, lillibullero, lero, lero, bullen-a-la.*

Then came a change. The Dutch had stopped even the mail packets, and no more news came from Holland, but a single dispatch from France said that the Dutch were now ready, that their army was embarked, and that the Prince of Orange waited only for a wind before boarding his frigate. But therein lay the trouble, for the wind was from the west, and it seemed to have settled there. It blew strong and steady, and no fleet could sail from Holland while it lasted, and in London, and perhaps in all England, impatience grew into a fever. Trade seemed to stop completely. Masters and men alike were for ever gathering round the churches, staring up at the weathercocks on the steeples, then going within to pray for an easterly wind. But obstinately the cocks faced to the west.

They stayed so till the nineteenth of October. On that cold grey morning the cocks had turned at last, and the wind was strong. It was not, indeed, quite steady. It wavered a little, and sometimes it gusted, but it was in the main south-easterly, and the streets were all but blocked by the exultant crowds who forgot all thought of work as they stared up, gave thanks to God, and burst into 'Lillibullero'. Only in the Pool were there doubts and some anxious faces. The sailors had noted those gusts and the wavering wind, and they spoke of a coming storm.

They were right. The wind stayed easterly through the day and the night. Then it backed to the north and the gusts became stronger. It backed further, the gusts began to merge, and by the afternoon it was in the north-west, rising to a furious gale. Londoners watched with dismay, which turned to consternation as they heard the howling of the wind and saw the smoke from their chimneys swirling across the roofs instead of rising. What, they asked, was happening to the Prince of Orange? Was he at sea in this, and how was he faring? Would he and his armament win safe to shore again? Or what? Dusk came upon the town, then the dark of night, and the wind seemed as strong as ever.

Morning came, a cold bleak Sunday, grey with scudding cloud

and spatters of noisy rain, and everywhere the churches were crowded. In all of them prayers were said for the safety and deliverance of men – not named – who might that day be at sea, and in all of them the roar and drone of the wind could be heard in the roof. It held its strength through the day and the night and half the next day, and then it began to moderate. By Tuesday it was no more than a breeze, and Admiral Lord Dartmouth, who commanded the King's fleet, sent frigates from the Nore to glean what news they could. London waited, and in the absence of news a rumour swept through the town that half the Dutch fleet was wrecked, and that it would be many months before the Prince of Orange could again be ready. Then, from France, came a single letter, and men believed it because they could not bear to disbelieve. The Dutch fleet, it said, had won back to its harbours with no loss or damage worth mentioning, and the Prince had not even gone ashore; he was still aboard his frigate, waiting only for a wind before he sailed again.

But there lay the trouble. He had no fair wind, and no sign of one. Day after wet October day the weathercocks faced obstinately to the west or south-west, as if they welcomed the driving clouds and the curtains of rain that were sweeping over England from the distant seas. Winter was coming fast, and it was all but too late for any fleet to sail. On the last Sunday in October Nick went to Bow church, in Cheapside, where half the wealth and power of London was in the congregation, and as they were coming out he saw Sir Thomas Mallory. They were soon on the inevitable topic.

'I'm not surprised that men worry,' said Mallory. 'There's cause for it. Another week or two of this and we can give up hope for this year, and then what? And the maddening thing – ' He threw his head back and glanced at the cock on the steeple, high above them. ' – is that it needs so little to make it possible. Another four points, say. It's south-west now, but that little difference is enough. Orange could perhaps get out, but he'd never make the coast.'

'We can only pray for a wind.'

'It seems to be the papist prayers that are being answered.'

He sounded gloomy, but he was none the less right. The Fates were in the wind and the wind was in the west. It veered that afternoon exactly to west, and there it stayed. The last three days of October went slowly by, and they brought nothing but the west wind, banks of cloud, and squalls of driving rain. Then came November, which even Richard Gibson had declared to be almost too late for a campaign, and suddenly, many said miraculously, the weather turned about. Nick, coming out of the Temple that Thursday morning, was aware of it at once. The rain had passed, the clouds were lifting and breaking, and here and there was a patch of blue and a gleam of sunlight. Best of all, the wind had dropped, and the morning was cool and still, as if it waited for some new weather to begin. Expectancy was in the air, and men stood staring up, scanning the sky above the roofs, and trying, hoping, to feel a wind.

An hour later a light air stirred, gently, almost imperceptibly, then strengthening till it could be called a breeze, and by the time Nick came out of Westminster Hall for dinner it was a wind, fresh and steady. He felt it on his face, and saw the ripple of it on the sunlit river, and then a whole tangle of thoughts came rushing at him. It was coming to him across the river, and it was therefore from the east. In Holland it would be a wind for sailing; and even now the trumpets might be sounding as sails were loosed and cables hauled short. It was the wind so many had been praying for.

All through the afternoon it freshened, exactly from the east, and by evening it was strong and steady, and London seethed and quivered. No one supposed that the Prince would miss the chance, but there could be no news yet. He would need three days at the least, perhaps four or five, to make his landfall, and then from the north a courier would have to ride, which meant another day or two. A week at least of suspense seemed certain before London could have the news, and even then it might be good or bad. The King had sent strong forces to the north, both English and Irish, but no one knew where they were or how they would behave, or how prepared and resolute the men of the north would be when the moment came. It was all for guessing, and far into the night the taverns and coffee houses were hot and noisy. The streets were even noisier, and time and time again, rising above the cheering and shouting and the tramping of feet, came the lilting tune and the drums of 'Lillibullero'.

The next day passed, and the night, and then Saturday. The wind was still steady from the east, blowing at nearly a gale, but no news came, and nerves were becoming stretched. On Sunday, as soon as Nick was up and about, he found that even the courts of the Temple were full of talk and excitement. There was news, he was quickly told, and not of the kind expected. At midnight an exhausted courier had come clattering into Whitehall with a despatch for the King, and soon the Palace, dark and silent for the night, was lit again as men of every rank were called from their beds. Horses were saddled and men sent riding everywhere, and at three o'clock in the morning the King had himself been in Hyde Park for a torchlight review of regiments before they marched away. Then had come a brief announcement that on Saturday morning the whole Dutch armament had been seen from Dover, running westwards before the wind; and the loyalty of all good men was now required by the King.

That took Nick to Westminster, but John was for once unable to tell him much.

'I've picked up what there is,' he said quickly, 'but it isn't much. The tale's true, of course. The despatch did come from Dover, and the whole Palace seems to have been roused. Those regiments who marched from Hyde Park, by the way, are bound for Portsmouth, so it looks as if the landing is expected there.'

'That's not certain, I suppose?'

'How could it be? It rests with Orange, and he has the whole English Channel in front of him and the wind in his tail. He can do what he chooses.'

'We all thought he was for the north.'

'So did James. He sent a dozen regiments there, and now he'll have to call them back again.'

'I don't like this. I thought Judith was as safe as anyone when Orange was expected in the north. But if he now lands somewhere in the west country, we could have another Sedgemoor, I suppose?'

'It won't be a Sedgemoor. Not ploughboys fighting regiments. Orange is in strength, it seems. That despatch judged his fleet as six hundred sail. Some of his ships may be pretty small, but even so it's a lot of men.'

'That means a bigger battle if he lands. So – '

'Nick, don't get alarmed. If Orange lands at Portsmouth, and then marches on London, he won't be within fifty miles of Salisbury.'

'We don't know it will be Portsmouth.'

'Perhaps the King does, since he's sent his troops there. You'll have to wait for news before you can decide anything.'

Edmund Innes said the same thing when Nick went to him that

evening. He was as concerned as Nick for both Judith and her mother, but he agreed with John that they must wait for more certain news.

'No,' he said firmly. 'You must *not* go rushing off to Salisbury tomorrow. For one thing it isn't needed – yet – and also you've your work to do, with Mr Pollexfen. You've no right to leave him until it is necessary.'

'No, but – '

'Also – ' He looked Nick straight in the eye. 'You would not wish it to be said of you that you had taken fright and were seeking safety in the country. Yet it might well be said if you were to leave us as soon as this. You know the way of gossip, and it's the hurtful gossip that travels fast.'

That seemed all too likely, and Nick gloomily agreed that he would have to stay where he was, at least for a few more days, till matters became clearer. Then he walked back to the Temple, buffeted by a wind that was as strong as ever, and as steadily from the east. He could feel it in his back, driving him down the dark of Ludgate Hill; and that made him think of the Prince of Orange and his officers, who at this moment would be driving down the English Channel, with the dark of impenetrable night in front of them, and the wind and a rolling sea astern. They had staked their lives on this. They could not return against this wind, and they could not even be sure that it would allow a landing anywhere. It might grow stronger, or even back to the north.

Another thought came, asking where his cousin was, Tom Culley, who served in a King's ship. Where *were* the King's ships? They had been lying at the Nore, ready to sail when the moment came, but they would never get out against a wind as strong as this, and they were probably still at the Nore, with officers fretting as they waited, knowing that the Dutch were clear away. Or were they perhaps not fretting at all? Protestant officers might have some other thoughts, which they would not speak aloud.

In Fleet Street a company of men were marching, two or three hundred of them with some flutes and drums, singing 'Lillibullero,' and Nick suddenly became aware of an oddity. They were singing the same verse over and over again, the first line softly, and the second line roared with all the force they had. They were plainly emphasizing the words, shouting them into everyone's notice:

'Arra, but why does he stay behind?
Lillibullero, bullen-a-la.
Ho, by my shoul, 'tis a protestant wind.
Lillibullero, bullen-a-la.
Lero, lero, lillibullero, lero, lero, bullen-a-la.'

The words came hammering, and the point was entirely clear. It mattered nothing that the verse had been written a year ago and referred to another wind. The Prince of Orange was at sea, sailing fast, and a protestant wind this was. The phrase was perfect to describe it, and the men were using it so. *'Ho, by my shoul, 'tis a protestant wind.'* The words came again from the distant dark as he paused by the Temple lane, and he found himself repeating them. A protestant wind indeed.

Another night passed, and then it was Monday, the fifth of November, when every church would have the required service of thanksgiving for deliverance from the intended massacre by gunpowder eighty years ago. But few had their thoughts on that this morning. They had more present things to think of, and already there was news that early on Sunday morning the Dutch had been off the Isle of Wight, still running to the west. The announcement from Whitehall was brief, but it was enough to set men talking and guessing again. It was not to be Portsmouth, and the King would have to countermand his orders to those marching regiments. But where would he send them now? Above all, what *did* the Dutch intend?

Then the wind changed, the cherished protestant wind. In the morning it had been as strong as ever from the east, but by noon it had veered to the south and dropped to a gentle breeze, soft and pleasant. But where was the Prince of Orange? Had he made his landing? He *must* have made it. Men said this fiercely, and insisted on it, unwilling to believe that the protestant wind, after so much, could play them false.

Late on Tuesday afternoon the next despatch came in, all the way from Devon, and it said that a little after sunrise on Monday, when some morning mist had cleared, the Dutch had been sighted south of Dartmouth, apparently making towards the land. That was all, and it roused the talking and the guessing to a fever yet again. Another day passed, and it was Wednesday morning before the details came. That Monday morning had been dull and misty in Devon, and the Dutch had been unable to see the land. They had run too far to the west, and when the mist had cleared they had been off Start Point, or a little to the west of it, and in the strong east wind it had been impossible to turn about. They must, it had now seemed, think of a landing at Plymouth, where the King had a garrison. And then the protestant wind had shown what it could do. It had behaved as it had done in London. The gale from the east had abruptly stopped, and then had come the lull, the breaking cloud and the shafts of sunlight, followed by the soft southerly wind; and the fleet had put about, rounded Start Point, and made an easy passage to the north round Berry Head to a safe anchorage. Then even the gentle wind had died away as ships lowered boats and began to set men ashore. The Prince had been the first to land, and had said that his forces would march at once to Exeter.

Londoners had scarcely taken this in, and were still marvelling at a wind that could, at each stage, so exactly fit the needs of the Prince of Orange, when their own streets grew noisy with wind again. Since Monday they had had only the lightest of airs, and now a wind was rising again from the west. It strengthened, the rain came back with it, and by dusk it was near a gale, with sheets of rain spattering on the roofs and splashing from the gutters. Thoughts of bonfires had to be abandoned, and there were few who wished even to march and sing in it. But in the taverns the rejoicing and the marvelling grew even keener as they saw that this wind, too, was in the service of the Prince of Orange. He would have landed his men and stores by now, and his ships would be safe in Torbay. The King's ships were known to have left the Nore. They had been seen off Beachy Head, steering to the west after the Dutch, and now they would have to forget pursuit and run for any harbour they could reach, while the Dutch lay safe under Berry Head. Londoners drained their glasses, listened to the storm, and gave thanks to God. *'Ho, by my shoul, 'tis a protestant wind.'*

But Torbay was west of Salisbury, and no one knew which road the Prince would choose. Nick, deeply troubled, went to see Edmund Innes.

19 *Royal Headquarters*

Innes stayed calm, entirely refusing to be ruffled. He agreed that there was cause for concern, but he insisted that it was not immediate. Salisbury was not yet in the path of an advancing army, and it might never be.

'Orange,' he said, 'has a choice of roads by which he may advance, and he may pass far from Elizabeth and Judith. We must wait till we know his choice.'

'I'd be happier if they were away from Salisbury.'

'But where would you take them? You'll hardly wish to bring them here, where Orange must certainly come?'

'Of course not. But I'd thought of Bridgwater, where they're invited already. This Mr Moore and his wife. I think they should now accept that invitation and go there.'

'That's a good thought, and it may be useful. But again – not yet.'

'Why?'

'Because Orange, as I've said, has a choice of roads, and some men are saying he will next make sure of Bristol. It's the second city in the kingdom, and if he marches there from Exeter, he must go through Bridgwater. Ought you to take them there until we know?'

So Nick had to wait, as thousands of others did that week. He had to wait for what the Prince of Orange would do, and what the King would do, and neither of them seemed to be doing anything. They stayed where they were, in Exeter and Whitehall, and no news came. Nick went urgently to John, who might have heard something at the Court, but John could only shake his head.

'There's talk all day,' he said, 'but it's only talk and guessing. Nobody knows anything.'

'Does the King do nothing?'

'I doubt if he can, just yet. He keeps giving orders about guns and wagons, but he sent some good regiments to the north, and now he must have them back. I'm told they're marching, but what do you think the roads are like, after all this rain?'

'Does Crosedale say anything?'

'He's plain Mr Crosedale now, so he isn't told anything. His old regiment is somewhere in the west, and that's about all he knows.'

'How about Harry?'

'He's with the regiment, or so Crosedale says, and I think he may be unhappy. It seems that when Crosedale resigned, Harry wanted to resign too, but Crosedale told him he was too young to do things like that. So Harry obeyed orders and stayed. But he can't be as happy as he was, and I wish we could hear from him.'

'Any word from home about Father?'

'None. Of course they'll only just have had news there of this landing. But it does look as if they had a plan ready in the north, so Father is probably looking at pistols and getting a valise packed. We needn't ask about Gibson.'

'How of yourself?'

'I'm caught in it properly. Churchill's with the King, on duty. Mumford's disappeared, and I much suspect that he's at Exeter with the Prince. Likewise with two others, and I'm now the only one left with the Princess who's been with her long enough to be trusted. So if she has to go away, I'll have to go with her, wherever it is, and I'm keeping boots and a sword at the Cockpit now, and a horse in the stable there.'

'That seems to account for the whole family, except me and Nick Culley.'

'He'll be in it somewhere. He's more or less in the danger path, and this affair is going to catch all of us, even if we haven't a glimmer of what it will do to each of us. I once said something like that to Gibson, and he gave me his old-soldier look and told me that that's the way of war, and that nobody knows what it will mean till it comes. I didn't quite understand him then, but I do now.'

So did Nick, and he had the unhappy thought that he alone was committed to nothing and was offering no sort of service. He was thinking only of Judith and of his wish to be with her. He saw it clearly, and he knew that once he had her in safety he would have no more excuse. He would have to take a part himself, though he did not yet know what it would be. It would probably rise in front of him, as Gibson had said.

Another Sunday passed. Regiments were marching south. Wagonloads of ball and powder, of beans and bacon and all else that might be needed, were moving west from London, and it was clear that the King was making ready. The Prince of Orange stayed quiet at Exeter and seemed still to be doing nothing, but letters from the west told of gentleman after gentleman riding in to join him. Sir Thomas Mallory spoke crisply about this.

'It's what was needed,' he said to Nick. 'He can't conquer England with fifteen thousand men, and he mustn't even look as if he's trying to, or he may set everyone against him. It's a rising of the English that must sweep James away, and here's the beginning of it. These few who join him now will show the way to others, and they'll soon come in thousands. It's like priming a pump.'

'Ye-es.' Nick nodded, and had thoughts of Nick Culley; and possibly, a little later, of himself.

'Apart from that, he must have some English companies to do the scouting for him, perhaps the skirmishing, and the collecting of food and fodder and so on. That's best done by the English. They'll know the ground, and be better received by the people.'

Again Nick nodded, and he began to see himself as one of those volunteers – after he had dealt with Judith. It would be a decent and honourable service, perhaps with others of his rank and age, and it would let him look his brothers in the face when all was done. He began to feel more cheerful. Then, on the Thursday of that week, being the 15th of November, came an announcement that flung him into plain consternation. The King was ready at last, and it was briefly announced that he had chosen Salisbury as his headquarters and as the general rendezvous of his armies. He was himself going there at once, to take command.

The thought of it seemed beyond all bearing. Salisbury of all towns in the country! The armies would include those new undisciplined Irish, who might be loose in the town at night – and some of the English regiments might be bad enough, if things should go wrong with them. Nick went to Edmund Innes, but this time he had his mind made up. He would go to

Salisbury and have Judith out of the place, whether Innes agreed or not.

But this time Innes did agree, and he had given more thought to the details than Nick had done. Mother and daughter must certainly be taken out of Salisbury, he said, and to Bridgwater, if it were by that time clear that the Prince of Orange would not march that way. Otherwise, Nick must take them to any quiet town he could reach, and there find them a lodging, and Innes produced a bag containing a hundred pounds in gold. It might be needed, he said, for a lodging; or perhaps as a bribe to somebody. One never knew.

Nick was away as soon as there was light the next morning, and at once he met trouble. He was stopped by a patrol of soldiers who told him that passes were now needed on the western roads, and when he returned to London to get one he found that there were as yet no arrangements for giving them. It took him a full two days to get one, and when he at last set out again his progress was maddeningly slow. The road was choked with carts and wagons, companies of marching men, and even guns, slithering in the mud as they were hauled by teams of eight and ten horses, and he took twice his usual time for the journey. It was Friday afternoon, the 23rd of November, when he came in sight of Salisbury, and it was not the sight he knew. It looked now like an island, set in a sea of white.

It was a town ringed with camps. The water meadows had been flooded for the winter, which added to the look of an island; but beyond them, on the rising ground, and even on the steeper ground to the north, he could see nothing but tents and baggage carts, the tents in orderly lines and the carts arranged to make boundaries between one encampment and the next. Regiment after regiment must have come marching in, to be given a patch of ground on which to do the best it could. Twenty-five thousand men were camped round Salisbury, and as he drew closer he could see them between the tents, crowded together, and seemingly having little to do. He wondered which encampment the Foot Guards had, and whether Harry was in one of those tents.

The men had no doubt been ordered to stay in their camps, but inevitably, on one pretext or another, some were in the town, and they had it almost to themselves. The inns and taverns were busy and some shops were open, but there were few civilians to be seen. Some of the soldiers, particularly an officer or two, looked ill humoured, and Nick thought he had better be careful. They might deal roughly with a rider whose horse touched them, and he turned aside, finding a way through the outskirts as best he could, till he came in the end to the quiet street, overlooking the Avon, where Judith lived. It was lifeless now, seeming utterly deserted, and all the windows in Judith's house were shuttered, upper as well as lower. He plied the knocker, and again, and a third time, though he was already sure that it was hopeless. But then a shutter creaked in an adjoining house, and a man looked out whom he remembered having met on an earlier visit. He recognized Nick, and made no difficulty about answering the urgent question.

'They're away,' he said briefly. 'Mrs Allinson, and Judith with her. Since Monday.'

'Where to?'

'They didn't say. But Sir Nicholas Culley came for them in a coach, and took them.'

'Oh!'

He was suddenly thankful that Nick Culley had had so good a thought and had taken them away in time. They would be safe at his house, and the sooner Nick could join them, the better. He spoke quick thanks for the news, and then made his way along the fringe of the water meadows till he came to the road and the river bridge. It was familiar going now.

He came to the house at sunset, and the last gleam of gold was leaving a November sky. There was not even a barking dog to greet him, let alone the noisy welcome his uncle usually gave. He had to knock, and when the door was opened his aunt came from her parlour to receive him. There was no one with her, and no sign of Judith.

'Your room's ready,' she said calmly. 'I've been expecting you for a week past.'

'Blame roads and passes. But where's Judith?'

'Bridgwater, I hope. Nick went off with them on Wednesday.'

'But – '

'Get out of your boots, and wash some dust off. Then we'll talk.'

He came down the stair to find spiced cakes and October ale in front of a cheerful fire, and he soon had the rest of the tale. Nick Culley had been keeping a careful eye on the Allinsons, especially when he saw the growing concentration of troops at Salisbury. Then, last Sunday, when he heard that the King was expected at any moment, he had thought it time to act.

'He thought they'd be safer somewhere else,' she went on, 'so he brought them here the next day. Judith was willing enough, but her mother was difficult. She didn't like being uprooted.'

'Then what happened?'

'He was short with her. So was Judith, and they brought her here. Then she started talking about Bridgwater, which she'd always wanted.'

'She has an invitation there.'

'Exactly. And Nick was soon saying that if those people wanted her they might as well have her. He wouldn't move at once, though. Orange was still at Exeter, and some people thought he'd go next to Bristol. But on Wednesday we had news of him on the march to Axminster.'

'Where? This is new to me.'

'Axminster. It's almost on the south coast, so Orange isn't going near Bridgwater, and that was enough for Nick. He went off with them yesterday morning.'

'How about you, alone here?'

'Oh, this is quiet enough. We aren't on a road to anywhere.'

'Then I think I'll go to Bridgwater.'

'In a day or two, perhaps, but give them chance to settle first. Besides, Nick will wish to see you.'

'But when will he be back?'

'He said he wouldn't stay with the coach, coming home. He'd ride ahead and let it follow. So he might be here tomorrow night, or perhaps Sunday.'

'How of passes for riding west? Are they needed?'

'I've not heard of them.'

'They're strict enough out of London. But of course I'll stay till he's back. How is he?'

'Well enough for his age, but he has it in his head that he must now do something to help the Prince of Orange, and I suppose he's right, if something comes that he can do. But he's too old for war, and I've been telling him so. But how of yourself, Nick? What view do *you* take?'

'That I'll have to do something. I think my father will, and both my brothers. And that reminds me – is there any word of Harry here?'

'No, though we thought he must surely be in one of those camps around Salisbury.'

'I'm told his regiment is there. So if I've a waiting day tomorrow, I think I'll inquire for him.'

'Do. It should be quite in order for you to ask for your brother.'

Nick therefore rode into Salisbury again the next morning, as fine and sunny a morning as November could give. He had first to learn where the Foot Guards were, so he went carefully into the town, and at what seemed to be a principal inn he rode through the arch into the stable yard behind. Almost at once a young officer rode also into the yard, and Nick took the chance and put his question. He was given the brief answer that the Foot Guards were camped to the north of the town, where the road climbed to the plain.

He had no great trouble in finding it, a pleasant site by the Avon, with a row of baggage carts to shut it off from the road. A gap between carts made an entrance, and here sentries were posted. Nick rode boldly up to them, dismounted, and asked for Lieutenant Burnaby. The sentries were civil. They called a sergeant, and Nick was soon taken to the Officer of the Day, whom he recognized at once; a Lieutenant Brinsley, whom he had once met when with Harry.

'Ha! I'm glad to see you.' Brinsley had obviously remembered it too. 'Harry did say you sometimes came here.'

'Whenever I can. But where is Harry? Can I see him?'

'Not today, I'm afraid, but I expect he'll be free tomorrow. You know the King is here?'

'I'm told so.'

'He came on Monday, and he's lodged in the Bishop's Palace, yonder by the cathedral. He's keeping some state there, which means a strong guard round him, and this is Harry's day for it. He'll be on duty till dusk, I'm afraid, and busy. But if you could come back here tomorrow – '

It had to be accepted. Nick rode slowly back into the town, and decided he would call again at the inn for a mug of ale. He dismounted in the yard, and he was telling an ostler to water his horse when a man came out of the inn. He stopped, and they stood staring at each other.

'Lory!' Nick was the first to speak. 'What the devil are you doing here?'

'Much what you'd expect.'

'Would I, indeed? Can we talk?'

'Not in here. It's full of officers.'

'Just so.' He was noting that Lory, like himself, was in boots and country russets. 'Get your horse, and we'll talk in a country lane.'

20 *The Unexpected*

Of course I'm with Orange,' said a bright-eyed Lory. 'Where lse should I be for the day of reckoning? I was in the fleet with im, then ashore at Brixham, and thence to Exeter – for a rest, hank God!'

'Why?'

'Those ships, in that wind. We could have fought nobody, hose first days, till we could look at food again. I don't really now how we got to Exeter.'

'You seem to have recovered now.'

'Oh, it passes. But it needs time. The whole army needed time, ven Orange himself, and perhaps that's why he stayed so long at Exeter.'

'But of yourself?'

'I even managed a few days' leave, home at Bridgwater, to how them I'm still alive.'

'How is Bridgwater? Is it quiet and safe?'

'Perfectly, and murderous too. They haven't forgotten Jeffreys, nd I was almost a local hero when they knew I was with Orange. But of course I had to rejoin, and then I was sent here, and hereabouts. I'm to gain intelligence, if I can – and so far, I can't. Nick, I'm in as much need of help now as I was when we met in London.'

'How?'

'It's the same work again. I think Orange was pleased with the eport I took him from London, and perhaps that's why he's iven it me again. It's not military. I'm not to talk to officers, or ven soldiers. It's the ordinary folk again, in the towns and in the illages, and what he needs to know is how they'll behave if he rings his army here. Will it be a hostile country to him? If not, re they too frightened to do more than sit and watch, while ffering nothing? Or will he get meat and bread brought in, if he pays for it? And hay for horses, and wood for fires? And the Justices? Will they continue in their duties? And the clergy? Will they preach for him or against him? It's like that, and I can learn nothing.'

'Why not?'

'You saw how it was at that inn, officers everywhere. I'd have been taken up at once if I'd tried to ask such questions. I've tried in villages, and nobody will talk to me at all. They don't know who I am, of course.'

'You're probably right. But – ' Nick thought for a moment. 'You'll now ride with me to the house of my uncle, Sir Nicholas Culley. He's a Justice in these parts. He knows everyone, and is well thought of by most, including the dissenters. He isn't a Whig, unless the King has made him one, but I think he could answer those questions.'

'Nick!' It came with sudden eagerness. 'But would he?'

'Why not? He's too old to ride to war, or so his wife tells him but he wishes to serve, and answering questions is something he could do. Now turn about, please. I'll tell you more as we ride.'

Mary Culley, when Nick had presented Lory, and had told most of the truth about him, approved of this arrangement The Prince of Orange, she said emphatically, must certainly be given whatever help he now needed, since if he failed in thi enterprise he would be most unlikely to try again. As for he Nick, helping Lory was certainly something he could do, and she thought he had better do it. Otherwise he would probably do something less useful and more dangerous. So Lory must stay for the night.

But Nick Culley came riding in that same evening, looking pleased and buoyant. He had had no trouble at all. The roads had been dry, none had asked him for a pass, no part of the coach had broken, and in Bridgwater the Moores had made no difficulty about their unexpected guests. So all was well, and he now needed supper; after which he would by all means talk to Lory.

It seemed quite simple, but it soon took a twist. He and Lor settled into talk after supper, and within half an hour they wer saying that tomorrow they would ride together to Axminste and the Prince of Orange. Nick's knowledge of local affairs wa so complete, and so full of detail, that Lory could not store it i his memory in so short a time, and it would be much better fo

Vick to go himself and answer whatever questions might rise. 'hey settled happily on this, and Mary heard it at first in silence. 'hen she agreed also.

'Of course I can see the reason for it,' she said later to the ounger Nick. 'It makes quite good sense, but that isn't why he's oing it.'

'Why then?'

'He keeps talking about these passive obedience men, as he alls them. He says they're going to stay at home in safety while thers do the work for them, and he isn't going to look like one f them. So it's not enough that he should do something. He ıust be seen to do it, and that is why he'll go with Lory. But how f you, Nick? You're not going with them?'

'There seems no reason to. I'd thought of Bridgwater next, and udith.'

'Quite right. But will you spare a day or two first, to be with ıe while Nick's away?'

'Of course I will.'

Nick Culley and Lory rode away together the next morning, 'hich was splendidly bright and sunny for late November. Nick ırned to his aunt and asked if she could spare him for the mor-ing.

'It's Sunday,' she answered. 'Aren't you going to church?'

'Just for once, I think I'm not. I'd sooner go in search of Iarry. I've not seen him for weeks past, and I think I ought to. Ie could be in battle at any time.'

'I suppose he could. Yes – go by all means.'

It was almost ten o'clock when Nick came to Salisbury, and efore he had crossed the river he knew that something was foot. In half a dozen fields, which yesterday had been white with ents, he now saw the green of grass, and while he watched he ıw tents wobble and collapse in another field. The army was riking camp, hurriedly on a Sunday morning, and he wondered hat news had come in the night about the Prince of Orange. nd what of Harry? He could not yet see the Foot Guards' camp.

The town was full of people, out to see what the excitement 'as, and at corners drums were beating and trumpets blaring, as to call all stragglers back to camp. Some senior officers must have ›dged at inns, and through the archways he could see the inn-ards busy, as ostlers led out horses and soldier-servants struggled ith valises. From one of the inns a two-horsed cart was pulling away, piled high with bags and boxes and escorted by dragoon as if it held the furnishing of a general. Nick had to pick his wa slowly, wondering all the time whether the Foot Guards ha already gone.

They were still there, but they were busily striking cam Most of the tents were down when he reached the place, an the baggage carts, now drawn into a line, were already ha loaded. Men were scurrying everywhere, sergeants were bus and here and there an officer stood alone and watchful. There wa no longer an entrance between carts, but there was still a guar and Nick was quickly stopped by a sergeant and told that h could come no closer. He demanded Lieutenant Burnaby, an the man hesitated and looked uneasy, as if he did not know ho to answer. Finally he said that Lieutenant Burnaby was not i camp, and Nick, finding something odd in this, demande Lieutenant Brinsley. This seemed to be easier, and the sergea made no more difficulties. A message was sent, and a minute o two later Brinsley appeared, looking a little harassed, but sti calm and friendly.

'An awkward moment,' he said pleasantly. 'I'm sorry to recei you like this.'

'Not at all. But where's Harry?'

'Gone.'

It was terse, and a vague suspicion of something wrong flare suddenly into a certainty. Brinsley nodded, as if to confirm wh he had said.

'Gone,' he said again, 'and not the only one.'

'But what – '

'Have you heard what happened in the night?'

'Of course not.'

'We've had some desertions. And not by chance. They mu have been organized.'

'Desertions?' Nick echoed the word, not quite taking this i 'Men going, do you mean? Deserting the colours?'

'Or the King. Whichever you please.'

'But – Are you telling me that Harry – '

'Yes,' he snapped, and then the tone changed and softene 'I'm afraid so. But don't blame him. He was one among man and he had some reason. He took it hard when Colonel Croseda was cashiered, but I don't think he'd have gone even now if I hadn't been asked to.'

'Asked?'

'He must have been.' Brinsley stopped, and for a moment he ɔoked away. 'It wasn't casual. It was a big affair, three or four undred of them, as far as we've counted, and Lord Churchill as the leader.'

'Who?'

'Churchill – the best general we have, and the one closest to the ing. If *he* goes, why blame Harry? Churchill had been good to im.'

'I know. But – '

Nick was trying to make sense of it. Lord Churchill was close ot only to the King but to the Princess of Denmark. He was uch at the Cockpit, and he had procured John's appointment ere. The Princess leaned on him for much, and on his wife ven more, and she might one day be Queen. The thoughts came rting, one after the other and in no clear order, as if they must ɔw be put together to make a pattern which would not quite rm. Lord Churchill was a far-sighted man, and the soldiers ought he was their best general. And now he had deserted in e night. He had taken Harry with him, and many another, and had ridden away to – where? The question rose sharply, and ick turned again to Brinsley.

'Where have they ridden to?'

'Orange. That isn't a guess. Some of them left letters to us. hey'll ride in his train, I suppose.'

'And fight for him?' Thoughts of Harry were flickering again.

'Ugh!' It sounded like suppressed anger. 'If there *is* any fighting. ut it looks now as if there won't be. We're falling back.'

'What!' Nick looked round, seeing that the last of the tents as down. 'Aren't you ready to advance?'

'Back, I said. We're retreating. It's Andover today, and then, suppose, anywhere.'

'But what does the King do?'

'He's gone already. The first to leave.' Brinsley's voice seemed t and without expression now. 'We've twenty-five thousand en here, more or less, and Orange has about half that. We uld have swept him into the sea.'

'Did you wish to?'

'Not all of us. But we're soldiers – or we thought we were – d if the King had trusted us, and led us boldly forward, I n't think we'd have failed him. For very pride as soldiers we couldn't have done. And what's left of pride now, do you think We're deserted by Churchill. We're deserted by the King, an we're falling back before half our number. How many will wis to fight now, or have the heart to?'

A trumpet blared behind him, imperiously sounding a com mand, and he had just time for a quick farewell.

'I must go,' he said hurriedly, 'and I'm sorry if I've been out o humour. Commend me, please, to Harry. And may we all mee again, some happier day.'

He went off at nearly a run, and Nick stood watching for moment. Then he swung into his saddle and rode quietly hom where his aunt was waiting with some look of impatience. Sh wanted the news, of the King, of the army, and of Harry, an Nick told her all he had heard from Brinsley. She listened wit concentrated attention and with her eyes half closed, and h knew that her clear mind was taking in all the pieces of the tal and fitting them together. She sat quite still, never interruptin him, and when he had finished she was silent for some momen longer, not even lifting her head. Then she opened h eyes.

'We've known a dozen reasons,' she told him, 'why we shoul help Orange if we can, and now we've another. If he wins th tussle, Harry will be in credit, and he'll have his commissio back, perhaps with promotion. But if Orange fails, and has return to Holland, how will the King see an officer who desert in time of war?'

'I've thought of that.'

'It's a pressing reason for helping Orange. So what have yo in mind? Where do you go now?'

'Bridgwater, I hope. Not at once, of course. I'll wait here till –

'You should not wait here. Nor should you go to Bridgwate

'But please! What – '

'Should you not be riding hard, to the Prince? It could chan all his plans, and urgent's a small word for it.'

'But – ' His own thoughts were moving now. 'If Harry Churchill and the others – if they left in the night they should there by now, so he'll have the news already.'

'Of the desertion, yes, and that's important. But it isn't a It's even more important that the King isn't pressing forwar That he's ordered a retreat and was the first to go, and that t army's sick at heart from this, and has scarcely a wish to figh

Churchill was away before these things were known, and Orange *must* be told, and at once. They could change his whole campaign.'

'Oh – of course.'

It seemed beyond dispute. He would have to do it, if only for Harry's sake; and it meant that he too had been caught in a way he had not expected. It would be irrevocable. If he once rode to the Prince on such an errand, he would be a declared adherent, and he would have to stay as one. Here was his Rubicon.

'How far to Axminster?' he asked.

'Sixty miles, or a little more. Too much for one horse, so you'll have to find another.'

'If I can. But with armies about, men who have horses may keep them close.'

He was away an hour later, when he had dined, and he took it steadily, not pressing his horse at all. But the road was firm and dry, and in a quiet and sunny afternoon he made good progress. At five o' clock, when dusk was deepening into night, he thought he had done nearly half the journey, and it was not quite six when he rode slowly into Sherbourne, knowing that his horse had done enough. He found an inn and asked, none too hopefully, for a fresh horse, and to his surprise he had no difficulty. The innkeeper looked hard at him, asked how far he had to go, and evidently guessed that it was Axminster; and that was enough. This was Dorset, within a mile or two of Somerset, and memories still burned of Monmouth, of Feversham's dragoons, and of Lord Chief Justice Jeffreys, and a man who rode to the Prince of Orange was reckoned here as a friend. They quickly came to terms about the horse, and it proved to be a good one, perhaps the best in the stable. He went on after a quick supper, and it carried him easily, under clear bright stars, and with a quarter-moon setting in front of him to light the road. It was near midnight when he came to Axminster, and a mile from the town he was stopped by a patrol of soldiers, who had only some halting and broken English; and he guessed that they were Dutch.

They sent him under guard into the town, to the house where the Prince was lodged, and here he had the wit to ask for Lord Churchill, who would know him. In no long time, for all the lateness of the hour, Lord Churchill appeared, and remembered him at once.

Nick told his tale, and Lord Churchill listened with unruffled calm. But then he nodded.

'This is news indeed,' he said, 'and you have done great service by bringing it. Stay here, please, while I go to the Prince.'

He was away for some minutes. Then he came quietly back.

'Come now to His Highness,' he said. 'I have told him of it.'

The Prince of Orange was still at business in spite of the hour. He had a secretary with him, and he was pacing up and down as he dictated a letter, but he stopped as they entered the room. He was small of stature, short and slight, and though he was not yet forty he seemed a man of fifty, aged by ceaseless work and worry. He was pale of face, his breathing sounded troubled and asthmatical, and some grey hairs were plainly showing. But there were qualities in him that overcame all this, and Nick, stepping back after making his bow, was for a moment uncomfortable, ill at ease, as he met the scrutiny of two vivid eyes, the sharpest he had ever known, that seemed to look right through him, seeing in an instant anything of falsehood or pretence. Above the eyes was a wide forehead suggestive of intelligence, below them a strong and aquiline nose and lips that met in a firm clear line. Nick steadied himself, and knew already that this was not a man to be trifled with, even by King James.

'I am glad to see you, Mr Burnaby.' The Prince spoke carefully, as if he were picking his way through a language that was not his own. 'You bring me news that is important, and I thank you.'

'Sir!'

'You did see yourself this army break its camp?'

'This morning, sir.'

'And march to the east, away from here?'

'Some were going, sir, as I left the town.'

'And then you rode here? You have – how do you say it? – not lost the time. I thank you, and make you welcome.' He turned to Lord Churchill. 'We can give a bed to him?'

'I will arrange it, sir.'

'Good.' He gave a slight nod, and his eyes came back to Nick. 'Then go to sleep. Other gentlemen are here, whom you may now ride with.'

He turned away abruptly, with the air of one who has spent enough time talking, and there was nothing for it but to bow and go. In the passage that had to serve as an ante-room, Lord Churchill turned his understanding eyes on Nick.

'You thought it short?' he said quietly. 'But that's his way. I've not known a man as sparing of words as he, and you may think yourself favoured. He said more to you than he does to most, and he's in good humour with you.'

'Or with the news?'

'Both, of course, and so he should be. There could hardly be news more pleasing to any general, and you bring it fine to the moment. I will tell you that he has had letters today from the midlands and from the north, and it seems that all England is in arms for him.'

'Oh?'

'Indeed yes. The Earl of Danby is in arms in Yorkshire. The Earl of Devonshire has taken Derby, and marches now on Nottingham. Others are in arms at Oxford. And in Lancashire and Cheshire the Earl of Delamere is up. He says he has secured those parts and is about to ride south to the Prince, bringing some troops of horse. I do not know who they are, but – ' He stopped for a moment, and was smiling. 'You may soon see someone you know.'

'What! You mean – '

'Who knows? Anything is possible. But you've been overlong in your boots, and it's time you were abed. Time I was too, for I was riding through half the night.'

'Yes. But where's Harry? They told me he rode with you.'

'So he did, and he'll be easy to find in the morning. And glad, no doubt, to see you.'

There was too much to think about, and Nick did not fall quickly asleep. He was given a bed, but he was too tired to find full comfort, and thoughts seemed to come and go, though he wished for none of them. They were all caught up in it now, and in ways they had not expected. He had meant to ride to Judith, and he had ridden to the Prince of Orange. He had been received in audience, and told to ride with the others who had joined; which made him a rebel in arms. Harry was here too, and a greater rebel. Nick Culley, as wayward and impulsive as ever, had surely never intended it, but he would be here with Lory, and as like as not would stay. But the north was up, the Earl of Delamere was out, and it was to this that his thoughts kept turning. For the Earl of Delamere was Henry Booth, son of the Sir George Booth who, thirty years ago, had raised a revolt in Cheshire against the Commonwealth, for the restoration of King Charles. In that brief and disastrous adventure his adjutant had been young Hal Burnaby, who had ended in the Gatehouse prison. It would be old times come again if he were now riding with the son as he had done with the father. It was likely enough, and it would mean that they were all caught up in it now – except, perhaps, John. There was no word yet of disturbances in London, so perhaps he was still quietly at the Cockpit, in his smooth attendance on the Princess.

It was long past midnight, into the thin small hours of the morning. The moon was down, and under the stars a mist was rising, deepening the dark and making it safer for those who would not be seen. Nick fell asleep; and in that same hour, at the Cockpit, John was coming slowly down a discreet back-stair in boots and riding coat, with a cloak wrapped over all, and his sword hilt pushing through its folds. He held a dim horn lantern, showing the stairs to the two women who followed him, tight wrapped in cloaks and hoods. One was Lady Churchill, the other the Princess of Denmark. In silence he lighted them to a side-door, and they passed through it into the cold dark and the mist blowing from the river. He followed, and locked the door behind him.

He covered the lantern and led them, under the stars, to a door in the Palace wall that led to St James's Park, and again he had the key. He opened it, and two men were waiting, cloaked and booted like himself. They bowed low, sweeping their hats, and the Princess waved impatiently. Then she followed them, along the wall and round its corner till they came to the street, and here a coach was waiting, too far from Whitehall Gate to be seen by the sentries there. The lantern gave a gleam of light as the ladies were handed in, the men standing bare-headed. A servant had their horses ready, and they mounted to escort the coach. One, who led the way, was the Bishop of London, riding now like the soldier he once had been, with his sword ready, and pistols in his holsters. At one door of the coach was the Earl of Dorset, and John was at the other.

The coach rumbled away, and its journey was to end at Nottingham, where the Earl of Devonshire was in arms against the King. The Princess had made her choice, and she was putting herself under his protection, which meant that of the Prince of Orange. John was still with her, riding by her coach with the Bishop and the Earl of Dorset. He, too, had been caught in this, perhaps in a way he had not expected.

21 *The Broken Hope*

Harry was delighted the next morning, when he found that his brother, too, was in the Prince's camp, and then his one wish was to explain and justify himself. He was deeply troubled by his desertion, seeing all too well what could be said about it, and yet not knowing how he could have stayed to fight, as he put it, against his own people and his own religion, and he did not hide his relief that the same thoughts had led others to the same decision. He listened intently when Nick gave him the news from Salisbury, and it was plain that he understood Brinsley's feelings.

They had to wait till past noon for Nick Culley, who had been giving to Lord Churchill his detailed account of the affairs and loyalties of Salisbury. Then, with Lory, he had been taken briefly to the Prince, who had thanked and commended both of them. Nick was thus in high good humour. He was reassuring to Harry, and he told the younger Nick he had better take the chance while he had it, and go to Bridgwater for a word with Judith.

It did seem a chance. The Prince of Orange gave no order for an immediate advance, and no one had much to do. The campaign, as Nick remarked to Lory, seemed to be a leisurely affair, and they had no difficulty in getting leave to go to Bridgwater. It would be enough, they were told, if they were to rejoin during the following week, when the army would probably be at Salisbury. So off they went the next morning, going first to Sherbourne, where Nick had to return a hired horse and reclaim his own. But by Friday afternoon they were in Bridgwater, where Mr Moore and his wife were hospitable, and both Judith and her mother showed some memories of Lory from earlier days. But this was general talk, and it was the next day before Nick could talk to Judith alone. Almost at once she became purposeful.

'Nick, I'm more glad than I can tell you that you've come, and

I've a special reason for it. You say you'll go next to Salisbury, you and Lory?'

'We're to rejoin there.'

'Will you take me with you, as far as your uncle's house?'

'Of course. But – '

'I never wished to come here, but of course I had to. It was a matter of getting my mother here.'

'She seems well after it.'

'She's well enough to do what she's always said she would do, and that's look for a house here – her own place, she says, and Richard's. She wants to start *now*, and by the way she's going I think she'll soon find one. And then what?'

'Tell me.'

'Oh, I'll tell you. It will be Salisbury all over again, getting a house ready and preparing it to suit her, and then her furnishings to be brought and put in – and I'll have to see to it, all of it.'

'You've said plainly that you won't.'

'What's the use of saying that when I'm here? Is it for the Moores to do it, while I sit in the house – *their* house – and watch? Of course I'd have to do it, and once I'd started I'd have to finish it. I couldn't stop in the middle and throw it at the Moores, half done, just because it suited me to go somewhere else. I don't know how long I could be kept here, and I won't risk it. We've waited long enough, you and I, and you're not going to be kept waiting longer by anything that's my fault. I must get away while I can, and that's why I'm for Salisbury, please, and quickly.'

'How quickly?'

'Just a day or two, out of politeness, though I don't suppose the Moores will mind if I go. It's my mother who's their friend, not I. I'll be ready on Tuesday.'

Nick went off to tell Lory of this, and found him in high excitement over a newsletter that had come from London. The King had not stayed in Andover but had hurried back to Whitehall, where he had consulted with some peers of high rank. He now declared that for the sake of peace and unity he would again make large concessions. He had therefore ordered that writs be prepared for the election of a new Parliament, and he had issued a proclamation of pardon to all who were now in rebellion against him. He had agreed also to send commissioners to the Prince of Orange to treat for terms on which fighting might be avoided. The newsletter added, almost by way of afterthought, that the

Princess of Denmark, who had disappeared from the Cockpit a week ago, was now known to be safe at Nottingham, with the Earl of Devonshire and many others.

'The Princess!' said Nick blankly. 'Has she joined the rebellion? And John? He must be with her, surely?'

'Very likely, but she'll be safe enough now, and so will he. This is what matters.' Lory stabbed a finger jubilantly at the letter. 'Nick, it means surrender by King James. It's nothing less than that. It can't be.'

'Not so fast, Lory. It isn't finished yet.'

'But we can see what the end will be. Do you think a Parliament will leave him with a dispensing power, or the control of an army? Will the Prince, or anyone, accept his so-called son? It's Prince and Parliament who'll command now, not King James, and our campaign's as good as over.'

He was still in that jubilant mood when they rode away on Tuesday with Judith. They were into December now, but the days were still fine and sunny, and Lory raised their spirits even higher by firmly declaring that another week or two, or three at the most, should see London safe and quiet, and therefore fit for anybody's wedding. The roads were pleasant, and with no sort of hurry they finished their journey in the middle of Thursday afternoon. Mary Culley looked at them with some surprise, and then gave them her usual calm welcome. Nick hastily explained about Judith, and his aunt seemed to approve.

'Quite right,' she said. 'You'll be much better here, Judith, and I'll be glad of your company. I don't think I'll have any other till this is over.'

She explained that better when she had them in the house. It was true that the King was sending commissioners to the Prince, who had said he would receive them at Hungerford. His army was already moving in that direction, and he had himself ridden away that very morning. There were now no troops in Salisbury, which was quiet and peaceful again. Some two hundred gentlemen volunteers had ridden with the Prince, and one of these was Nick Culley, who had insisted on taking what part he could, and not leaving others to do it for him.

'He'll feel better if he does,' said Mary calmly, 'and I don't see why he shouldn't. It won't be dangerous now, and not very arduous. But how of yourselves, you and Lory?'

They had promised to rejoin, so they rode off together the next morning, which brought them to Hungerford at nightfall. Here they found all quiet, no commissioners yet from the King, no news from London and none from the north. Everyone was quietly waiting.

But the commissioners arrived the next morning, the Lords Halifax, Nottingham, and Godolphin. They presented their credentials, and were received by the Prince. Discussions began, and were still going on in the afternoon when the Earl of Delamere came riding in from the north with a company of gentlemen and a strong troop of horse, already looking soldierly and disciplined. With him rode his Adjutant, Sir Harry Burnaby, doing now for the son what he had done in his youth for the father. The troop of horse was commanded by Colonel Gibson.

That led to a gathering that was almost a family party. Nick took Lory with him, to be presented to his father. Harry arrived a few minutes later, and then Nick Culley, with his usual boisterous greeting. Gibson, looking sure and confident, was already there, and he was the first to give assurance to Harry that he had done right to join the Prince. Only John was missing, but no one doubted that he was safe at Nottingham with the Princess; or that the tide of events would soon bring her, and him, to the Prince.

But the commissioners were still in Hungerford. The next day was Sunday, and it was known by afternoon that the Prince had given them an answer. He had accepted a proposal from the King that all matters in dispute should be decided by the Parliament that was to meet in January; but he insisted that it should be left to deliberate in freedom, and that he would therefore keep his regiments at least thirty miles from Westminster, if the King's regiments were withdrawn to an equal distance to the east. The commissioners wrote of this to the King, and then could do nothing but wait for his answer. Monday passed, and more men came riding in from the north. Tuesday came, and men rode in from Oxford and Nottingham. A mood of happy confidence began to spread to everyone; and then, late on Tuesday evening, when some were already abed, a message came to Lory that he was to go at once to the Prince. He hurried off, puzzled and disturbed, and Nick waited impatiently to know the reason why.

Lory was soon back, looking even more disturbed, and with a clear glint of anger in his eyes.

'You can pack your valise,' he snapped. 'We're for London, you and I, and I don't know whether we can wait for daylight or not. He's played us false again.'

'*Who?* What do you mean?'

'James, of course.' Lory drew a hard breath, steadying himself, and then he spoke more calmly. 'I was taken to Lord Churchill first, and he told me that four peers have just come from London, in great haste, from a full meeting of the Lords there. James has disappeared, in the night, and it's believed he's taken ship for France. The Queen's missing too – a day earlier – and the child with her, so they're probably in France too, and we're left without a government.'

'Lory!' Nick had not quite taken this in. 'But these commissioners here?'

'They've been finely fooled. We all have, even the Prince, and it was all a pretence, done to win him time to get away.'

'The devil it was! But why have *we* to go to London? We aren't important.'

'Churchill soon told me, and it's worse than I thought.'

'I'd have thought it good, if the King has left it to Orange.'

'What he has left is chaos, deliberate and wicked, done of intent from sheer spite, murderous and – '

'Don't rant. Get your breath back and tell me what you mean.'

'Oh!' Lory stopped short. He nodded ruefully, and then spoke quietly and sensibly. 'There's no lawful authority left. There's no Parliament, and the King's gone – and the Great Seal's gone too. They can't find it, so he must have made away with it to complete the chaos.'

'Go on.'

'Something had to be done. With no law and no authority, you can guess what sort of creatures would have come from the stews of London to make a hell of everything, and the Lord Mayor had sense enough to ask all peers and bishops who were in town to meet him at the Guildhall. That was this morning, and they sent this deputation to the Prince, begging him to be with them as soon as he can. In the meantime they'll assume authority and take it on themselves to keep what order they can.'

'Excellent. So if the Prince – '

'Listen.' Lory's voice hardened again. 'Just before the deputation left London they learned that James has disbanded his army – or told Feversham to do it. Some troops in London had already been turned loose – just dismissed on the spot and then turned loose, with no pay, no food, no anything. But – ' He drew sharply at his breath. 'They've been allowed to keep their weapons. They're still fully armed, so if they get loose in London, or anywhere else, what's to be expected? And what sort of a King is he who deliberately, and of cold intent, puts this upon his people? Is it anything less than – '

'You're ranting again. And you still haven't told me why *we* are to go to London.'

'I'll try to.' Lory visibly steadied himself again. 'The Prince, of course, will be there as soon as he can. He'll go first to Windsor, and then his question is, can he go to London? The last thing he must do, remember, is to battle his way in with his Dutch troops fighting the English. He must be sure of a proper welcome in a peaceful and friendly London – and now you'll see our work. To report on the ordinary people, the merchants and shopkeepers, how they think and feel. We've done this twice before, and to his liking, and he said that's why he's chosen us again.'

'I'm glad it's no worse. It shouldn't be difficult.'

'It might be dangerous. We don't know what London will be like, or the roads either, if the Irish are disbanded.'

They talked of it further, and decided on an early start. Nick wrote a short note to his father, to say where he had gone, and then they were away at two o'clock in the morning, resolved to make as many miles as they could in the dark. They rode steadily, sparing the horses, but they met no one, seeing no sign of the Irish or of anyone else, and by daybreak they had done half the journey. They stopped at an inn, staying there till noon to rest the horses, and then they went on, finding that the roads were not quite so deserted now. Twice they met parties of Irish, still in their uniforms, but they looked too forlorn and bewildered to be a danger to anyone, and they accepted eagerly the bread and cheese that Lory had the wit to hand to them. Then, later in the afternoon, some English soldiers appeared, riding as a disciplined patrol under the command of an officer who was positively friendly. His colonel, he told them, instead of disbanding his regiment, was using it to keep peace and order until the arrival of the Prince of Orange, whom he now regarded as the only authority he could recognize. Lory looked jubilant.

It was past five o'clock, and all but dark, when they came to London, and at the City gates they were stopped by a guard of the trainband, all wearing orange favours, and they were admitted only when they insisted that they were protestant and English, and were willing to wear orange favours in their hats. In Fleet Street they separated, Lory going in search of Sir Thomas Mallory, and Nick of Edmund Innes, in a London that was anything but quiet. Groups of excited men were everywhere, all with the orange favours, and all armed with whatever they could find, from swords and knives to clubs and flails, and as often as not they were bawling 'Lillibullero'. In Lombard Street the doors were locked and the shutters in place, and Nick had to knock harder and harder until he was at length admitted; and before he had even a foot on the stair he heard the door made fast behind him.

'What brings you here?' said Innes sharply. 'And where's Judith?'

'With my aunt, at Salisbury. You had my letter?'

'Yes, and I thought it well that you should take her to your aunt. But what brings you here?'

'To learn how things go.'

'They go very badly. You've seen the City?'

'I came in after dark.'

'You'd think that in parts it had been sacked and burned. When will Orange be here?'

'In a day or two, I hope.'

'Thank God for that. He's our only hope. You know the King has gone?'

'Yes. Is there any word of him?'

'None. And affairs are now as bad as we can remember.'

'What's this of sacking and burning?'

'It was last night.' Innes spoke unhappily, almost unwillingly. 'The day was bad enough, with authority gone and rumour running mad, but at nightfall we had all the vermin in London creeping out, thieves, cut-purses, and footpads, and all the common rabble too, and between them they raised a tumult there was no quelling. They started on the Romish chapels that have sprung up these last years, and they burned each one of them, and then the King's printing house, with all its books and tracts. The houses of some papists came next, and then the houses of ambassadors from papist states. The Spanish ambassador hadn't a spoon or a blanket left this morning, and he's had to be lodged in Whitehall. You can guess what a dawn we had.'

'What of today?'

'The trainbands were out, and they were helped by having daylight. But no sooner did the streets seem safe than we had another alarm. Jeffreys was found in Wapping, in an alehouse there, dressed as a dirty sailor. He was trying to escape, but someone knew him, and that was enough. The rabble dragged him into the City, and you may guess what an uproar that was. Now he's in the Tower. But what comes tonight, I wonder?'

'Some sleep, I hope.'

'You look as if you need it. You'd better stay here.'

Innes was insistent, saying that Nick was in no state for a lonely walk back to the Temple through streets that might be disturbed and dangerous, and Nick, after a night and a day of riding, was willing enough to stay in comfort. He went to bed early, hardly caring by then whether London burned or not, and he was asleep before he had given another thought to anything.

There was daylight in the chink of the shutters when he woke, and he must have slept through the night almost without moving. He roused himself and dressed, and when he went into the parlour he found Innes sitting limply by the fire, looking tired and strained. But he was still very calm and controlled.

'You've slept well,' he said, 'and you may be the only one in London who has done so. Did you hear anything?'

'Not a thing. What?'

'I came to your room about one o'clock, but you were so dead in sleep that I did not wake you. It might wait, I thought, till things grew desperate. We had been roused by a trainband, hammering very loudly. Intelligence had come, they told us, that the dismissed Irish soldiers had joined all together in a great force, and would soon be at the City gates, sworn to kill every man, woman, and child they could find alive. We were all to stand to it with whatever arms we had, and to sell it dearly to the Irish when the moment came.'

'And you did not wake me?'

'There would be time enough for that when we heard sounds of fighting. But the rest of us stood to it. We had pistols in the house, and a fowling piece or two, so we watched and listened.'

'Hearing what?'

'Shouting, tramping feet, and "Lillibullero". Many were in the streets, and I'm told that by two o'clock there were twenty thousand men in arms.'

'And what happened?'

'Nothing. Not an Irishman appeared, and the whole thing was a rumour, or perhaps a hoax. But I tell you of it because I think you'll hear little else spoken of in London today. What do you think to do this morning?'

'I should perhaps go to the King's Head, to see how Lory fares.'

'He'll probably be asleep, if he was as tired as you, and if they kept him up all night. Leave him till afternoon.'

It was therefore past one o'clock when Nick walked into the King's Head, to find Lory sitting over the remains of dinner with Sir Thomas Mallory. But Lory, he noted, was in riding boots.

'Why these?' he asked.

'Because I'm for Windsor. I've no wish to, after a night spoiled by this Irish foolery, but I think I must. Orange could be in Windsor by tonight, and he'll want our report.'

'What's it to be?'

'That he'll be more than welcome in London. He's awaited impatiently, and is sure of a fine reception. Can you agree?'

'Certainly I can. The sooner he's here, the better.'

'You sound decided.' Lory broke into a smile as he turned to Mallory. 'That's because he waits for a wedding, and the wedding waits till it's safe to bring her to London. Hence the impatience.'

'You need not tell me,' said Mallory with a pleasant ease. 'I was at his betrothal, and his Judith is very charming. But now – ' He looked steadily at Nick. 'I do not think it is for much longer. A few days at most. James, we may hope, is now in France, and I do not see how he can return. Orange and the Council will quickly come to agreement, and whatever form it takes, it's bound to leave Orange in command. Nothing else is possible, and he'll most certainly restore the law and keep good order. Say within a week from now. May I then be invited to the wedding?'

'Indeed yes. And Lory too.'

Nick was doing some quick calculations. This was the 13th of December. The week that Mallory suggested would last until the 20th. Even allowing another day or two before all was settled, there could still be just time to get to Salisbury by Christmas Eve, and Christmas with the Culleys and Judith seemed a fair approach to heaven to him now. Then they might all return with him to London, where they would find his father, and Innes, and Gibson. John and Harry would surely be in London by then, and a wedding might be possible by about the beginning of January. It was perhaps time to be seeing about a licence.

He walked quickly back to Lombard Street, eager to talk with Innes about this. But Innes had gone to the Guildhall to learn about the alarms in the night, and it was another half-hour before he returned.

'Have you heard the news?' he asked abruptly. 'About the King?'

'No? What – '

'He isn't in France at all. He's at Faversham, in Kent, under some sort of guard.'

'Guard!'

'It seems he reached the Isle of Sheppey, and boarded a hoy. There was a delay in sailing, and some local men pulled him ashore and took him to Faversham. The Council have just heard of it, and they say that while he's here he's the King. They've sent a troop of Life Guards to set him free.'

'Then what's going to happen?'

'Who can know? He could come back here, I suppose.' Innes snapped it angrily. 'But the hopes we had this morning have been broken.'

22 *Twelfth Night*

It was known the next day that the Prince of Orange was at Windsor, and that King James, freed from his rustic captors, had been escorted by the Life Guards to Rochester, where he seemed to be staying. He and Orange, as Innes remarked, were sitting at opposite sides of London, glaring at each other, and not knowing what to do next. Nick began to care very little what either of them did, if only they would leave London safe enough for Judith. But London was quarrelsome and noisy, with men angered and disturbed by this starting again of troubles they had thought were over.

Lory came in at noon on Saturday, having had to wait till that morning to make his report. The Prince, said Lory, was believed to be as angry as anyone at this new turn of events, and when Lord Feversham had arrived at Windsor that morning with a letter from the King, he had at once been put under arrest, nominally because he had come without a safe-conduct; actually, perhaps, because he had so recklessly disbanded the army, unpaid and not disarmed.

'What was the letter he brought?' asked Innes.

'We're not told. But the whisper is that the King now invites Orange to London to meet him, and that Orange isn't going to be fooled a second time. It's thought he'll answer that James is to stay where he is, and not come nearer to London.'

'Did you,' asked Nick impatiently, 'see anything of my father and the others?'

'Oh yes. Lord Delamere, being a strong Whig, was with the Prince, and your father, being still called his Adjutant, was at Windsor with him. Colonel Gibson was there too, with his troop, and your Harry had somehow attached himself.'

'How are they?'

'Very cheerful. It's Sir Nicholas who isn't. He blows hot and cold now.' Lory puckered his forehead. 'He's a royalist at heart, of course. Loyal all his life, and so on. He joined Orange because he thought he had to for the Church, but as soon as it was done he began to have doubts. Wondered if he should have done it. Now, with James lifting his head at Rochester, he doesn't know what he should think, and he changes his mind every ten minutes. There'll be others like him.'

The next day was Sunday. Nick was at Bow Church in the morning, and the talk after the service was that St James's Palace was being hurriedly prepared for the Prince of Orange, who had been invited by the King to lodge there. But then things went wrong. The Prince, who had been invited to Westminster, did not come, and the King, who had been pressed to stay at Rochester, did come. Doraty had been upriver with the Crosedales, and Nick went again that afternoon to see if she had returned. He found that she had not. But as he was walking back to London he met in the Strand a troop of Life Guards, escorting a coach-and-six, and King James could be seen in the coach as he acknowledged some wavings of hats by a few spectators. But most of those who were in the Strand showed him no welcome, and not all of them even doffed their hats. It was not a triumphant return to the Palace of Whitehall.

Thursday morning was cold and windy, with frequent showers of rain rattling on the windows. Nick had not long finished breakfast when a note was brought to him from his father, who wrote briefly that he was now in Westminster, at the Angel in King Street, and that he hoped Nick would go there for dinner. Then Lory arrived in high excitement. The town, he said, was seething with news. Late last night, at past ten o'clock, three battalions of Dutch infantry had arrived at Whitehall, where only a single company of Foot Guards had been on duty. The officer commanding the Foot Guards, though he was hopelessly outnumbered, had refused to withdraw, and serious trouble had been averted only when the King had himself ordered that the posts should be surrendered to the Dutch. He was now virtually a prisoner in his own Palace, surrounded by the Dutch army.

Lory told this with a satisfaction that Nick did not entirely share. He did not much like the thought of the Dutch, or anybody else, putting sentries round the home of the kings of England. Then it occurred to him that his father's sudden arrival in Westminster might be in some way connected with this, and he decided not to wait till dinner time. He would go at once to the Angel and learn as much as he could. He said so, and Lory promptly asked if he might come too.

They decided to go by water, and they walked down to the Temple stairs, where the wind seemed stronger and colder than in Fleet Street. They were between showers, and over the choppy windswept river the light was clear. It showed them the royal arms on a barge that was making a steady way downstream, and the soldiers, in blue Dutch uniforms, crowded into two escorting barges. Lory stopped in his walk, and for a long moment he stood stiffly. Then he clapped a hand on Nick's shoulder.

'Look well,' he said slowly, and his voice was less sharp than usual. 'It's the passing of King James. It could be nothing else, and we're here to see it.'

The barges went steadily on, with flecks of white water leaping up as the oar-blades rose and fell, and Nick stood in silence. He did not doubt that the guess was right. The royal barge, and an escort of such unusual strength, left no room for doubt, and if the King had done it by his own choice the escort would have been in scarlet, from his own Foot Guards. It was all too plain, and it was necessary that the King should go. He had made it impossible for the nation to continue with him, but Nick was not happy that it should have come like this. His thoughts were with the man – the man rather than the King – who had left his home, and was sitting in the barge this wet and stormy morning, having what would perhaps be his last view of London. It was a bleak cold morning for King James, and it was within a week of Christmas.

'Better call a boat,' said Nick abruptly, and he was still watching the receding barge. 'We're for Westminster.'

'You are. But I think I ought to tell Mallory of this, and at once.'

Lory had become the Whig again, ardent and conscientious, and Nick was still thinking of the barge. It would be off the Tower by now, passing the long grey wall and the Traitors' Gate, where the bishops had been sent by the King's order. Another squall of rain was coming down the river, grey and heavy, blotting out everything, and in a few minutes more it would be upon the barge, blotting out the Tower, and all London too; which might seem symbolic to the King, if he had enough imagination. Probably he had not.

The squall reached them, the rain came spattering, and Lory, turning hastily, hurried off in search of Mallory. Nick took boat alone, thinking that he would have been less drenched if he had stayed ashore and walked. He arrived at the Angel wet and bedraggled, and not caring very much about either, and he found his father looking warm and comfortable by a fire in the wine-room. Nick told of the barge, and his father nodded without surprise.

'I knew he'd gone,' he said quietly. 'I was on the Privy Stairs to see him go, and I thought that perhaps I should not have been.'

'Why?'

'What took me there? To salute him? Or just curiosity, and to say I'd seen him go? But at least I pulled my hat off.'

He was plainly unhappy about it, and he sipped at his wine, staring gloomily at the fire, before he turned to Nick again.

'There's no mystery of why he went,' he said. 'There were a lot of peers at Windsor, and last night they told Orange that if he meant to come to Westminster he mustn't leave James at Whitehall. Of course that suited Orange, and he sent three of them at once to convey it to James. They were Halifax, Shrewsbury, and Delamere, and since I'm in some sort of attendance on Delamere, I had to ride with him. It was past midnight when we reached Whitehall, and James had to be roused to receive them.'

'And what happened?'

'I didn't go in with them. It seems he didn't like it, but understood at last that he must go.'

'Where to?'

'Rochester again, at his own choice, and that's easy to understand. He's right on the Medway there, and he can take ship at any time.'

'With all those guards around him?'

'I don't think the guards are meant to hinder him. They are surely to see that he isn't brought back a second time by local busybodies.'

'Hmm!' Nick considered it thoughtfully. 'I still don't know why he went. If he'd said firmly that he was King of England, that he was in his own Palace of Whitehall and wasn't going to be ordered out of it by anybody, I don't see what Orange could have done.'

'Nor do I. Nor, perhaps, does Orange. So if James chooses to go, I don't think he'll be hindered. All the same, I did *not* like to see him go off like that this morning. He *is* our King, and we owed him a loyalty which we haven't given.'

'How could we, after the way – '

'I know all that, but I still don't like it, and I hope I did right to join like this with Delamere.'

'Surely you did.'

'I hope so, but I don't find it as easy as Gibson. He, of course, has no doubts. He's jubilant, and your uncle, Nick Culley, is deeply troubled. He'd like to disown the whole thing, if he could, and pretend he never rode to Orange.'

'How does Gibson take that?'

'He's being tactful, more so than I thought he could be. But be careful about it yourself, when they come here.'

'When will that be?'

'Any time. Orange is expected here today.'

He arrived that afternoon. He sent some regiments slow-marching into Westminster, where it was at once supposed that they were escorting him. Crowds gathered round them, shouting, cheering, waving orange favours, and climbing to any vantage point they could reach, and while their attention was thus diverted he drove to St James's Palace in a small calash, with only a trifling escort. As soon as this was known the crowds surrounded the Palace, drawing attention to themselves with 'Lillibullero', and then, as dusk fell, lighting bonfires wherever they could. Inside the Palace it was scarcely possible to move, so great was the press of gentlemen who had hurried to make their bows and profess their duty to His Highness. There was a mood of high excitement and great expectation, even among those who should have known better. The Prince could not, with tact and propriety, make any announcement about the future of England while the King of England was a mere thirty miles away, and had done nothing to abdicate his sovereignty. Nick understood this, but most people did not, and the next morning the crowds around St James's were as dense as ever, all of them seeming to expect something at any moment. Nothing came, and impatience grew.

That day passed, and the next. Then came Friday, and the Prince broke his silence at last. But he merely asked that all peers who were at hand should meet to consider affairs and advise him, and that all gentlemen who had served in the Commons during the last reign should do likewise; which plainly meant that any change of sovereignty should be suggested by the English and not by himself. If was very proper, and no doubt wise, but it would take some days, and it did not allay impatience.

Nick was becoming as impatient as anyone. He had had a letter from Judith, who was plainly impatient too. She had been left with Mary Culley as a temporary arrangement, and she said it was now growing tedious. They had nothing to do, they were short of news, and they would both be glad when their lives began to move again. Nick wished for nothing more than to get life moving again, but he did not see how he could do it until affairs were more settled than they were at the moment.

Then, on Friday evening, Harry came to him, looking not quite himself in civilian clothes, and perhaps not pleased with them. But he sounded cheerful enough.

'John's back,' he announced abruptly, 'and he's riding very high.'

'Oh?'

'The Princess came back on Wednesday, it seems, to the Cockpit, and they've had the Prince of Orange there to see her. You should hear John about it.'

'Was he presented?'

'He certainly was. He came tonight to tell us about it. He's in high favour with his Princess, after the way he's been escorting her, and she presented him with some very gracious words. So now he's in favour with Orange too, and he's pretty sure he can expect something.'

'So he's riding high?'

'A lot higher than the rest of us. And he, mind you, had the easiest lot. No risk worth mentioning, and he didn't even have a decision to make.'

'There's nothing like serving near to someone. But how are the others? I thought they weren't at all high.'

'They aren't – except Gibson, of course. The rest of us keep asking if we did right. We know we did, but we keep asking.'

'How's Nick Culley?'

'The worst of all, and that's what brings me here. He says he was compelled to support Orange. But the Church looks safe enough now, so he'd like to change sides if he could, and be loyal to his lawful King again.'

'It's too late for that.'

'Exactly. So the best he can do is to say he won't stay here to see Orange triumphant. He says he'll go home, where things are different, and make what he can of Christmas.'

'What a thought!'

But a further thought came quickly, that Nick Culley was providing a home for Judith, as well as for Mary; which seemed to put more sense into it. Nick began to wonder about possibilities.

'He can't go at once,' went on Harry. 'He says he must have the latest news of all of us, or he won't hear the last of it when he gets home. Doraty and her brood aren't back yet, and John's going upriver to get them tomorrow. Old Nick says he must wait for them, and he must see you as well, and the short of it is that he'll be off at crack of dawn on Monday. But before then he invites us all to dinner on Sunday, at the Angel, and I'm sent to bid you to it.'

'Of course I'll come. Pray tell him so.'

London became quieter, as if men had understood at last that nothing could be expected for a day or two. On Saturday Nick went for wine with Lory and Sir Thomas Mallory, and found them uneasy to the point almost of distraction. It was crazy, they said, but true, that despite all that had happened it still lay with King James. He was still at Rochester, and there was no saying what would follow if, even at this late hour, he were to announce that he would abandon his dispensing power, remove papists from offices they were not qualified to hold, and thenceforth govern in accordance with the law. Nick Culley was not alone in his misgivings, and there could be an enormous return to loyalty. Sir Thomas expatiated gloomily on this, Lory was hardly better, and Nick was glad to leave them to it. They made poor company.

He went again to Bow Church on Sunday morning, and he noted that after the Collects they had the Litany, which avoided the prayer for the King, and that before the end of the Litany they had the General Thanksgiving and the thanksgiving for deliverance from enemies. Then came an hour-long sermon on 'Render unto Caesar', which brought hums of approval from the crowded congregation. All in all it took longer than usual, and when Nick reached Westminster he thought he would be the last to arrive at the Angel. But Nick Culley, alone in a quiet room, looked pleased when he walked in.

'I'm glad you've come,' he said. 'I'm still waiting for the others. They went to St James's Chapel for service, and to see Orange there, and that's just why I didn't go. I'd no wish to see him at all, so I went to the Abbey and was back at a decent time. I don't know what's kept them.'

He poured wine, perhaps a little jerkily, and the usual exuberant confidence was not in his voice. There was a tightness in his face, as if he was disturbed and unhappy, and was trying hard to control it.

'Doraty's not coming,' he said abruptly. 'She's in her house again, and very happy because John's done well, but she said we'd be all men here today and she'd keep out. Sensible of her. Did they tell you I'm going home for Christmas?'

'Yes. I – '

'I'm not staying here while the King's sent away and Orange moves to Whitehall. I know we couldn't go on as we were, but I don't like it and I'm not staying for it. What do you say to coming with me, to Christmas and Judith?'

It was even more abrupt, and it sounded almost angry, as if he expected a refusal. But Nick did not hesitate. He had been thinking of this since Harry had first mentioned it.

'I'd like to,' he said quickly. 'I've not much to stay for here, and – '

The door opened, and his father came in, followed by Gibson and Harry, and then Colonel Crosedale. Only John was missing.

'Here we are,' said Hal, 'and I'm sorry we've kept you. There was a crowd this morning, and we couldn't even get seats. We had to stand, and the sermon was overlong.'

'You'd have been better at the Abbey. But here's the wine. Where's John?'

'He said he must call at the Cockpit before coming here.'

'Keeping it warm, I suppose, now he's in favour there, and it's wise of him, if that's what he wants. Young Nick's wiser, though. He's coming home with me for Christmas.'

'Splendid,' said Crosedale promptly, and Hal, after a quick and surprised glance, turned to his son.

'Yes,' he said simply, 'I think you could. There's nothing to keep you here, and you'll be happier with Judith. Go by all means.'

'So he should.' It was Nick Culley again, and he still sounded aggressive and challenging. 'We've pretty well broken the country to pieces these last days, and it's time to pick up the pieces and try to live decent lives again. Christmas is at hand, and that's where we should start.'

'I think that's true,' said Gibson, and he was toying with his wineglass as he looked at Nick. 'We should not keep men longer than is needed, and you have done your part and may have honourable discharge. Go to Judith, and find your life again. We all wish you well. So – ' He lifted his glass. 'Your health and happiness, and Judith's too!'

He got no further with it. The door was flung open again and John burst in, looking as if he had hurried.

'He's gone,' he said quickly, and without waiting for any of them. 'On the night tide, from – '

'The King?' cut in Gibson, all thought of his toast forgotten. 'Do you mean – '

'Yes. The Prince has just sent the news to the Cockpit, and I heard it there.'

'Any details?'

'This morning, in the dark, perhaps about two o' clock. That's when the tide would ebb at Rochester, so he's probably clear away by now. He had a house with a garden to the river, and the Guards weren't near it. They had proper orders.'

'Yes.' Hal checked him with a word, and then stood in thought, none too happily. 'How long to France from Rochester?'

'Two days, or thereabouts. He's thought to be in a fishing smack, which will be slow, and they'll want to keep out of sight, well clear of the Foreland, so it could last till Tuesday.'

'Christmas Day!' Nick Culley snapped it at him, and sounded hardly believing. 'You tell me the King of England creeps away in a fishing smack, and goes ashore in France – on Christmas Day?'

'It looks like it.'

'And you don't feel sick?' He glared angrily at John, and then swung as angrily to the others. 'Go home, did I say, for Christmas? What's left of Christmas now?'

'Not much, this year,' said Crosedale quietly. 'Though it will come another year. But Culley – '

'Yes?'

'I was much with the King in my duties, and I can share your feeling. You're perhaps right about Christmas. But pick up the pieces was what you said, and back to decent lives. Please remember it. We must all do that now, and particularly, we must not spoil it for the younger ones. Nick, it's time you and Judith were wed, and more than time. When do you see to it?'

'I – ' Nick was confounded by the suddenness of it, and for an instant he all but stuttered. 'Any time. It couldn't be too soon. But I can't quite speak for Judith.'

'Good.' Crosedale looked round. 'Who helps?'

'I do.' Nick Culley was suddenly tempestuous, and he seemed to have grown even larger. 'We'll all help, and we'll all find life again. Now, young Nick – ' He turned in his most overpowering style. 'You'll come home with me as I said, and I'll answer for Judith. *She'll* not keep you waiting, by what she's said to me. So where will you be wed? At Salisbury, or come back here?'

'Whichever you – whichever Judith pleases.' Nick managed at last to catch his father's eye. 'But what, please, do *you* say to this?'

'It's certainly being thrust upon you. But if you wish it soon, I won't say no to you.'

'I should hope not,' said Nick Culley, and he seemed to dispose of all possible objections with one sweeping gesture. 'Since the girl's at my house, it would be handy to have her wed from there. Will you make a journey for it, all of you?'

'Yes,' said Crosedale cheerfully.

'Don't rush it so,' said Hal. 'I can't leave here at present, and nor can Gibson. The old Commons are to meet, and that means both of us.'

'Politics again! All right then. We'll have to come here for it, and I don't think Judith will mind. Mary won't, either, if there's a wedding at the end of it. Now what about a date?'

'You *are* in a hurry.'

'Isn't it time to be? Haven't they been put off long enough? They'll never be wed if we don't fix a date.'

'But – '

'Stop making objections. Apart from these two, it will be good for all of us to have something proper in our minds. It could make us sane again. So what about a date? Nick, if we ride tomorrow, and are home on Christmas Day, how long to get two women to London?'

'A week, perhaps, allowing them time to pack.'

'Pack and chatter. But that means the first of January. Allow a few days longer here, and – ha!' He sounded suddenly triumphant. 'We'll say the Saturday, and that's Twelfth Night! Twelfth Night, do you hear, and what could be better? Of all days in the year! We'll have something of Christmas after all, so are we agreed on *that*?'

'I suppose we are,' said Hal, who had just caught Crosedale's eye, and was beginning to see amusement in it. 'But you've still forgotten two of the most important.'

'Who?'

'Innes.'

'He'll be no trouble. Nick, you can deal with him, can't you, and persuade him to it?'

'I expect so.'

'Do it today, then. And who's the other?'

'Alison, of course. She's his mother.'

'Oh!' For a moment he seemed put out, and even contrite. Then the confidence returned. 'Harry, that's your work. The weather's fine and the roads are good. Will you be off tomorrow and bring your mother here, in time for Twelfth Night?'

'Yes,' said Harry simply. 'If she'll come.'

'The wedding's the carrot. Dangle it in front of her. Now then – ' He looked round the circle. 'John – you and Doraty?'

'Yes.'

'Good. It just leaves Gibson?'

'I'm not of the first concern. It's not my family. But if I'm asked – '

'You are.'

'Why then – ' He was toying again with his glass. 'The Lord grant thee according to thine own heart, and fulfil all thy counsel.'

'Mine?' It came delightedly.

'Yes. And for me, I'll go back to what I said before.' His voice sharpened, and then his glass rose in salute. 'Gentlemen, from all of us! To Nick, his health and happiness, and Judith's too!'